TRINITY UNITED CHURCH
NORTH BAY, ONTARIO

About the Author

Lilly Bartlett's cosy romcoms are full of warmth, quirky characters and guaranteed happily-ever-afters. Lilly is the pen-name of *Sunday Times* and *USA Today* best-selling author, Michele Gorman, who writes best friend-girl power comedies under her own name.

D1383031

Also by Lilly Bartlett

The Big Little Wedding in Carlton Square

The Second Chance Cafe in Carlton Square

Michele Gorman writing as
LILLY BARTLETT

TRINITY UNITED CHURCH
NORTH BAY, ONTARIO

A division of HarperCollins*Publishers*
www.harpercollins.co.uk

Harper*Impulse* an imprint of
HarperCollins*Publishers*
The News Building
1 London Bridge Street
London SE1 9GF

www.harpercollins.co.uk

A Paperback edition 2017

First published in Great Britain in ebook format by
Harper*Impulse* 2017

Copyright © Lilly Bartlett 2017

Lilly Bartlett asserts the moral right to
be identified as the author of this work

A catalogue record for this book
is available from the British Library

ISBN: 9780008226602

This novel is entirely a work of fiction.
The names, characters and incidents portrayed in it are
the work of the author's imagination. Any resemblance to
actual persons, living or dead, events or localities is
entirely coincidental.

Set in Birka by Palimpsest Book Production Limited,
Falkirk, Stirlingshire

Printed and bound by CPI Group (UK) Ltd, Croydon, CR0 4YY

All rights reserved. No part of this publication may be
reproduced, stored in a retrieval system, or transmitted,
in any form or by any means, electronic, mechanical,
photocopying, recording or otherwise, without the prior
permission of the publishers.

The book is dedicated to my friend, Fanny Blake – author, editor, unerring support and amazing woman. It was your idea to unleash Lilly Bartlett. Thank you, and here's to many more years together in the park.

Chapter 1

Stop the Convict Café!!

Concerned neighbours: Don't let our homes be overrun by criminals!

Are you worried about the untrustworthy people lurking around the Second Chance Café day and night?

Do you want your children and grannies threatened and intimidated?

Would you like to have homeless people sleeping in your doorway??

HAVE YOUR SAY!!
Wednesday at 7 p.m.
The Other Half Caff
Tea and cake will be served

I can't keep my hand from shaking as I reread the crinkled notice. What a complete load of rubbish! Criminals?! They're only children, for heaven's sake. Most of them haven't even been to court yet. Intimidated grannies? Have you *seen* the old-timers around here? I wouldn't fancy my chances against any of them down a dark alley.

This really is the last straw.

All publicity might be good publicity, but the leaflet that's been pushed through every letterbox on the square won't exactly bring the punters in for a cuppa, will it?

'They were up all over the main road too,' says Lou, chewing on the end of her pale blue hair. She knows it's not attractive – or hygienic – when she does that, but who can blame her? She's only worried for me. For all of us.

'You want me to send the lads round to 'ave a word?' she asks. 'You know it's *her* behind it.' She punches her fist into the palm of her hand, like I wouldn't catch her meaning otherwise. Fat chance of that. Lou's about as subtle as an armed robbery. The last thing we need now is for her to go over there and prove everyone right.

Of course I know it's her behind it. It's been her behind it ever since we opened the café. But sending the kids around is only going to make the situation worse. And Lou knows that as well as I do.

I can feel tears welling in my eyes as I scan the leaflet again. It's not sadness, though. It's pissed-offness. I stare hard at the strings of calico bunting that criss-cross the ceiling until I'm sure I won't weep in front of my employees. Every single person in here, I remind myself – sipping their hot drinks, chatting, laughing or quietly enjoying the warm cosy ambiance – *loves* our café. So get a grip on yourself. Sticks and stones and all that.

One of the walkie-talkies crackles to life on the countertop. 'Emma, Emma, come in, Emma.'

I'm not sure why I ever thought it would be clever to let the customers upstairs give us orders over those things. Most of the time they use them to ask the answers to stupid trivia questions that they're too lazy to look up on their phones.

I'm in no mood for trivia right now. 'What is it, Leo?' I'm sure my annoyance comes through loud and clear despite the static.

'We need you upstairs.'

'Do you actually need me to bring you something or is this your usual afternoon plea for attention? Because I haven't really got time right now.'

There's a pause. 'It's just my usual plea for attention. Sorry to bother you. Over and out.' The walkie-talkie goes dead.

Now I'm cross *and* I feel bad. I'm absolutely definitely not treating Leo any differently than usual. I'd have been just as short with him yesterday. It's the situation that's changed, not me. And definitely not my feelings.

Something tells me today should have been a duvet day.

Two months earlier…

I'm sitting at our solid old dining room table, oblivious to the fact that I'm about to make a mortal enemy. I don't even know Leo yet, or Lou or Joseph or most of the customers who will become my friends. Morning sun streams through the wide bay window in the front room, throwing a long rectangle of light along the floor. It'll reach my chair in another hour, but I'll be long gone by then.

That window is my favourite part of the whole house. It's where Daniel and I looked out over our wedding reception at everyone in the world we love. It's also where we took Auntie Rose's advice not to wait till after the party to christen our new marriage. While it's beyond mortifying to hear bedroom suggestions from your seventy-something great aunt, she was right. And there wasn't even a sofa there yet. We used to live life on the edge.

Now our edges are blunt and you don't really get any view from the window unless you stand up to look out over the window boxes – crammed full of colourful pansies and winter primroses – past the wrought-iron fence and over the quiet road into the garden square beyond.

I can't claim credit for the flowers. Mrs Ishtiaque comes over every few months to plant new ones after I've killed the previous lot. It was involuntary plant slaughter, Your Honour.

Mrs Ishtiaque has lived next door to my parents my whole life. She looks out for me like I'm one of her daughters. She says that newly-weds should always have blossoms in their lives. Blooming flowers, blooming love, she claims.

Though we're not technically newly-weds anymore. I'll have been married to Daniel two years in July. Sometimes it feels like two decades.

The twins are in lockdown in their high chairs, happily finger-painting stewed apples over everything. They're a couple of Picassos, those two.

It's a surprise to see them both painting, actually. They almost never do the same thing at the same time. If one is sleeping, the other's awake. One's breakfast is the other's playtime. The only things they seem to synchronise are tantrums and bowel movements.

I wouldn't believe they were related if they hadn't put me through thirty hours of labour.

'Mama! Mamamamamamamamamama!' screams Grace, blinking fast to dislodge a bit of apple from her eyelid. She couldn't care less about the smears all over her face. It's the attention she wants.

'Have you made a mess, my love?' She squirms but lets me wipe her chubby cheeks. By the time I've got most of the stewed fruit off her, the cloth is filthy.

'Grab another wet cloth for Oscar, will you?' I call to Daniel as I spot him weaving his way towards us through the piles of laundry and strewn toys.

Changing direction, he calls, 'Clean-up in aisle six,' from the kitchen.

'Clean-up in aisles one through five as well,' I mutter, looking around.

No one would ever call me house-proud – Mum holds that title every year running – but even *I'm* getting fed up with the mess. 'Could you please fold the laundry while I get them cleaned up?' I ask Daniel. 'It's the pile on the sofa.' As opposed to the ones on the floor, the chair or the coffee table.

He plants a swift kiss on top of my head and plonks a soaking wet cloth into my hand. That'll need wringing out before I assault our child with it. I want to clean Oscar, not drown him.

'Can't I have my brekkie first? I'm rahly running late for work,' says Daniel.

My lips twitch when he says brekkie. And *rahly*. He's still trying to speak commoner like the rest of us do around here, but his posh accent really shows up the difference in our upbringings.

He didn't need to utter a word the first time I saw him for me to know he was different. Picture the scene: I'm twenty-five and it's our first day of class – an architecture course at City Lit in Central London – and everyone shuffles in to find a seat. The classroom is functional and bare aside from the battered plastic chairs and scarred desks – no oak-panelled walls, antique tomes or dreaming spires for us mature students. Most of us are huddled into wool coats against the bite of January, laden with satchels and rucksacks and nerves.

It wasn't Daniel's strong jawline or wavy blond hair that I first noticed, or his broad shoulders or long legs or the way his face crinkled into a friendly smile every time he caught someone's eye.

It was his vivid green trousers as he stood to take off his duffel coat. Then he pulled off his dark V-neck jumper to reveal a bright yellow striped work shirt underneath. By the time he'd tied the jumper around his shoulders, the rest of us – clad in T-shirts or sweatshirts and jeans – were staring at him.

Mistaking our curiosity for friendliness, Daniel did what no one ever did on the first day of class. He started talking to strangers. You'd think he was catching up with old friends the way he asked everyone how far they'd travelled and whether this was their first course. Daniel was on a first-name basis with everyone within a few hours.

And that sums him up, really.

It's not his fault he dresses the way he does. He grew up in one of those five-story white-fronted mansions in West London, with rooms stuffed full of masterpieces and precious artwork and a pond in the back garden. They had people who answered the door for them and made them their meals. They count most heads of state as friends and Daniel's godfather is a lord. It took me a while to realise that his parents are very nice people, despite sounding like the upstairs family from *Downton Abbey*. What a world away from the council house where I grew up with Mum and Dad. Our furniture is more Ikea than iconic and our friends drink pints, not Dom Pérignon. I don't run across many poshies in my day-to-day life, except for the ones who occasionally come this way to stuff fivers into G-strings at the local strip club. And I don't date them.

With such an upbringing, Daniel sounds like he should be spoiled or at least a bit of an arse, right? It's hard not to make assumptions when you hear about someone's giant house and their servants and gap year holidays. But like I said, he's kind and easy-going and generous, totally unflashy and not the least bit judgmental. It helped that I got to know all these things about him before I found out he was stonking rich. Otherwise, naturally I'd have presumed he was a wanker.

That doesn't mean we're not from different worlds, only that the differences are more about our accents and experiences, not the things that really matter. That's why I do give him full marks for trying to fit in, even if the slang sounds wrong with his plummy pronunciation. Besides, he totally ruins it with his next remarks.

'I'll just put the seeded bloomer in to toast, yah? It's the last of the loaf before Waitrose delivers again. I think we're out of hummus too.'

He sounds straight off the estate, doesn't he?

I stop wringing the sopping cloth into my half-drunk coffee cup. If I'm ever kidnapped, the police will be able to trace my last movements through the string of unfinished hot drinks I've left behind. 'Having your seeded bloomer toast before or after you fold clothes won't make a difference to your lateness, you know.'

When his face breaks into a cheeky smile, one dimple appears on the left side. That dimple! It hints at a mouth that's usually lopsided with merriment. He can make me laugh at myself like nobody else. It's one of the things that's always charmed me. It would probably work now, but I'm too tired. 'I think I'll be more efficient, energy-wise, if I eat first,' he says, glancing at his phone. 'You're right as usual, though. Just let me answer this one email. I'll be quick.'

But he's not quick enough. By the time he finishes his toast I need him to change Grace while I do Oscar. Our children are messy at both ends. So the laundry will sit in a heap for another day as my award for Homemaker of the Year slips further away.

Daniel waits till he's at the front door to break his news

casually to me. He thinks it cushions the blow to kiss me when he does it. Kisses or not, it feels like an ambush.

'I've got to meet with Jacob quickly after work tonight.' He nuzzles my neck. 'Are you wearing a new perfume? It smells so good.'

That would be the tea tree oil for the spot that's come up on my forehead. 'But you were out just the other night.'

'That was last week, darling.'

'Was it? Still, do you have to? I'll be working at the café all day with Mum. I thought you could do tea for us tonight.'

'Yah, I could have if you'd told me before now, but I've already said yes to Jacob. He says it's rahly important, otherwise I'd cancel. I won't be late, though. And don't worry about supper for me. If it's easier, I can grab a bite with Jacob while I'm out. I love you!'

Yeah, sure it's easier. Easier for him. 'Love you too,' I say quietly.

And I do. I'm crazy about him. I just wish he was, I don't know, more helpful. No, that's not the right word, because he is almost always ready to help. It's his follow-through that needs work.

When the twins were tiny we were such a solid team: cuddling, changing, feeding, fussing, staring for hours in wonder and bewilderment. We did it *all* together. Even though he hasn't got the feeding equipment to be of much practical use, he'd sit with us while I nursed our babies so that I wasn't the only one awake.

Now that they're toddlers, he sleeps through the night even when we don't. He will do what I ask of him, usually without grumbles. But I've become more of a lead singer to his backing vocals and the thing is, I never wanted a solo career.

Grace raises her arms and mewls for a cuddle as soon as Daniel leaves, fixing me with the same long-lashed blue-eyed stare that he has. She's as irresistible as he is, with her golden hair and dimples. Oscar's got my family's red tinge, which thrills Mum. It would be nice, though, for one of my children to have my dark hair or even the cowlick at the front that I can't do anything with. Not that one should ever wish a cowlick on their children.

There's no time on the walk to my parents' house for a proper grizzle about Daniel getting to go out tonight. Even walking slowly, it only takes fifteen minutes, plus time to stop for the toys, dummies and shoes the twins jettison from the pushchair along the way.

It'll be no use whinging to Mum when I get there either. She didn't manage to hold our family together – raising me, making ends meet and looking after Dad while working her cleaning jobs – by being soft. She'll only be her usual sensible self and tell me that I'm overreacting. It's not like Daniel is out every night or comes home pissed. You heard him. It's a once-a-week thing at most. And the world won't end because he didn't fold our pants. I'm just overtired. Looking after the children is a lot harder than I imagined.

Says every parent in the world. Still, I wouldn't trade them for anything. Well, maybe I would, just for half an hour so I could have a bath without an audience. I'd want them back, though, as soon as I was towelled off.

'Good morning!' I call into Mum and Dad's house as I let myself in with my key. 'You have a special delivery: two toddlers, fairly clean and ready to play!'

They're all in their usual spots in the lounge – Mum and Auntie Rose on the settees and Dad in his old reading chair that Mum has tried to get rid of for years.

Dad's face creases into a broad smile when he sees his grandchildren. 'Come 'ere, me loves!'

It's hard to unbuckle them with all the wriggling. They're in Dad's lap as fast as their little legs will carry them across the lounge floor. 'There's me angels,' he murmurs as he kisses the tops of their heads.

'Hah, you should have seen them at breakfast.'

'They're angels to me.'

He means it too. I don't know what happened to the strict father I had to deal with growing up. He's turned into a giant marshmallow of a man. 'How come you never spoiled me like that?'

'I would have if you'd smelled like biscuits,' he says.

'That's not what they smelled like an hour ago.'

You'd have thought Mum and Dad had won the lottery when I asked if they'd look after the twins for a few hours a day till I can get the café ready to open. Mum had the whole house baby-proofed, including Dad. She saw her chance with his chair, reciting a litany of childhood diseases that might lurk in its nubbly striped fabric. But Dad offered to get it cleaned and she hasn't thought up a way around that. If she ever does manage to get rid of it, I just know Dad's going to go too.

He glances up. 'How are you, love?'

'Okay. Just tired, Dad.'

'She's burning the candle at both ends,' Auntie Rose says. 'It's too much, if you ask me. Not that anybody ever does.'

Auntie Rose likes to say that, but she knows how important she is in our family. We joke that that's why we keep her under lock and key. It's not really the reason. It's just nice to have a laugh about it with her. Otherwise it's a bit sad. 'You're right, Auntie Rose, but I can't stop now. Besides, it's not for much longer. Mum and I are stripping the tables and chairs today. We're nearly there.'

'You'll be just as busy after the café opens, you know,'

Mum reminds me as she goes to tidy up around Dad's chair. She never sits still for long. 'You keep talking like it's all going to calm down suddenly. I just hope it's not too much.'

Of course it's too much, but Mum knows what it means to me to open this café. I didn't spend five years getting my degree not to use it just because my uterus decided it suddenly wanted to play host to a couple of embryos. There's a lot at stake. Not least of which is the wodge of my in-laws' money that's going into the business.

Being as rich as they are, they invest in all sorts of things, though Daniel doesn't like to rely on them. We didn't even accept help from them for our wedding. But that's another story.

When they offered to loan me the money for the café officially, there was a lot of discussion about it before Daniel and I agreed. I thought it would be better to borrow money from family instead of an impersonal bank. Now I'm not so sure.

They're not putting pressure on me or anything. I'd feel better if they did. But every time I promise to pay them back, Philippa waves me away with a cheerful 'Don't worry about that', like they've already kissed their investment goodbye. Sometimes I think I should have risked the bad credit rating with the bank manager. At least I wouldn't have to spend every holiday at *his* house worrying that he thinks I'll never come good on the business.

I know I can do this. I'll have to, won't I? A year ago I wouldn't have thought I could handle having twins and look at me now. Frazzled, exhausted and barely managing, but I haven't screwed them up too badly yet.

When we hear the knock at the door, Auntie Rose says, 'That'll be Doreen.'

Mum opens it with the key from around her neck. I wasn't kidding about the lockdown around here.

'Where are the babies?!' Doreen exclaims, not waiting for an invitation inside. ''Ere, for elevenses.' She hands Mum a carrier bag full of biscuits. 'They were on special, two-for-one. Ha, like these two!'

Doreen is one of Auntie Rose's lifelong best friends. She smokes like a wet log fire and there are questions over exactly what happened when her husband disappeared back in the eighties, but beneath her over-tanned cleavage and lumpy wrap dresses there beats the heart of an angel. Just don't cross her or try cheating at cribbage.

There used to be four of them, till my gran died eight or nine years ago. She was Auntie Rose's sister. Now it's Auntie Rose, Doreen and June, whose husband hasn't disappeared, so she mostly does her visiting with everyone in the evenings at the pub.

Both twins scramble off Dad's lap to see what Doreen's got to offer. Oscar doesn't come empty-handed, though. Shyly, he holds his stuffed duck out for Doreen's inspection.

'He's just like you, Emma,' Auntie Rose says.

'Not Grace too?' I say, though I'm just fishing for compliments. Greedy me, wanting credit for all the best traits of my children. But Grace has Daniel's outgoing nature.

'Nah, she's a tearaway like your mother. It skipped a generation.'

Mum ignores my questioning smile. I love when Auntie Rose lets slip about Mum's younger days. When I was a child it gave me useful ammunition against her rules. Now I'm just curious to know more about my parents.

Auntie Rose gathers Grace up onto her ample lap while Doreen settles next to her with Oscar, and Dad tries not to look too jealous that they've got his grandchildren. 'Off you go now,' Auntie Rose says to Mum and me. 'That café ain't opening itself. We'll look after the wee ones.'

'Okay, but we'll be back at lunchtime,' I say as Mum hands me a bag full of paint stripper and brushes. 'I've got my phone if you need me. Mum does too.'

Mum manages to get me into the car after I kiss my babies about a hundred times and remind everyone about the nappies, bottles, extra clothes, extra nappies and the bottles again.

'It's only for a few hours, Emma,' Mum reminds me on the short drive back to Carlton Square.

'You were probably just as bad when you had to leave me.'

'I couldn't get away fast enough,' she says, smirking into the windscreen.

'Liar. I remember Gran telling you off for being a hover mother.' My gran was cut from the same no-nonsense cloth as Auntie Rose and my mum.

'Oh, she was a great one for repeating whatever she read in the *Daily Mail*,' Mum says, still smiling.

'The skip's arrived,' she notes as she carefully manoeuvres the car into the free spot just behind it. 'Let's take up those carpets before we do the furniture.'

Chapter 2

The café isn't much of a café yet, but it's perfect in my imagination. In reality it's still just the old pub that sits across the square from our house. It did have a brief life as a café before I took it over, but the owners never really got rid of its pubness. That's a blessing and a curse.

The waft of stale beer hits me as usual when I unlock the double doors at the front, though it looks better than it smells. There's a big wraparound bar at the back and shiny cream and green tiles running waist-high along all the walls. It's even got two of those old gold-lettered mirrored advertisements for whisky set into the walls at the side of the bar. When we first came to see inside, Mum climbed up the ladder to inspect the ceiling. It's pressed tin, though like the rest of the place, stained by about a hundred years of tobacco smoke.

She throws a pair of work gloves and a face mask at me.

'Put your back into it. Start in a corner where it's easier to get it up.'

That's easy for her to say when she's got muscles on top of muscles from all her cleaning jobs. She can even lift Dad when she needs to. Luckily that's not too often these days.

The carpet pulls away – in some places in shreds – setting loose a cloud of God-knows-what into the air. 'Open the windows, Mum!' I shout through the mask.

When the dust settles, there's no beautifully preserved Victorian parquet floor underneath. This isn't one of those BBC makeover programmes where gorgeous George Clarke congratulates us on our period features.

The floor is made up of rough old unfinished planks.

'That's even uglier than the carpet,' I tell Mum when she comes over for a look. 'We can't afford a whole new floor.' Even if we had the extra money, there's no way I'd hand that capital improvement to the council, who owns the lease.

'Let's have a think about this,' she says, leading me to one of the booths by the open window where, hopefully, the slight breeze is clearing away whatever was in that carpet.

The booths are as knackered as the rest of the pub, but at least they're wooden so they won't need re-covering. Unlike all the chairs piled in a heap upstairs. I don't even like to think about what's stained their fabric seats over the decades.

Suddenly Mum reaches into my hair. 'Hold still, you've got something– It's a bit of ... I don't know what it is.' Then she squints at my head. 'Is that a grey hair?'

My hand flies to my head. 'NO! It can't be.' I'm only twenty-seven.

'It's only because your hair is so dark that I noticed it. I started getting them at your age. Don't worry, it's only one ...' She reaches for my head again. 'Or two. 'Ere, I'll get them.'

'Ow, don't pull them out! You'll make more.'

'That's an old wives' tale. Let me just get—'

'Get off me!'

As I twist my head away from my mother's snatching fingers, I look out the window and straight into two strange faces. They look about as old as God and his secretary and as surprised to see us as I am to see them.

'Oh! Excuse us,' says the man. 'We thought we saw someone inside ...' He grasps the woman's hand. 'We're terribly sorry to disturb you.'

'No, no, don't be sorry,' calls my mum through the window. 'We're renovating the pub.'

The man hesitates. 'It's been decades since we've been inside.'

'It smells like it,' I murmur, then realise how rude that sounds. 'Since it's been open, I mean.'

'Would you like to come in?' Mum asks. 'You're very welcome.'

'We shouldn't bother you,' says the woman, but I can see that she's dying for a snoop.

'It's no bother, really, come in. Just a sec, I'll open the door.'

They're even older than they looked outside, but they come nimbly through the door like they own the place. They're both wearing long dark wool coats against the February cold snap.

'I always hated that carpet,' says the woman, seeing the pile I've made in the corner. 'It stank to high heaven. But then so did a lot of the men who drank 'ere.'

'Present company excepted.' The man removes his flat cap and bows, showing me the top of his balding, age-spotted head. 'Carl Brumfeld. Pleased to meet you. And this 'ere's Elsie.'

Their accents are as local to East London as my family's is. After I make introductions, Elsie asks, 'Are you the new land-lord?' Her face is nearly unlined, but her hair is snowy white, spun into an intricate sort of beehive on top of her head. Auntie Rose would say she'd look younger with it coloured, but she says that about everyone because she does hair.

'It's going to be a café,' Mum tells them. As she relays this, her pride even tops her bragging about me going to Uni. And that was monumental.

'Oh,' they chorus. 'That's a shame,' Carl says. 'We were hoping to get the old place back. This is where we met, you see.'

'When was that?' I ask. Just after the dawn of time, I'm guessing.

'Nineteen forty-one,' says Elsie. 'We were children during the war. We used to sit together in that booth right there.'

'Wow, seventy-five years.' Mum whistles. 'What's that in anniversaries? Diamond is sixty. Of course you couldn't have been married so young!'

'We're not married now either,' Carl says.

'Carl is my brother-in-law,' Elsie adds.

Which does make me wonder why they're holding hands. 'You'll come back when we're open, won't you?' I ask. 'Maybe you'd like to sit in your old booth for a cup of tea.'

Where I'll be able to winkle their story out of them. A café is the perfect business for a nosey person like me to run.

'We'd like that, thank you,' Carl says. 'You're keeping the booths, then? It would be nice for someone to take account of history around 'ere instead of tearing everything down to build flats.'

'The booths are staying,' I assure them.

Carl's words stay with me after they leave. It would be a shame to strip the pub of its history if we don't have to. Except for the carpet. The history of spilled pints and trodden-on fag ends will have to go.

'Daniel's out tonight,' I tell Mum as we pull up the rest of the carpet together. Despite my promise to myself, the words are out before I can stop them.

She halts her ripping to glance at me. Her gingery bob has come loose from its hair tie and she keeps swiping it back behind her ears. She is pretty, though she doesn't usually wear much make-up. Only when she's doing things like trying to impress Daniel's parents. Then she goes for full-on slap, even though my mother-in-law doesn't bother with it herself.

'And you hate him a bit, right?' she asks.

Instinctively I want to deny it, even though I've just brought it up. 'I'm trying not to, Mum, and I know you're going to tell me I shouldn't.'

But Mum shakes her head. 'I was going to say that I understand. After you were born, when your father got to go out in his taxi every day, I wanted to puncture his tyres. I wanted to puncture *him* sometimes. He used to complain about how hard it was driving around all day. I would have bloody loved to trade places. Believe me, you 'aven't got the monopoly on resentment.'

Resentment. Is that what I've got? 'It's just so hard,' I say.

'I know, love, but it gets easier when they're in school.'

'Nursery?'

'University,' she deadpans.

I guess I shouldn't be surprised that Mum understands. She and Dad didn't wait long after their wedding to have me either. Everyone keeps telling us how lucky we are to be young parents. We've got more energy, they say. We'll still be youngish when the children are grown. But what about the decades in between? At the moment, it looks like a long time between now and then.

Mum gathers me into a carpet-dust-filled hug. 'It's always harder than you think it's going to be. Thank goodness I had your Gran and Auntie Rose. Your Granny Liddell was no help.'

'Thank goodness I've got you and Dad and Auntie Rose now,' I say.

Mum nods. 'Your Dad's a dark horse, isn't he? He's so much better with the twins than he ever was with you. He's got more confidence now than he did then. He was terrified of making a mistake with you.'

'Weren't you terrified?' I'm constantly worried that I'm

doing it all wrong or that I'll damage the twins somehow. I could be feeding them too much, or not enough, leaving them to get too hot or too cold, smothering them with cuddles or not paying them enough attention, pushing them to learn new things or being too laid back, letting their faces get too dirty or wiping them so much that they'll end up with allergies. They might be underdressed or over-stimulated, under-cuddled, over-coddled, disgruntled or disappointed. Just off the top of my head. I could give you another ten lists like that every single day.

'Of course I was afraid to mess up,' Mum says, 'but I didn't have a choice. You had to eat and be held and changed. If I didn't do it, who would?'

That's exactly how I feel. It's not that Daniel can't do it too. He's just not as good at it as I am. And lately he's seemed to leave more and more to me while he gets on with his life.

I always seem to have toddlers hanging off me when I try getting on with my life. Just try being glamorous with ladies who lunch when you're saying, 'Get that out of your mouth,' every two minutes.

Not that I've ever been glamorous. And my friends aren't ladies who lunch, but you see my point.

Today it's my turn to host everyone at the house, so

despite having had to shove most of the toys under the sofa and the unfolded laundry into the closet, I've got the easy part. Just try going anywhere with the twins. Trying to move a circus is less challenging.

'Maybe if they didn't act like they'd invented nuclear fusion every time they changed a nappy, I wouldn't mind so much,' my friend Melody says, talking about husbands as she shifts her child to her other breast. Speaking of having children hanging off you.

Melody and Samantha, Emerald and Garnet – four women who at first had no more in common with me than leaky boobs and sleepless nights – are the reason I'm holding on to my sanity. But when your world has shrunk to leaky boobs and sleepless nights, that can be enough.

We're covering our usual ground – what we've done since we saw each other last week and who's aggrieved about what – and, also as usual, I've got to keep my eyes glued to Melody's face and away from her feeding daughter. Not because breastfeeding embarrasses me. Not at all. When I was breastfeeding my boobs came out anywhere the twins needed to feed, and we're only in my house anyway. When they legislate against boys wearing their jeans so low that you can see their bollocks from the back, I'll agree that we should be hiding feeding babies under tea towels and table-cloths to protect the public's sensibilities.

It would be perfectly normal for Melody to feed her toddler, Joy. Which she does. She just happens to also like to feed her five-year-old, who's not even sitting in her mother's lap. She's got her own chair. Her feet nearly touch the floor.

'Because it's such a huge favour to care for his own child,' Samantha throws in.

I'm not the only one who thinks that nearly school-age children really ought to be drinking milk from cups. Samantha doesn't bother trying to hide her eye roll. Melody doesn't bother pretending to ignore it. Samantha won't say anything with Melody's daughter here, though. She may be one of the toughest women I've ever met, but she's never cruel.

'Well, that's not really fair,' Emerald points out, brushing a non-existent speck of something from her pristine top. Not that a crumb could have come from any of the food on the table. She never eats the buttery croissants or packets of biscuits that the rest of us scoff. 'The men do work all day.'

I wince at her terrible choice of words. What is it that we're doing all day – and night – if not working? But Garnet, Emerald's sister, nods, adding, 'My Michael works late into the night sometimes.'

'Boo hoo,' Samantha bites back.

'Not to mention weekends.' Emerald ignores Samantha's dig at her sister. 'Anthony's a workhorse too.'

When Emerald and Garnet sit beside each other they look like someone has taken the same drawing and just coloured them in differently. Their eyes are almond shaped and they have identical long slender noses, angular faces and full lips. But Garnet's got nearly black eyes and her thick straight shoulder-length hair is cut in a heavy blunt fringe and coloured a russet red. Emerald has the same haircut but her colour is even darker than mine – almost a true black – and her eyes are nearly black too. It's very striking against her pale skin.

'Poor Michael has even had to cancel holidays,' says Garnet.

Melody covers her daughter's ears when she catches the look on Samantha's face. Samantha doesn't disappoint. 'Oh, for fuck's sake, at least they get holidays,' she replies. 'Not to mention sick days and bonuses and at least some bloody idea about all the hours they'll have to work. I'd trade places in a heartbeat. They're not sitting around with their friends feeling sorry for us, are they?'

When I first met Samantha in antenatal class I mistook her abruptness for rudeness, but she's just very honest and efficient. She used to be a high-powered consultant before having her first child and she never really lost the drive. It was her job to go into companies and restructure them (efficiently, of course). Now she hasn't got anywhere for all that energy to go so she channels it into everyday life and her marathon yoga sessions. The rest of us might dress to camouflage the baby tummies we haven't quite lost yet. Samantha's got thighs that could crack walnuts.

Naturally, it gets Samantha's back up when Garnet and Emerald try excusing their husbands, which happens a lot.

It's not just Samantha's lack of employment that frustrates her. It doesn't sound like her husband appreciates her thighs, walnut-cracking or not, any more than all the work she does. Like I said, she channels a lot into yoga.

And Garnet and Emerald are very nice women once you get used to their rivalry. They only ever turn it on each other and have a long-running disagreement over which precious stone their parents think is more precious. That sums them up, really.

Not only were their first babies due within days of each other, but their husbands work for the same bank and their houses are one road away from one another. Both think theirs is the better neighbourhood. And the better husband.

Garnet was over-the-top smug about getting to the finishing line first in the maternity ward, pushing out her ten-pound daughter a day and a half before Emerald. But Emerald had the better time when her son was born in under six hours, and they've been competitively parenting ever since.

The sisters are closest in age to me, twenty-seven and twenty-eight, and both think they're the perfect age. Samantha is in her mid-thirties and Melody's age is anyone's guess, so of course we all do. I think she's well over forty because of her long frizzy brown and grey hair, but since I've got a few greys too (thanks to Mum for pointing those out), maybe she is younger.

'It will be all right, you know,' Melody says, fixing me with her pale blue, wide-set eyes. Combined with a longish face and big-toothed smile, they make her look a bit like a goat. I don't mean that in an insulting way. It's just so you can picture her. Because her hair is salt-and-pepper, though, instead of goat-coloured, the resemblance ends there.

Melody is even more of a tree-hugging yogurt-knitter than I thought when we first met, the kind of person who makes her own baby food and sews up holes in socks even though there's usually an uncomfortable lump in your shoe after, instead of just buying another pack of twenty for a fiver.

You won't be surprised to know that she gave birth to her daughter in an inflatable paddling pool in her lounge, with the sound of wind chimes and whale noises for pain

31

relief. All her friends were there to see it and it sounds like it was a bit of a party between contractions. She claims it was the most magical three days of her life, especially when her then four-year-old cut the umbilical cord and her husband made an afterbirth smoothie for Melody. I imagine the other guests stuck to the hummus and kale chips.

I wouldn't have been much of a hostess at my own birth party. I cried through most of my labour because, holy hell, it hurt. Daniel did too, come to think of it, in solidarity and helplessness at seeing me. We were basically that nightmare couple in labour for the first time. But anyone who tells you it's not that bad is either lying or has had their memory erased by those post-birth hormones.

'I hate to be the one to break this up,' Samantha says, 'but I've got to pick up Dougie. It's been fun as always. Same time next week at my house?'

She doesn't need to ask because I wouldn't miss these get-togethers even if I ended up in hospital with appendicitis. I'd crawl on all fours with tubes hanging off me and a packet of biscuits clenched in my teeth. And to think that when I first had the babies I thought I didn't need the mums I'd met in antenatal class. Naïve, deluded Emma.

'Thanks for coming,' I say. 'Sorry we were out of milk.'

Everyone starts to shift as Samantha perfects her lipstick without looking and pulls out her hairbrush to give her chestnut tresses a swipe. Which reminds me that I forgot to brush mine this morning. At least I cleaned my teeth. I'm a winner.

'We should be going too,' Garnet says to her sister.

Their toddlers are already in day care, though that's not what they call it. 'It's pre-Montessori, like Eton is a feeder for Oxbridge,' they explain.

'I bet you'll be excited to start school in the autumn, Eva,' I tell Melody's five-year-old, who is busy drawing orange trees on her sketch pad. She's got her mum's clear blue eyes and long face.

'I can't wait for school!' Eva says, but Melody looks troubled. I'm not sure what she'll do then. Will she turn up at snack time in her nursing bra?

Chapter 3

Talk about putting the cart before the horse. Or the staff before the café, in this case. My glance falls on the stack of boxes leaning precariously beside the bar. One more thing to put away. It looks messy, unfinished and unprofessional. Ditto the half-painted walls, filthy window glass and stripped but yet-to-be refinished tables and chairs. It looks like a building site.

It *is* a building site. But in four weeks it needs to be a welcoming café. With staff.

So far none of this has seemed altogether real, despite the loan from Daniel's parents or the official two-year extendable lease from the council. Just paperwork, I've convinced myself. If it all goes pear-shaped for some reason, I can always find a way to pay my in-laws back and cancel the lease. No real harm done to anyone but me.

Until now. As soon as I put teenagers into the training

positions they'll be depending on me for the job. And they deserve the chance to do something that could give them a leg-up in life. Lots of charities do after-school programmes and run youth centres and activity groups, not to mention everyone campaigning to get more funding. But training programmes are harder to come by.

I never imagined I'd set one up myself, yet here I am fidgeting over a stack of CVs and notes from Social Services, checking the door every two seconds for my first interviewee.

The lady at the council who has been helping me was uncomfortably vague about the applicants' details. I know they've all had reason to catch the attention of the authorities, which is why they're being put forward as potential trainees. But when I asked her what they'd done – just to know whether I'd be dealing with someone who's run red lights or run drugs – she went tight-lipped. And she wasn't exactly chatting like my BFF to begin with.

'We can't disclose any details about the cases,' she'd said, rapidly clicking the top of her pen. 'I'm sure you understand.'

I nodded like I did. 'When you say *cases*, do you mean their Social Services cases? Or their court cases?'

'Both,' she said. 'Either.'

'Uh-huh, I see. Would those be criminal cases or civil ones?'

She just stared at me over her reading glasses. 'Everyone we're referring has needed intervention by Social Services, and in each situation we feel that the opportunity to work, to get training, will benefit them.'

I felt like such a dick then. Here was this lady, working with troubled kids every day, probably for little pay and little thanks, and I was swanning in sounding like I only wanted the cream off the top of the barrel. 'Yes, of course, of course, that's why I'm here,' I said as my face reddened. 'To offer them that chance.' I took home every one of the files she'd prepared for me to consider.

Just the bare bones information I've got is enough to break your heart. A catalogue of foster care, school disruption and instability. I wanted to hire them all, so how was I supposed to choose between them to make a shortlist? I'm not exactly opening Starbucks nationwide. I've only got room, and money, for two trainees at a time.

I'm not looking for the *best* candidates, per se, like you would for a regular job. I'm looking for the ones who most need the help, and the ones who most want it. It's like going into a bakery and asking which cakes taste okay. No, no fancy decoration or mouth-watering icing. Someone else will gladly have those. I'll take the ones that are irregularly shaped or might have fallen on the floor, please. They're still perfectly good, just not as obviously appealing as the perfect ones.

A hulking form suddenly blocks most of the light from the open doorway. 'Yo. This for the interview?' his deep voice booms.

'Yes, in here. You must be Martin. Hi.'

He doesn't look like a Martin. He walks in with a sort of half-skip, half-lumber, as if he's got a bad limp on one side. 'Yo, I'm Ice,' he says, putting his fist in front of me for a bump. I must not do it right because he sucks his teeth at me. The kids are always doing this to me – when I don't get out of the way fast enough at the Tube station, or dither over the bowls of fruit at the market or hold up the queue in the local Tesco. Basically, whenever they judge me hopeless, which is a lot. 'Wagwan?' he asks.

He means what's going on. 'Well, we're renovating the café to get it ready for the opening, as you can see!'

He looks around as I look at him. His file says he's fifteen, and his face looks babyish, but he's huge, man-size. There's a thick metal chain snaking into the front pocket of his jeans, which are so low they're nearly around his knees, and his mini Afro looks too old for his spot-prone brown face.

I know he's trying to be intimidating, but it's so clearly bravado that I just want to say '*Aww*!' and pinch his babyish cheeks. Though he might break my arm if I did.

He keeps looking around as I explain about the six-month training scheme and what would be expected of him. Eventually he says, 'Why you making it a café, not a pub? It'd be banging working in a pub.'

'Aren't you a minor? You can't work in a pub.'

He sucks his teeth again. 'True dat.'

'Maybe you could tell me why you'd like to work here?' He shrugs his answer. 'Can you think of *any* reason you'd like to work here?'

'It pays, yeah?'

'Right, yes. Any reason beyond the money?' Though at trainee rates he wouldn't really need that chain on his wallet.

'Nah, man, my social worker say I got to come.' He pulls a crumpled paper from his non-chained pocket. 'She said sign this.'

I take the short, photocopied statement from him and add my signature to the bottom.

Ice snatches it off the table and leaves without a backward glance.

By mid-morning my hand is starting to cramp from signing so many attendance forms. Some of the kids bother to sit down and a few even humour me by answering a question or two. Others turn up with their paper already in hand, waving it for a signature.

I'm in so far over my head that I should be in a submersible. I may have grown up in a tough part of London and be on first-name terms with PC Billy Bramble. I may have seen the fights break out down the market when the gangs kick off. But I've never lived that life myself. I like to think I'm street. I'm really just street-light.

Take the kid who rumbled me for gawping at the purplish blood droplet tattooed on his arm. It had a triangle above it, like a gang symbol. 'You starin' at my tatt?' he'd said.

I could feel my face go red. 'Erm, sorry, I was just interested. Is it supposed to be blood, or a gang sign of some kind?' I couldn't sound more lame.

'Teletubby,' he said.

I'd never heard of them. The Teletubby Massive? I didn't want any gang members in my crew.

He pointed to the red blotch beside the drop. 'Tinky Winky.'

'You mean it's an actual Teletubby?!' I tried to bite down my smile.

'Joker blud did it to me.' He shrugged. 'I wanted a stopwatch.'

Just as I was starting to wonder if this boy with a children's character on his arm might be worth another look, I asked him why he wanted to do the training programme.

'Everybody likes coffee, yeah? I can drink that shit all day.'

'Well, yes, but you'd actually be working, not drinking coffee. And hopefully it won't be shit.'

'I can slip it to my bluds though, yeah?'

He really thought I'd pay him to hand out free coffee to his mates all day.

'I can let you know by next week, okay?' I said, scribbling my signature on his form.

Mum and Dad would have cuffed him on the side of the head for answers like that. I can hear Dad now. *Lazy sod.* My parents were working by the time they were teens, and not just making their beds for pocket money, either. Mum cycled all over London to pick up and drop off clothes for my gran's tailoring customers. 'Join a Union if you don't like the deal,' Gran used to say of the sweatshop wages she paid her daughter, but she bought Mum off by letting her keep any tips. Mum was slightly easier on me, and she'd never let me cycle across the city. She often took me with her to help when she cleaned houses, though. There was less risk to life and limb but the wages were still crap.

On his way out, my latest applicant passes a boy just coming in. 'Yo, Tinky Winky, 'sup?' says the boy.

'Fuck off, dweeb.'

'That's Professor to you,' he says.

I watch this brief exchange with interest. Not because the new boy, with his tall lanky frame, looks as if his brain has no idea what his arms and legs are doing, or that he doesn't seem frightened by his tattooed rival. His close-cropped wavy black hair and mixed-race complexion don't differentiate him from most of the other kids.

It's his three-piece suit and the fatly knotted blue tie round his skinny neck.

And his briefcase, which he sets on the table between us.

'I'm Joseph.' He sticks his hand out for me to shake. His long-lashed brown eyes are the first to look directly at me all morning. 'It's your lucky day,' he says. 'You can cancel the other punters, because you've found your future employee.'

'Well, I hope I have, but I'll still need to ask you some questions, okay?' Who told him to be so cocky in an interview? I glance at his file. Lives with his mum and older brother, who seems to be mixed up with one of the local gangs. 'You're seventeen?'

'Yeah, but don't let that fool you. I can do anything you can, and I'm really *good.*'

His suggestion is unmistakable.

That won't do him any favours and the sooner he realises it, the better. Just to prove the point, I ask him if he can drive. No? What about buying alcohol legally? Are you registered to vote? No again? 'Then you can't quite do anything I can,' I say, 'so let's stick to the interview, okay? Why would you like to do this training?'

There's a scattering of hairs on his face where he's been trying to shave, and his suit sleeves cover his knuckles. I bet he's borrowed it from his big brother. He might have borrowed the razor too.

Joseph clears his throat. That doesn't stop his voice from cracking. 'I see the position as a stepping stone for my future as a CEO.'

'A CEO … here?' We both look around the pub. 'That's not really the position I'm recruiting for.' Unless CEO stands for Chief Egg-on-toast Officer.

'Well, then, what *are* you going to do for my career progression?'

'It's a six-month traineeship, so you'll learn all aspects of working in a café. Working with colleagues, serving customers, making coffee and tea …' I sort of run out of steam. It's just a café, not Microsoft.

He sits forward in his chair. 'Sales and marketing?'

I thought I might put up a few posters around the bus stops. 'Sure.'

'How 'bout customer complaint resolution?'

'I expect so. Tell me, Joseph, what would you like to be a CEO of?'

'A company with good benefits,' he says right away.

'Any particular kind?'

'Definitely stock options. And a gold-plated pension.'

'No, I mean any particular kind of company?'

'I'd be happy at Apple. Or Xbox.'

I like that he's dreaming big. My most ambitious goal at his age was getting a real pair of Dr. Martens. 'Well, maybe you'll get there. It would have been easier if you'd stayed in school, you know.' He finished secondary school but doesn't want to go on for college.

'I like to think of myself as a student of life,' he says. 'Steve Jobs dropped out. So did Bill Gates and Mark Zuckerberg, and they all became CEOs.'

'Mark Zuckerberg dropped out of Harvard,' I point out. 'If you get into Harvard, then you can feel free to drop out.'

'That's what my mum said.'

'I think I'd like your mum.'

Who can blame Joseph for not wanting to be in school? Not everyone is a swot like I was. I only left at sixteen because I needed to help Mum and Dad with the bills. And I went back to graduate from Uni.

If it hadn't been for the twins' unplanned arrival scuppering the job plans I had after university, I'd be the one on the other side of the interview table now, trying to get a charity to hire me and probably sounding as naïve as Joseph does.

There but for the grace of god, and my in-laws...

Joseph's heart seems to be in the right place, underneath the cocksure attitude. He needs a lot of help with his interview technique and he'll have to learn that people aren't just going to hand him a job as CEO because he asks for it.

He might not know a teabag from a tea towel, for all I know, but that's the point, isn't it? If he can already do the job, then he doesn't need the training.

'You've got the job if you want it,' I tell him. 'Congratulations. We'll open in four weeks.'

His face splits into a beaming grin. 'Yeah, that's well good! Are you for reals?'

'I'm for reals. You'll need to come in for training and stuff before the opening.' I consider my very first employee. My employee! 'Can I ask you a question before you go? Your briefcase. You didn't open it. What's in there?'

Joseph takes a second to answer. 'My lunch. Mum packed it for me.'

And just like that, the CEO-in-the-making becomes young Joseph again.

I've just finished putting away all the boxes piled near the bar when Dad turns up with Auntie Rose wheeling the babies in the pushchair. 'I'm glad the ramp works!' I shout to them as they come through the door. We just had it installed last week and it's only about three inches high, but it means Dad can come through in his wheelchair without having to pop a wheelie.

'I've actually hired someone!' I tell them.

'Wayhey!' Dad whoops, meeting me halfway for a hug. 'You're on your way now, me girl. Mind the wheels. This deserves a proper stand-up job.' Slowly he lifts himself from his wheelchair so I can throw my arms around him.

The twins stop their babbling to stare. They're not used to seeing my dad standing, and especially not without the crutches he uses to walk. 'Look at them,' I say. 'Astounded.'

'It's a bloomin' miracle, me angels.'

What a difference a generation makes. When Dad first came down with the multiple sclerosis that keeps him mostly in the chair these days, I was fourteen and mortified at having a disabled family member.

Typical teenager, thinking about myself instead of Dad, whose whole life changed in a matter of months. He'd had tingles in his arms and legs for a while but assumed it was from driving round in his cab every day. He might not have said anything if his vision hadn't started going funny, and the disease had already taken hold by the time he got the diagnosis. He stayed out of the wheelchair for a few more years – a few more years than he should have, really, but he's stubborn like that. Now he uses it most of the time, and it's completely normal for Oscar and Grace.

He sits down again. 'Let 'em loose, Rose. Emma, love, Kelly's right behind us with fish and chips.'

His announcement makes my mouth start watering. It's one of the advantages of having a fishmonger for a best friend. Kelly's worked a deal with the local chippy who fries up her leftover fillets sometimes. She throws the owners a few free portions of fresh fish to cook her tea for her, and they throw in the chips.

'Mum's gone to work?' I ask, reaching for my babies. I might have fantasies about child-free baths and cups of tea that I actually get to finish, but a few hours away from them starts the longing that pulls from my gut and makes me feel breathless.

That was a rhetorical question about Mum anyway. She cleans every weekday afternoon and evening. They're mostly commercial office contracts, with a few houses whose owners she liked enough to keep as clients over the years.

Just in case Daniel wants some fish too, I ring his mobile but it goes straight through to voicemail. He's probably in the Underground on his way home. I know Kelly. She'll have a portion for him when he gets here.

My best friend comes through the door, as usual, with

about as much grace as a tipper truck. Kelly's not a big woman. She just makes big entrances. That sometimes tricks people into assuming she's tough, so they're not always as considerate as they could be. A perfect example is when her family decided she should be the one to take over the fish van instead of her sisters. They just assumed she'd do it, like a sixteen-year-old would naturally want to give up any chance of living a life that's wider than her local market.

'I figured you needed this after dealing with the little bleeders all day,' she says, clearing one of the booths to make room for our meal.

Kell takes a different view than me of the hoodies who hang around the market where she works. I can understand why, when she sometimes gets caught up in their skirmishes. She'd like to fillet them and I'm trying to save them.

'I've hired one of the little bleeders,' I tell her. 'You should see him, Kell, he's adorable. He wants to be a CEO.'

'Just watch the till. Rose, I got you extra chips.'

'That's kind, but I really shouldn't,' Auntie Rose says, looking up from where her hand is already elbow-deep in the carrier bag. 'I'm watching me girlish figure.'

Auntie Rose pats her hip with her free hand as she chews on a chip. She's a generously proportioned lady, in stark contrast to her sister, my Gran, who was always skinny like

Mum. She's got the same smiling eyes and sharp mind, though. Except when she wanders.

That's why our doors are all locked from the inside and why we can't leave her alone anymore. For years, she's had little strokes that make her mind skip sometimes, which was okay when she stayed in the neighbourhood. But we had to take drastic measures after she turned up on the A12 with no idea how to get back home.

She's pretty relaxed about being incarcerated. She and Dad do everything together these days and she's as much a help to him as he is a minder for her. At least Mum doesn't have to worry about either of them when she's at work.

By the time we lock up the pub we're full of fish, salt and vinegar. Daniel's portion is soaking through the bag under the sleeping twins' pushchair. His phone keeps going straight to voicemail.

'Are you worried about him?' Kell asks, walking beside me.

'No, not worried,' I say, rubbing the phone in my pocket. 'More like disappointed. Don't get me wrong, Kell. I don't begrudge him having a night out. Lord knows, I wish I could do it any time I wanted too. It's just that, I feel like—'

'He's having his cake and eating it, the bastard,' she finishes for me. 'I'd be pissed off too.'

'Don't put words in my mouth, Kell. I didn't say pissed off. I said disappointed.'

'Really? Not pissed off when he gets to have these gorgeous children, the perfect family, plus you to look after it all while he goes out on the lash whenever he feels like it. Why does he get to be the only one? Shouldn't you get to do it too? I say hand the twins over to Daniel for a few hours and let him be the one to sit at home covered in sick, being jealous of you while you dance on the tables.'

'Kell, when have I ever in my life danced on a table?' She is right, though. He should be the responsible parent for once. At least for a few hours. 'You know what? I will.'

'Tomorrow. Do it tomorrow,' she says. 'We'll go out.'

'I can't tomorrow. I'm not sure what Daniel has on after work.'

'You mean like he didn't know what you had on tonight, yet just assumed you'd be there to look after the twins? Have I got that right?' Her stare challenges me to disagree.

'Fine, tomorrow night then. I'll tell Daniel.'

Chapter 4

Daniel was home by eight o'clock. Not out on the lash, just working late with a dead phone. But I've avoided Kelly's questions anyway. She's been too prickly about him lately. Besides, I'm supposed to be having fun tonight, not whinging about my marriage.

It's crowded as usual at the Cock and Crown, with Uncle Colin and Uncle Barbara pulling pints behind the bar. The vicar is tinkling sing-a-long show tunes on the piano and we've squeezed on to the end of a table where a couple around our age are either on their first date together or having a job interview. It's kind of hard to tell. So far there's no sign of a CV, but he just asked her where she thinks she'll be in a year.

'What's that for?' asks Kell.

'What's what for?'

'That sigh?'

'Oh, did I? Just happy to be here, I guess.'

The pub has been my home from home literally since I was born. Every picture, poster and random piece of football memorabilia on the walls is familiar, and I could sing most of the jukebox songs in my sleep. Like the green swirly carpet, they haven't been updated since the eighties.

Uncle Colin took over the business from old Fred nearly twenty years ago when he retired without an interested heir or successor. Colin had paid his dues behind the bar for years by then. The only consistent thing about Fred's managerial style was his bad mood. It seemed to be a trait he carried home too, judging by how few people turned up at his funeral, even with the free beer on offer.

Mum and Dad had their wedding party here. Uncle Barbara did too (before he started wearing dresses, when he was still Uncle Mark). And I used to fall asleep in Mum's arms transfixed by the blinking lights on the fruit machines.

This is exactly the kind of atmosphere I want the café to have – where people will feel a connection. They can stroll in with friends or on their own and always find someone for a conversation or at least a smile.

Not that most of the punters in here are what you'd call fans of the café culture. Somehow, I can't picture Uncle Colin or the vicar sipping skinny soy lattes from dainty cups. And the men downing pints along the bar probably won't trade their ales for Assam tea. But the atmosphere. That's what I want.

'Feckin' hell, will you watch it!' Kelly shouts at a shaven-headed man who's just jostled the pint in her hand.

Without the language, ideally.

'So, how's Daniel doing?' she asks.

I check my phone. 'Twelve minutes since the last text. I guess he figured out how to open the talc.' Just as I say it, my phone buzzes in my hand.

Sorry! Does it matter which twin gets which onesie? Dx

I sigh again. This time it's not from happiness.

They have their own clothes. Get one from each of their drawers. x

Which drawer is which? Dx

I turn my phone for Kell to read. 'Bloody hell,' she says, snatching it.

Figure it out and stop bloody texting, Daniel!

She presses send.

'He'll think that's from me.'

'Puhlease, when do you ever swear? You've got to put your phone away. It's up as loud as it can go. You'll hear it ring. Because you know it will,' she murmurs.

I tuck it into my bag. 'Is Calvin meeting us?'

I watch the bashful smile sweep across her face. A boyfriend has never had that effect on her before. No one would accuse Kell of being a romantic. Where I've always jumped head first into the deep end, she wades around with the water around her knees. Sometimes she doesn't even bother getting wet.

'Nah, it's just you and me tonight,' she says. 'I can see him any time I want. Who knows when I'll get you to myself again?'

'That's not fair, Kell. I see you almost every day.'

'Not like this, sans children, like the old days.'

She's right. We hardly ever get to talk now without the children. Which means we hardly ever finish a conversation. Sometimes we don't even get to start them. Dancing on tables. Hah! Falling asleep under them, more like. I'm yawning into my beer and it's not yet 9 p.m. It's not exactly like the old days, and don't think I don't miss them too. I can't remember the last time I felt like my normal self. I might look like any other twenty-something woman sitting in the pub with her best friend. I've even got make-up on and my top has no visible stains. But it's a façade. My head is back at our house worrying about whether Daniel will remember not to pull down the blinds all the way in the twins' bedroom or that Oscar sleeps with a blanket but Grace doesn't. I can't stop thinking about them. And Daniel's texts aren't helping.

When do mothers get to turn off their worry? Just give

me some kind of time frame, so I've got something to look forward to.

'Things are good between you and Calvin?' I ask, as if the smile hasn't already told me.

Calvin came like a bolt from the blue thanks to his gran, one of Kelly's most devoted customers at the fish van. He had moved from Manchester to live with her for a year, because she's not as steady on her feet as she used to be. He took one look at Kell – with her white coat smeared in fish guts and her no-nonsense ponytail tucked up under the dorky white fishmonger's hat her father makes her wear – and now he's most devoted to her too.

Kelly blushes, again out of character. She's never been a girly girl, and not only because she wears jeans all the time and doesn't usually bother with make-up. Being the youngest of four daughters, all a year apart, she didn't get the luxury of being the pampered baby of the family. There wasn't a big enough age difference to make her siblings feel like protecting her, or enough attention to go around. She had to hold her own early on, and that means she doesn't show her soft side to many people. I only get to see it because we've known each other all our lives.

'He's been really over-the-top lovely lately,' Kell says of Calvin. 'You know, flowers and surprise dinners and stuff. Now he's talking about meeting my parents.' She takes a big gulp of her pint. 'But if he meets them, then he'll have to meet my sisters too, because they're such twats like that. And you know they'll just take the piss out of me till they turn him off me.'

'No, they won't.' I'm just being nice. They totally will. 'You'll let them meet, won't you? You can't put it off forever.'

'Probably. I think he might be working up to a big question,' she says.

'YOU'RE KIDDING! Sorry, sorry. I just mean that that's fantastic. You're nuts about him. You mean *the* big question? You'd say yes, right?'

She laughs. 'I don't know! I haven't known him long.'

'Daniel and I were engaged in six months. You've known Calvin that long.'

'Nine, actually.'

'So you're counting. Is he still planning on Spain?' He postponed his job abroad to help his gran, but his sister is coming to take over sometime in the summer. Calvin's question might change his plans, though. If he's thinking marriage, then hopefully he's thinking of staying in London too.

My phone starts ringing before she can answer me. I snatch it out of my bag. 'Daniel, can't you leave me in peace for two minutes?!'

... Daniel's voice is far away. 'Say it, sweetheart, go on, like we said, remember?'

'Nigh', Mama,' comes Grace's little voice as Oscar giggles. *I'm a horrible mother.*

'I'll be home in twenty minutes,' I tell my husband, making a sorry face at Kell. At least we nearly got to finish our pints, if not our conversation.

I get home to find talc all over the bathroom floor and a knife on the side of the bathtub.

'I'll clean that up,' Daniel says. 'I was going to but then ... the twins. I don't know how you do it every day.'

'I don't have much choice.' I don't mean it to come out quite so snappy.

He pulls me into a hug, tipping my face up for a kiss. 'I suspected it before but now I'm sure: mothers are super-humans. You're doing an amazing job.'

This superhuman will need to pick up some more talc tomorrow. 'Did they go down okay after their book?'

'Book?'

He leads me by the hand into the lounge so we can cuddle on the settee. I throw my legs across his lap and he curls me into his arms. The blinds on the bay window are open to the old-fashioned streetlamp outside. It throws a gorgeous glow over us.

'Didn't you read to them?' I ask, feeling myself start to tense up. I'd better check that he's put the right clothes on them too.

'Oh, I did. I read them about a dozen books. They kept pointing to more. They're extortionists.'

'They're East Londoners, Daniel. They know a soft touch when they see one.' I yawn. 'Can you take the morning shift tomorrow? I'm exhausted and I'll have to do interviews all day.'

He nods. 'Of course, darling, I'm happy to, but do you think it might be time to talk again about getting a nanny? It would make things so much easier for you, especially now that they're mobile.'

Not this again. Just because his parents had cooks and maids and nannies doesn't mean that it's right for our family. Besides, not even Mary Poppins would work for free and the last time I checked, our bank account balance doesn't have many zeros on the end. It has, occasionally, had a minus at the start, though.

I swing my legs off his lap. 'I've told you, Daniel. I don't want to outsource our childcare. I'm just asking you to take the occasional morning. I don't think that's unreasonable.'

'Of course it's reasonable, Em, and I said I'm happy to. I loved having them to myself tonight. Don't misunderstand me, but isn't that still outsourcing, if I'm doing it instead of you? Next month I'll get my raise and then I think we can just about afford to get someone in for a few hours a day. So you could have help. I mean *proper* help.'

My blood might actually be starting to boil. 'How is it outsourcing to have you look after *our* children, Daniel? In case you've forgotten, the twins have two parents. Why shouldn't it be your job as much as mine? And the only reason I don't have proper help is because you're so ... Never mind, I'm tired. I'm going to bed. I'll put everything they'll need out on the table. Wake me by seven, please, if I'm not up.'

It's not that he doesn't try. He does. Then he thinks he's a contender for Father of the Year because he's changed a nappy. Meanwhile, I'm the mother every minute of every bloomin' day and I don't see anyone pinning a medal on me.

It wouldn't be so bad if I didn't feel like such an over-worked hamster on a wheel. The twins need me and there's no time off for good behaviour, or because Mummy might have a breakdown. My brain is mushier than the children's strained carrots and I need an oxygen tank to ascend the dirty laundry pile. They don't tell you that along with the high-inducing, all-consuming love comes work that just goes on and on.

* * *

The next morning, I wake with a drooly snort from a deep slumber. *That* hasn't happened since before I was pregnant.

Pregnant. The twins! But I can hear them babbling away downstairs, and Daniel's side of the bed's empty, so either they've kidnapped him or he's feeding them their breakfast.

Just two more minutes. I snuggle down into the bed. Daniel can call it outsourcing or whatever he wants to. This is bliss.

Until my phone starts ringing. 'Hi, Philippa.' My mother-in-law.

'Hellair, darling!' she says in her booming posh voice that makes everyone think she's really stuck up when actually she's just the opposite. 'I just had the most amahzing idea and I knew you'd be up already with the children.'

'Actually—'

'Picture this, darling: live birds for your café! You could have gorgeous little cages hanging everywhere. Right, I've already found an exotic bird handler who can get us anything we want.'

I picture the plants in our window boxes that I kill every few months. Those birds wouldn't stand a chance. 'That's an interesting idea, Philippa, but I'm not sure we should be using live birds as decorations.'

'Of course, darling, whatever you say. It's just an idea. I'll keep thinking, yah? Must dash. My masseuse is due any minute.'

These calls are my fault, really. I let her have her way with a baby shower for the twins and the live storks went to her head.

So much for a lie-in.

'Morning,' I call to my family on my way to the kitchen for a cup of tea. A cup of tea that I might be able to finish!

If I can find the kettle, that is. It looks like a bomb's gone off in here. There are eggshells and banana peels in the sink. Oats cover the worktop and the floor, every cabinet door is open and two of the pans are burnt on the hob. The remains of Daniel's bloomer lies mutilated on the cutting board and as I go to the fridge for milk, my left sock becomes soaked with ... I hope that's orange juice.

'Look, Mummy's up!' Daniel sings.

'Have we been under attack?' The twins are smeary with breakfast as usual.

'Hmm?' He aims a porridge-filled soup spoon at Oscar's mouth and mashes it into his cheek when he turns away. 'Sorry, darling.'

'The kitchen? How many people have you been trying to feed?'

'Right, yah, sorry, it's a mess, I know. I wasn't sure what they'd eat, so I tried to do a bit of everything.'

'I don't think he can get that ladle into his mouth.' I dig out the colourful spoons from the cutlery drawer, but Grace is happier with her hands plunged into her porridge bowl. 'Suit yourself,' I tell her. She burbles at me.

'Actually, now that you're up,' says Daniel with a mad look in his eye, 'could you take over for a minute? I need to, erm, badly ...'

'Ah, you've discovered that your bowels are not your own when you've got to look after children. Go ahead, I'll finish them up.'

I get a fleeting kiss before he disappears into the loo. 'Daddy needs a poo,' I tell our children.

But they're not interested in anything I've got to say. Oscar twists around to see where Daniel's gone, and Grace starts to whimper. 'What's the matter, babies? I'm here. It's okay.' But the more I cuddle them the more they squirm, till Daniel emerges from the bog. They crow at him with excitement.

'Aw, they're so sweet,' he says, kissing the twins' downy heads as they clamour for his attention. 'We've rahly had so much fun together.'

Sure, he's the main attraction at the circus for one night and suddenly I'm demoted to the one in the dungarees following behind the elephants with a shovel.

* * *

I'm feeling completely sorry for myself by the time I drop off the twins at Mum and Dad's house. It's the way they escape their pushchair to launch themselves on Dad, like they can't get away from me fast enough.

Mum notices, so I have to blame my grump on PMT. Then she points out that *of course* the twins are excited to climb into a wheelchair. It's the chair, not the person. Which just makes Dad feel bad too, so now we're both feeling like we don't measure up to the expectations of toddlers.

I guess Dad clocks my mood too, because just as I'm leaving he decides that he needs more Weetabix from the shop. 'Can you hang on to the children, love?' he asks Mum. 'I'll go up with Emma.'

Neither of us says anything as we leave the house.

'Give me a push, will you, love? My arms aren't awake yet.'

Now I know he wants to talk. He wouldn't let me push him otherwise.

We round the corner out of the estate on to the main road. It's noisy with morning traffic and people rushing to work.

'What time do you need to be at the café?' Dad asks. 'Let's go along the canal for a bit. The sun feels nice.'

I stare at the back of his head. Dad's not usually a nature-lover. And he's not a man for spontaneous chit-chat. Which means he has something important to say.

I just hope he's not sick again. It's been almost two years since his last MS relapse. I've been daring to think that the medicine is keeping it under control. I hope that hasn't tempted fate.

'Everything okay, Dad?' I finally ask when we've gone down the ramp to the canal towpath. Colourful narrowboats are moored along the path and the tang of woodsmoke fills the air. It's a pleasant smell, though. Dad's right, this is nicer than swallowing bus fumes on the main road. A lot quieter too.

'I'll ask you the same thing,' he says, twisting in his chair as I push him along. 'What's up, Emma? You can talk to me as much as your mum, you know.'

I let out the breath that I've been holding. It's not a relapse. 'I know.' He's got enough to worry about without having to take on my problems too. Though I can't tell him that. He hates being treated any differently because of his health. 'I'm finding it harder than I thought with the children. It's better with you and Mum and Auntie Rose helping, but it's still a lot to deal with.'

'You know it's okay to ask for more help,' he says gently.

'Thanks, Dad, but you're already doing so much. It'll settle down once the café is open and we get into a routine.'

He reaches over his shoulder to grasp my hand on the

wheelchair handle. 'Stop for a sec. I don't mean from us, love. I mean from Daniel. Is that the trouble?'

How does he know that? I'm sure Mum hasn't said anything. She doesn't like to burden him any more than I do. 'It's not been easy,' I finally say.

'Do you want me to 'ave a word with him?'

'Oh god, no!'

'Then maybe you should do it.'

'I know, Dad.' It's on my to-do list. 'I never seem to say the right thing, though.'

He laughs. 'That's a family trait you got from me. You'd better ask your mum for advice there.'

'You usually do okay.'

'Only because your mum's trained me. I'd be hopeless without her.' He starts pushing his wheelchair along the path. I guess his arms have woken up. 'We'd better go to the shop or your mum will start wondering what's happened to me.'

There's a girl waiting in front of the pub when I get there to open up. She's hunched into her black sweatshirt with the hood pulled up, her hands tucked deeply into the pockets.

'Louise?' I ask, even though I know it must be her. There've been mostly boys on my interview list. The only other two girls came yesterday. One popped her gum at me for five minutes straight and the other one grumbled about how much she disliked espresso machines. Not espresso itself, just the machines. Something about the steam being bad for her nail extensions.

Louise nods but doesn't say anything. She doesn't offer to shake my hand, but she does sit opposite me in the booth and look me in the eye. That automatically puts her above Tinky Winky and Ice Lolly from the other day.

'Don't you want to take your coat off? The heat in here's pretty intense with those old radiators.'

'Nah, I'm all right.' But she does pull her hood down.

Her hair's blue. Smooth, shiny, pale silvery blue. It doesn't quite go with her girl-next-door, slightly freckled face, though the stud in her nose toughens up the look.

Not as much as her body language does, though. It's so obvious that she doesn't want to be here. From her frown to the way her shoulders are squared up to me, she's ready for a fight.

I glance through her file to jog my memory. That's right. She's the girl in foster care. 'So why do you want to do this traineeship?'

She doesn't return my smile. 'I need the money,' she says, 'and I'm used to looking after people.'

'Have you worked in a café before? Or retail maybe?'

'No, I mean at home,' she snaps. 'It's me that does their meals and that.' Her eyes slide away towards the window. 'It's nothing official. I just do.' She crosses her arms.

'That's all right, real-life experience is great.' Somehow, I can't picture Louise serving customers. Shouting at them, maybe. Giving them the cold shoulder, for sure.

I look again at her file, although I don't need the notes. I know what I've got to ask. 'Erm, about the referral. It says you've had some trouble lately? That you were arrested? Do you want to expand on that at all?'

Her eyes challenge mine. 'Do I have to?'

'Oh, well, no, of course not. It's just in case you wanted to explain the ... the theft? The alleged theft?'

Did you do it?! I'm dying to ask. *What did you steal? Where on the morality scale is the crime? Was it a lipstick from Boots or the life savings of a pensioner? Should I be watching my handbag?*

'Next question?' she says.

I can't force her to tell me. Social Services was very clear about that. She doesn't seem like the kind of girl I could force to do anything. 'You're seventeen? But you're not in school?'

'No, I'm finished with all that. Last year. But I've got to be in work or training. I thought I'd try something that uses my great people skills.'

Her eyes widen just a tiny bit and I see the shadow of a smirk.

'They do seem impressive,' I say with a slight shrug. 'You'd put anyone at ease.'

She finally allows herself to smile. 'Look, I need to work. I need the money and the government says I have to. I'll do a good job if you'll let me. I just need the chance.'

Well, what's the point of the café if I don't give kids the chance when they need it? 'I'm sure you will.'

I extend my hand over the table. Warily she shakes it.

'You've got the traineeship. Congratulations, Louise.'

'Call me Lou,' she says, standing to go. 'I hate Louise.'

Daniel meets me at our front door. There's a giant bouquet of pink roses hiding his face.

'What's this for?'

'It's for you, because you deserve flowers and I love you,' he says, helping to wheel the pushchair inside. 'Doesn't she deserve flowers?' he asks Grace and Oscar, who seem to agree. 'Just because you're amahzing.'

I smile. 'You must still be feeling guilty about not answering your phone the other night. Do you want to put those in water?'

'I would have, but I could only find the washing up bowl under the sink. I can get the twins out for you, though. Do they need feeding?'

'No, Mum fed them before I picked them up.'

'Good. Then we can relax.'

It's like he's never been in this house before. 'Yeah, right.'

Oscar wants a cuddle while he recites every word he's ever heard in his very own language, and Grace starts pulling all the toys out of the box in the lounge to show us.

'Glass of wine, Mummy?' Daniel says above the increasing din as I sink into the sofa with Oscar on my lap.

As soon as Daniel sits next to me, Oscar decides he'd rather straddle both parents than choose just one.

'I found my other trainee today,' I tell him, keeping my wine glass well clear of the twin tornados. 'She's going to be tough, but I think she'll work hard. Yes, darling, that's a lovely bunny. She's not going to take any crap from anyone, though.'

'She'll have to take crap from you,' he says, nodding along to Oscar's monologue. 'You're the boss.'

I wonder how that's going to work. I'm not really the authoritative type. I'd rather have everyone like me.

He shifts to face me. 'I'm so proud of what you're doing, darling. This is rahly something special and you're going to make such a difference in people's lives. You do know you're remarkable, right? I'm very lucky to be married to you.'

'You too,' I say. I love when he says things like this. Daniel can make me feel like the most important person in the world.

I do get a little embarrassed sometimes, though. He's so eloquent with his feelings, and while my family's never been one of those stiff-upper-lip, sweep-things-under-the-carpet type of families, we're not overly emotional sharers either. I'm still getting used to hearing Daniel talk like this.

His hands cradle my face. 'I'm rahly proud.' His kisses veer from appreciative to deep and urgent. 'Rahly, so proud.'

I kiss him back. How long has it been, actually, since we've had sex? Too long, if I can't remember.

'Sir, calm yourself in front of the children,' I tease. 'There are impressionable minds in the room.'

'We're good role models for them,' he says. 'Mummy and Daddy love each other. Let's put them to bed so I can show you how much.'

Grace releases a noise that makes us both turn to our daughter. She's squatting, sumo-style. It's her favourite position when she really wants to cut loose.

Oscar points at his sister, as if we don't notice her filling her nappy.

'Do you want to flip a coin for it?' I ask.

'I did get flowers. And wine,' he says.

Patting his knee, gently I shift Oscar to his lap. 'I'll do it.'

As I lift Grace into my arms, Daniel says, 'I shouldn't be jealous of my own children, should I? That's not nice to admit.'

'It's just that they need me.'

'I need you too.'

That's pretty obvious from the way he's shifting around uncomfortably in his seat. 'Yes, but they need me to wipe their arses. It's a bit more urgent, don't you think?'

Does he think I like being at the beck and call of these mini tyrants? 'This isn't my first choice for entertainment either. We may as well get them into the bath,' I say, and the first spark of romance we've had in months goes out with a soapy wet fizzle.

'Romance? You are joking,' Melody says the next afternoon at Samantha's. 'With Eva and Joy sleeping with us?'

We're sitting on Samantha's pristine leather sofas in her minimalist white cube of a house. I've often wondered what these old warehouses looked like inside, but Samantha's isn't a good example since they wanted all the space but none of the original features.

'Just be glad he's trying,' Samantha says, reaching for another chocolate croissant as I pull Oscar onto my lap. 'What I wouldn't give for those days again.'

This is the only time we ever see Samantha vulnerable, though she tries to turn it all into a joke – how she once wore a net body stocking under her dress to dinner and ended up looking like she'd been sleeping on a bed of tennis rackets. Her husband had teased her so much about the all-over red diamond pattern that the moment totally vanished. None of us can understand what's wrong with him, especially since Samantha will try anything to get him to sleep with her. What's great for our weekly conversations isn't so great for our poor friend's self-esteem.

'Couldn't you have taken care of the children and then gone back downstairs to Daniel?' Emerald asks. 'I mean, as long as the oven was already pre-heated, so to speak.'

'That's what I would have done,' says Garnet. 'Though I don't have to worry too much about missed chances with Michael.' Her smile is filthy, just in case we don't get her meaning.

'I know what you mean,' Emerald counters. 'Sometimes I wish Anthony wasn't so romantic.' Always a gold standard humble-bragger, she is. 'But we've got to remember that this isn't about us, Garnet, it's about Emma. We know we're okay. Are *you* okay, Emma?'

'Yeah, sure, I'm fine,' I tell them. 'It was just disappointing, that's all.'

'Ha, welcome to my world,' Samantha says, reaching for another croissant that, along with her frustration, she'll work off later at yoga.

Chapter 5

What do you get when you cross a vain Italian with someone who's probably drunk coffee from his baby bottle? Hopefully someone who can teach us how to use an espresso machine. The gleaming Gaggia has been hogging up bar space ever since the catering company delivered it last week. So far I'm hiring a machine to mock me in my own café.

I sneak another glance at Pablo, but he's too busy gazing at his reflection in the advertising mirror beside the bar to notice. Flick, flick, his hand tweaks another lock of expertly gelled dark hair till he gets the exact quiff he's going for.

Before Pablo turned up this morning, I'd never seen a man who plucked his eyebrows. Or one with such flawless skin. He looks like he's been airbrushed.

I really don't mind that he's so much prettier than me, as long as he's as good at coffee as he is at grooming.

'About those coffee supplies we'll need,' I say. 'You will have everything delivered in time? Because we open in—'

'Do not worry,' he says, smoothing the front of his perfectly ironed shirt.

Wrong answer, Pablo. I do not worry if I'm sunning myself on holiday in the Med. I do worry when I need coffee to serve to my customers in less than three weeks.

'Okay, I won't worry ... But you will have everything delivered?'

'*Carina mia*, you should listen to the great Ravi Shankar. "Worry is the enemy of love."'

Yeah, well Ravi wasn't about to open his café without any coffee. 'I don't need to love coffee, Pablo, I just want to make sure it's delivered in time.'

His smile makes the *Mona Lisa* look like an open book.

'Well, anyway, Lou and Joseph should be here soon,' I tell him, checking my phone. 'Can I get you a cup of tea while we wait? Sorry there's no coffee. That's why you're here!'

'I am fine, thank you.' He runs his index fingers along his eyebrows, in case a hair has dared to move out of place.

'You probably don't drink tea,' I say.

'I am Italian.' He couldn't sound more insulted by my offer.

All right, steady on, Pablo, I'm only suggesting tea.

He goes back to staring at his reflection and I go back to panicking.

This sounded easy when I first thought of it: open a café, train kids to serve good coffee, tea and food. Now I've got the café. I've got the kids, when they turn up. There's just the small issue of the coffee, the tea and the food.

The catering company that's supplying the Gaggia is also supplying Pablo. The days of sprinkling a few granules into hot water are long gone. Now, everyone supposedly wants fancy coffee from the other side of the world. If it's not harvested from an Indonesian cat's poo or a Thai elephant's dung or from a tiny volcanic island visited by Napoleon (though presumably not pooed by him), they don't want it.

I can't see Auntie Rose and her ladies enjoying coffee that's already gone through one digestive tract before it gets to theirs. But obviously I needed help, so I've got Pablo.

I've asked him to stick with Italian coffee, which pleased him down to the ground. Ha ha. Ground. Get it?

At least it's starting to look more like a café than a boozer in here, with all the furniture painted in mismatched pastels and the chairs covered in flowered oilcloth (thanks to Mum). Out of respect for old Carl, Elsie and history, I've left the booths stripped back to the bare wood, but we ended up staining the ugly rough floorboards throughout. Now they look like ugly rough stained floorboards, but no one will notice as long as there's lots of foot traffic.

'Yo, am I late?' Joseph calls as he saunters through the door in front of Lou. 'It was ten o'clock, yeah? Wassup, I'm Joseph.' He pumps Pablo's hand. 'You're the coffee dude? Sick job, bruv.'

He's still in his brother's suit and tie, which makes it seem odd that he's speaking like that and flicking air snaps at us.

'Lou, Joseph, this is Pablo. He's our coffee consultant.' I've got to bite down my smirk as I say this, but, really, it's a bit over the top, isn't it?

'How come you're dressed like an undertaker?' Lou asks Joseph, assessing him from beneath her blue fringe.

Joseph clearly doesn't think much of Lou's dress sense either. 'Yo, this is how professional people dress. Take lessons from the master.' He straightens the fat knot on his tie. 'No-hopers need not apply.'

Lou doesn't shift expression but shoves her hands into her sweatshirt pockets.

'Besides, I dress like a professional because I'm the Professor,' he says.

Lou scoffs. 'You can't give yourself a nickname, you muppet.'

'Do you two know each other already?' They shake their

heads. 'Really? Because I usually like to know someone for at least ten minutes before ripping into them. You can both wear whatever you want, as long as it's clean and presentable.'

It'll be hard enough training them without enforcing a dress code too. I don't care if Joseph wants to look like an undertaker or a professor or a circus clown, frankly.

'We can start whenever you're ready,' I tell Pablo.

He tears his eyes away from his reflection to say, 'So now we begin. Today I will open your eyes and your hearts. You will learn to love the coffee, to speak its language, to listen as it whispers its secrets to you. It will dance for you, it will caress you, it will transport you to another world. There is a sacred bond between the barista and his machine. You love it and it will love you back. But only after you have mastered the bean. Today we begin the journey together.' He aims his prayer hands at each of us and bows.

Lou's mouth hangs open. 'Mate, it's only a hot drink.'

She sounds challenging, but I can see the flash of humour in her expression. I wonder how many people look that closely, though?

Pablo puts his hands over his heart. 'It hurts me to hear these things. If you do not trust the process, the machine will not dance for you. It will not share its secrets. I cry for the bean.'

Puhlease. He'd never cry for the bean. He couldn't stand the puffy eyes.

At two hundred quid for Pablo's instruction, that machine had better dance for us. It doesn't have to win *Strictly*, but it should at least give us a tango that would make Len Goodman proud.

Pablo steers us to the Gaggia. Its buttons, knobs and handles are just as intimidating as when I last looked at it. 'Have you ever made coffee before?' he asks.

Lou says, 'Only instant. That Nescafé's not bad.'

Pablo shudders for his whole culture. 'I don't mean ...' He closes his eyes in pain. '... freeze-dried coffee. I mean proper espresso. THIS is real coffee.'

With a dramatic wave of his hand – actually, you can assume everything Pablo does is going to be dramatic – he pulls several sacks of beans from his satchel. Looking faintly orgasmic as he inhales from the first sack, he says, 'Smell the potential. Do you smell it?'

'I smell it,' Joseph says with a noisy sniff.

The beans do smell delicious, and I'm sure Pablo has a process, but I'm anxious to get to the part where coffee comes out of the little metal spout. We can't serve our customers coffee smells.

But Pablo will not be rushed. He explains all about the proper grind, steam temperature and exactly how many grams of beans go into each shot. I'm starting to nod off when, finally, he wants us to touch the machine.

He demonstrates. 'It is not that difficult,' he says, grinding the beans. Then he spoons the grounds into the filter, levels it off and tamps it down. He does this all with the kind of precision that makes the space shuttle look easy to launch. And we haven't even started on the milk yet.

We try copying him.

'Like this?'

'No, *carina mia*, like this.'

'Like this?'

'No, no, try again, like this.'

'Like this?'

'No, like this.'

'Like this?'

'No, like this!'

We go on (like this) for two hours. Pablo looks like he's about to risk those puffy eyes having a little sob in the corner, but finally we manage to coax out something that tastes like espresso.

By the time Pablo leaves, we've made enough coffee to fuel an army marching into battle. He's promised to return if we need him, like an over-caffeinated Nanny McPhee. And I get the feeling we will need him. I wouldn't say the Gaggia and I are friends yet, but we've got a tentative understanding.

'Well, that was fun,' Lou says, shrugging into her sweat-shirt. 'Let's be sure to do it again sometime.' She pretends to stab herself in the tummy.

'We aren't finished yet,' I say. 'We have to practise. Don't we want to be sure we can do it when we actually open?'

'Yeah, Lou, don't be so lazy,' Joseph says. 'I'm here for you, boss.'

'You don't have to call me boss.'

'We can always keep some Nescafé out back,' Lou suggests. 'Honestly, it doesn't taste bad.'

Don't think I haven't thought of that. 'Hopefully we won't need it. Lou, do you want to be the customer or the barista first? We'll take turns taking the orders and making and serving the coffee. You remember how Pablo did it?'

'I do!' Joseph says. 'I'll go first. Can I? I can be first, yeah?'

Lou shrugs. 'Knock yourself out.'

I'm intrigued and a little scared by her. She seems so self-contained, older than her seventeen years. I know she needs this job – she said so in her interview – but the question is: why? Does she just need the money like any other normal teenager, or is there something else?

I know it's still early days, but already the differences between them are stark. Joseph's got all the enthusiasm and

Lou's probably got all the skill. I just hope they draw even by the time we open.

Joseph goes behind the bar to wait for instructions. 'Lou, pretend you're a customer,' I say, 'and order anything we've practised today. Joseph, treat Lou like a real customer, not like Lou, okay?'

'Yes, madam, what would you like?' he says, imitating Pablo's prayer hands.

Lou thinks for a moment. 'A half-caff double-shot no-foam fat-free latte.'

'Boss!' Joseph whines. 'Tell her she can't do that.'

'Sorry, Joseph. She's the customer. Did you write it down? Lou, that's cruel.'

'The customer is always right,' she says.

I go behind the bar to help Joseph, who's starting to sweat. 'Lou, find a table, please. Joseph will bring your order when it's ready.'

She looks doubtfully at all the pastel before scooting into a booth. 'Those are nice.' She takes one of Mum's fancy teapots off the shelf above her head, turning it over to look at the maker's name. 'You've got a lot of these.'

'More than twenty. They're all my mum's. She's got a thing for old Staffordshire teapots. There's not really room for them at home so she's letting me use them to decorate in here. I'm not sure about using them for the customers, though. I'd hate to break one.'

'Why have them if you don't use them? You may as well sell them otherwise. They're probably worth something. Have you checked? I could look online for you.'

Alarm bells start ringing. I don't want Lou valuing my mother's teapot collection. What if that's why she's in trouble with the Old Bill? She might have been arrested for fencing fancy teapots. And I've plonked her right in the middle of another potential heist. 'They're quite fragile,' I tell her. 'I promised Mum we'd keep them on the shelf.'

That's a lie, but she takes the hint and puts the teapot back. Now I'm worried they'll get nicked.

Joseph finally gets the coffee right after the third go, but the whole order takes about ten minutes. Which is fine if we're only planning to have one customer at a time in the café. 'Good,' I tell him. 'We'll work on that some more, okay? Go give Lou her coffee.'

Carefully he carries the cup to her table.

She sends him back for a spoon.

'Certainly, madam, anything you want.' He gives her the spoon with a flourish.

'And a serviette? You've spilled a drop here.'

He trudges back to the bar for serviettes. 'Anything else?' he calls.

'No.'

He brings the serviette.

'Except sugar.'

'Boss!'

'Lou, thank you for making the important point that we've got to anticipate the customer's needs. Now it's your turn. Up here, please.'

Joseph can't stop grinning about their role change.

'What do you want?' Lou asks him.

'That's how you ask a customer for their order?' I say. 'I thought you said you were used to looking after people. Maybe you could be nicer.'

'This is me being nicer.'

'Then pretend you're talking to Father Christmas. Be *that* nice.'

'I'll have the same as you,' Joseph says. 'Half-caff no-foam fat-free latte, only don't make the coffee too hot and I'll have a triple shot. I'll just be over here when it's ready.'

He strolls to a table, brushes off the seat and sits down.

Lou's just about to start the grind when her phone starts ringing. 'Yeah? Okay. No, don't. I will.' Hanging up she says, 'I've gotta go.'

'But we're not finished yet. We're still training.'

'I'm sorry, but I've got to. Really, I'm sorry.'

'Are you okay, Lou? You look a bit—'

She rushes from the café.

Frantic.

'I hope she's not going to do that all the time,' says Joseph. 'It's hard to keep good help these days. But I can still get my coffee, yeah boss?' He nods towards the Gaggia, sending me off to make my trainee's half-caff no-foam fat-free not-too-hot triple-shot latte.

Chapter 6

I'm welling up again. This has been happening all the time lately. It doesn't even have to be one of those appeals on telly about the plight of orphaned children. An M&S food advert will do it. I made the mistake of watching *Four Weddings and a Funeral* the other day and it took me hours to recover.

Get hold of yourself, Emma, it's only bunting. 'A bit higher if you can,' I tell Kelly.

She stretches from the top step of the ladder. 'I'm as high as I can go.' She nails in the tail of the bunting. 'Which means it's as high as it can go. It looks good, Em.' She climbs down. 'Really good.'

I glance around my nearly-decorated café. It's hard to remember what it was like when I first walked in here. That was just before the wedding, nearly two years ago, when I was searching for a loo option on Carlton Square to keep my in-laws from having to squat behind the bushes at the reception. It was nondescript from the outside – clearly an old pub but long unused as one – with a few tables and chairs scattered inside and only a Daily Specials blackboard to hint that it had recently tried to be a café.

Not that I was thinking of being a business owner then. I'd had quite enough on my plate – an eat-all-you-like buffet piled with second helpings and a big fat bap teetering on top. Besides, I was still naïve enough to think that I could find a job to fit around my soon-to-be-born twins. Like I'd be able to stash them in my office drawer and take them out for a feed when I had my cup of tea for elevenses.

But how was I supposed to get interviews, let alone go to them, when I didn't even have time for a bath?

They say people often invent things to solve a problem they have. If that's true, then most inventors are probably new mothers.

There I was, at the mercy of two very demanding people who were at least fifteen years too young to be left on their own. I wanted work using the degree I'd just spent five years studying for. And I was running 24-hour room service for the twins anyway, so I knew something about catering for tough customers.

The idea came to me as Daniel and I sat at one of those outside cafés on the South Bank where you can people-watch for hours. Just a little further down the path along the river from the spot where he'd asked me to marry him, actually. Not that we were re-enacting an anniversary or anything. I guess we were just there enjoying being happy. The twins were still breastfeeding which, I'd only learn after the fact, were the easy days. Have boobs, will travel, that was my motto then. Now we need at least two bags full of gear for even the shortest of outings.

I haven't been to the South Bank since, come to think about it. I barely manage Uncle Colin's pub now, and that's just around the corner.

Anyway, the children were snoozing, giving us precious minutes to enjoy the rare winter sun and even speak in full sentences. Daniel was just starting to wonder if it might be better for him to stay home so that I could put my degree to good use, when it occurred to me that instead of looking for a workplace to accommodate our family, I might be able to create one locally. And wasn't there that old pub on the very square where we lived?

It was just a whisper of an idea, but the more I thought about it, the more sense it started to make. Luckily the vicar who drinks at Uncle Colin's has some influence with our councillor, who also drinks there. Everyone's better off not knowing the details about how he convinced the councillor to give us the pub's lease. Let's just say the vicar can be very persuasive when he wants to be. As an ex-con turned Godly, let's also say I wouldn't cross him.

Now it really does feel like a café in here – cosy and welcoming. We don't even need the lights on if it's sunny. The big old-fashioned paned-glass windows all along the front flood the room with light that's almost rosy. And when it's dim outside, the opaque glass wall sconces cast a yellowy glow. Even before we've served our first slice of cake, it feels like a vintage tearoom. And once we start brewing the hot drinks, it should stop smelling like fresh paint.

Mum and I went back and forth about the colours for the tables and chairs. She wanted pinks and blues to go with the flowered oilcloth she put on the seats. I've always been more partial to lilac and mint, so we compromised and used all the colours. It looks a little like Cath Kidston exploded in here, but the strings of bunting criss-crossing the ceiling and the different pastel patterns on the flags all add to its higgledy-piggledy welcome.

Mum sewed that bunting herself. It was one of her contributions to the wedding (cue more sniffles). That and my dress, which had been hers, handmade by my gran.

Kell peers at my face. 'Are you crying?'

God, what is wrong with me? 'Just a little misty. I guess I'm overly emotional. This is starting to seem like a big deal.'

'It's not a big deal. It's a huge deal! I'd be cacking myself if I were you.' She picks up the bags that had the bunting in them. 'It'd be one thing if I failed to keep the fishmonger's going, you know, a hundred years of family history and all, but at least that would have had a good run till I killed it.'

'Not helping, Kell.'

She pulls out her hair tie to redo her ponytail. She's got really nice hair – shimmery straight and light brown with a fringe that never goes wonky – but she always keeps it tied up. 'And it's not just about you, right?' she goes on, as if I need reminding. 'What about your trainees? You said yourself, the little bleeders need you. You can't fail them.'

'Really not helping, Kell.'

But she's right. Daniel and I can just about manage on his charity worker's salary, as long as we don't do anything too extravagant like go out to dinner. Or get a nanny (as if). His parents might be rich, but we stand on our own two sometimes-in-debt feet. If the café goes under, I can always try to find a job that would leave us a bit in the bank after paying for childcare.

I don't even want to think about not paying back my in-laws, but they're not exactly the Mafia. It would probably just mean a few uncomfortable family dinners, not broken legs.

What about Lou and Joseph, though? What happens if I fail them? Sure, Joseph is keen, but he's a terrible job applicant. He'll be up against others who've got work experience and don't think they deserve to be CEO straightaway. What chance will he have then?

And Lou. She's already been nicked for stealing. Who'd hire her with that smudge on her record and no work experience?

'You're not going to hang all these, are you?' Kelly holds up a big pile of cloth, pulling me away from thoughts of doom.

'No, don't you remember? They're the serviettes from the wedding.' Mum and I spent hours in Mrs Delaney's shop, drinking cups of tea and hemming dozens of squares of paisley, gingham and floral cotton cloth. I'd like to think my gran would be proud of me, as long as she didn't look too closely at the crooked hems. 'We may as well use them,' I say. 'Stick them on the shelves in the back and let's go to the pub.'

Daniel's looking after the twins again tonight, and he's promised not to ring unless there's an actual emergency. I did have to remind him that running low on Sauvignon Blanc doesn't count.

But instead of putting away the serviettes, Kelly is peering out the window. 'Who are those old people?' she wonders.

'Does he have a flat cap? That's Carl and Elsie. Invite them in.'

Kell flings open the door.

'Lord, you frightened the life out of me!' Elsie cries, grasping the brooch pinned at the neck of her blouse.

'Sorry, Elsie!' I say over Kelly's shoulder. 'Would you like to come in?'

Way to give OAPs a heart attack, Kell.

Carl takes his cap off when I introduce him to Kelly. 'Blow me, it's changed in here!' He sniffs. 'Smells better too.'

'Anything is an improvement,' says Elsie. 'You've got one of those doodahs, I see.' She points to the espresso machine on the bar. 'Look, Carl, like they did in Rome.'

'I couldn't get a decent cup of tea in Rome,' he mutters.

Elsie pats his arm. 'Now, it was only a week.'

'It's coming along,' I agree. 'We'll open in two weeks. Kelly, Carl and Elsie used to come in here when it was a pub during the ... Carl, are you all right?'

He's sunk to his knees near one of the booths.

'Carl?'

His head is under the table.

'Should we call 999?'

He mumbles something.

'I'm sorry, I didn't hear you. Do you need a doctor?'

91

His mobile lights up the underside of the booth. 'It's here! Elsie, look. I told you!'

Before I know it, Elsie is on the floor too with her head under the table. 'Oh, Carl. You really did. Come look at this!'

It's a squeeze with us all under there. Kell and I squint to where Carl has his phone light aimed. Amongst the decades-old wads of gum and who-knows-what-else, 'Carl Loves Elsie Forever' is carved into the underside of the table.

'After all these years, imagine,' says Carl. 'I told you, Els, you were always the one.'

If that's the case, though, then why did he marry Elsie's sister instead?

Carl and Elsie don't want to stay long after professing their everlasting love under the table. On my way to the Cock and Crown, I see another familiar face. Unfortunately, she's not as happy to see me.

I spot Lou's blue hair above the display case in The Co-Op. She's hard to miss. 'That's Lou, my new trainee!' I tell Kell. I've never seen her in this neighbourhood before. Hurrying across the road, I'm just about to raise my hand to rap on the window when she comes around the end of the aisle.

She's got a baby strapped to her front. Our eyes lock for a split second before she pulls up her hood and turns away.

'You never said she was a mother,' Kell says. 'That's tough. She's just a kid.'

'I didn't know.' That must be why she had to leave the other day after our espresso training. And I thought I had it hard with the twins. Imagine being seventeen, probably on your own, without a job, trying to take care of a baby.

'You think that's why she needs the work?' Kell asks as we make our way to Uncle Colin's pub.

'I guess so. She hasn't told me anything. Have you ever seen her around before?'

Kell says no, like everyone else I've asked about Lou. No one seems to know who she is.

It's like she doesn't exist.

With the weather turning nice now, there are just a few of the regulars along the bar in the Cock. Most are outside. Uncle Barbara is pulling the pints, so Uncle Colin must have the night off.

Uncle Barbara has really come into his own, wardrobe-wise, since being my bridesmaid. I guess wearing a flowy floral frock around all those wedding guests gave him the confidence he needed to really embrace his feminine dress

93

sense. He used to stick to wrap dresses. Now he wears floaty ones nearly every day.

But don't make the mistake of thinking he's feminine just because he likes to wear ladies' garments. Far from it. He looks like a rugby player in a dress. With a beard.

Uncle Colin and Uncle Barbara are my dad's identical twin brothers and they raised their families in the flats upstairs. My cousins are all grown now and Uncle Colin's wife spends a lot of time with her sister down in Cornwall, so we hardly ever see her. Uncle Barbara's wife moved out after she caught him in one of her dresses, so it's really just my two uncles who are my full-time family now at the pub.

As comfortable as it is having everyone I know in here – which is most of the time – it's nice when it's just me and Kell together like this. We've always been surrounded by people who know us. Sometimes I like to imagine that I'm a complete stranger somewhere. Then, instead of being Emma Billings née Liddell, Elaine and Jack's only daughter and the local pub landlord's niece, I could be anyone I wanted. I could even be exotic (-ish).

I suppose I got a taste of that when I took my course in town. Just being a few miles away from the neighbourhood seemed like being in a different world. And maybe I seemed like a different person by being there too.

Daniel saw me as a part-time Open University student,

juggling a job and coursework and hoping to work for a charity one day. I wonder who he'd have seen if we'd met here in East London, surrounded by my tribe, looking after Auntie Rose and Dad and spending most of my free time with Kell in Uncle Colin's pub. Would I have been just plain old East London Emma?

I was in the habit of keeping myself to myself in class since there wasn't much time in my life for socialising. But Daniel drew something out of me right from the first day we met. He made me want to be like the carefree students all around us. So, when he'd invited me for a coffee a little while after, I couldn't ignore the excitement in my tummy.

'What can I get you?' he'd asked as the aroma of freshly ground beans drew us towards the counter at the hipster coffee shop. 'Maybe an extra-dry cappuccino?'

I watched his expression. Surely he was taking the piss. I shook my head. 'Would I just chew the beans?'

The dimple I'd come to know so well appeared. 'I'm having a flat white.'

'Make mine hilly. I like to work for my coffee.' I spotted a cabinet full of games. 'Ooh, Scrabble.' I was nearly as good at it as Auntie Rose. Better, if you didn't let her cheat.

'Would you like to play?' he asked. 'If you've got time.'

I gazed at his happy, friendly face as I thought about the usual Saturday errands I should be running. There was also Dad's and Auntie Rose's tea to make later. But the world wouldn't stop spinning if I skipped the errands, and Dad was perfectly capable of feeding himself. 'I've got time,' I told Daniel.

By the time we'd had our second date, at a charity gig that he'd organised – for his work, not just for me – my excitement had turned to something significant and it had nothing to do with the living legend we saw onstage.

'Okay, so Calvin's asked me,' Kell says as we sit at one of the tables away from the TV.

That can only mean one thing. 'You're waiting till NOW to tell me this?! What did you say?' I glance at her hand. No ring. Though I'd have noticed it if she was wearing one. She's not a jewellery person.

'I said I don't know. He's asked me to go to Spain with him, Em.'

'To Spain. Oh. That's … nice.'

It's not nice. It's not. It's horrible. Kelly can't leave me. We're best friends. We've been in each other's lives nearly every day since we were seven. Her leaving would be like losing a limb. I *need* her.

'You're thinking about it, though?' I can't believe how calm I sound. Please say no.

'Yeah.' She snatches up her drink and takes a gulp. 'I love

him, and he's mad about me. Which is mad in itself, but there you go. And after I promised myself I wasn't going to get involved when I knew he was leaving. You remember. We were sat right here. You're the one who said I should go out with him. Now look what's happened.'

'Yeah, you're in love. I'm such a dick for encouraging that.'

'I couldn't help it,' she says. 'It crept up on me. One minute I couldn't be bothered and now I can't stop thinking about him.'

'Well, love does do that,' I say. 'You don't have to decide right away. This is a big move. It would mean leaving the business, right? Is there anyone else who can take over?'

We both know there's no one. We've known that since Kell was sixteen and her sisters all refused, leaving her as her dad's last choice to keep the fish van in the family.

I'm a terrible friend. I'm feeding her reasons to say no to Calvin, though mostly not out loud. You'll scupper your family's business. They'll be disappointed in you. And think how you'll miss them. Besides, you don't speak Spanish, you get freckly in the sun and airfares would be ridiculous to come home at Christmas.

Anything but the truth: that I selfishly want Kell to stay because I need her.

'Fancy seeing you here,' she says, looking pointedly past

me towards the door. 'Daniel's just walked in. S'pose he kept his promise. At least he isn't ringing you.'

Daniel? Daniel who is supposed to be minding our children?

He bounds over to kiss me, but I duck him. 'What are you doing here? Where are the twins?'

He pats his pockets. 'They were here a minute ago.' He – sensibly – decides to sit next to Kell instead of me. 'They're with your parents, darling. When I rang your mum earlier she asked if she could take them. I couldn't rahly deny a grandmother her wish, could I?'

'But I could have left them with my parents,' I point out. 'You were supposed to mind them.'

He grimaces sheepishly through his sigh. 'But it's rahly hard! Your parents are naturals.'

'I know it's hard, Daniel, I do it all the time, remember? How are you supposed to learn to do it if you don't *do it*?'

He reaches for my hand across the table. 'Just so I'm clear, Em, you're cross with me because I've let your parents have our children for an hour so I could be with you?'

'No! I'm cross because instead of just getting on with looking after them, like I have to do every single day, you foist them off on my parents the second it seems too hard.'

'I'll get us a round,' Kell says, escaping from the domestic that's brewing.

'It was only for a few hours,' I say. 'Couldn't you have managed instead of putting it on my parents?'

His normally jovial expression turns sour. 'I feel like you're trying to punish me, Emma, by having me look after the children. It's not supposed to be some kind of test, you know, for me to pass or fail. I didn't bring them to your parents because I don't love them or want to look after them. I just thought it would be nice to come meet you for a drink when your parents suggested it. We haven't done that for ages. Sorry for thinking that you'd like that.'

'What I'd like is for you to take responsibility sometimes instead of making me and my parents do everything. Why do I always have to be the one? If you're not texting every two minutes with questions, then you're getting my parents to do your job for you. What I'd like is for you to be a parent like I've got to be. THAT'S what I'd like.'

'That rahly hurts, Emma. I *am* a parent and I only wanted to surprise you.'

I sigh. I can't win. 'I don't want to hurt you, but I want you to know how I feel.'

Armed with our drinks, Kelly walks back into the chilly atmosphere. It's not exactly an ice age, but there's a notice-able drop in temperature.

Chapter 7

Just try holding a grudge against Daniel when he's being so sweet. I did my best, at least till we left the pub. He was right, though. He rumbled me when he mentioned punishment, because wasn't that what I was doing? I was testing him, at least. Besides, it *has* been ages since we've been out together. So even though it was definitely wrong to hand the children over to my parents, I've got to admit that I felt more like myself than I have in a long time. Maybe that's all I need, a little reminder every so often that I'm still in here. Underneath the puke-stained top and sleep-deprived stare and the faint aroma of dirty nappies, I am still me.

And while I'm being so critical of Daniel for taking my parents for granted, I should probably look at myself. Haven't I left the twins with Mum and Dad a lot lately? I didn't have much choice while the pub was under renovation. Social Services would have stepped in if I'd let Oscar and Grace toddle around in their Bob the Builder safety hats while we were stripping varnish and ripping up carpets. But that's all done now. The café is as safe and clean as it will be when we open.

Something tells me Mum and Dad aren't going to like the new arrangement I've got in mind.

They're all up when I get to the house. Dad's making a fry-up while Auntie Rose sits at the kitchen table calling out clues from the crossword puzzle. Not that she ever waits for anyone else to come up with the answer.

Back in the lounge, the twins are wriggling to get out of the pushchair. 'Come here, loves.' Mum goes to unsnap their safety belts.

'That's okay, Mum, leave them in. I can take them with me this morning.'

'What? Why?' she says, frowning. 'Have we done something wrong?'

'No!'

'Then I don't see why you're taking them away. Jack! Emma's taking the twins with her.'

Dad hurries in on his crutches. 'Why's that, love? They're no trouble. We love having them.'

If I tell them how guilty I'm feeling, then we'll have to

have a big long discussion about it and I'll be late to meet Lou and Joseph.

'I know you don't mind having them, but it's not fair to have you looking after them all day every day while I'm working. I'm going to need to figure out how to have them in the café with me anyway, and we're just doing some training today, so it's a good day to start. And speaking of being fair, I'm sorry that Daniel left the twins with you last night. He shouldn't have done that. He was meant to be looking after them, not you.'

Mum shakes her head. 'But we don't mind. We're just glad we're here to be in their lives. Well, you remember how nice it was having your gran around. We only wish that Philippa and Hugh were able to see them more.'

Mum likes saving us the trouble of pointing out all the ways that she's a better grandmother than Philippa, so she usually just does it herself.

Mum's right, my gran was the best. She and Auntie Rose were as big a part of my life as Mum and Dad were. When Gran died, Auntie Rose came to live with us. Home wouldn't be home without her here.

Dad's parents are another story. Even before they showed their true colours when it came to Uncle Barbara –that's what Mum calls them, and *true colours* aren't a compliment

– they were unpleasant, paranoid people who smelled of Pot Noodles and kept the heating on all summer just because it came free with the rent. I definitely didn't miss having them around.

'Even so,' I say, 'can you please not offer next time? I know you want to help, but why should Daniel miss out on all those fun nappy changes?'

'Whatever you want, love,' Dad says. 'But I'll miss my little sidekicks. You'll bring them round tomorrow?'

I smirk. 'Shall I just drop them off or will I be able to stay too?' But he knows I'm not offended that he might prefer my children to me.

When I wheel the twins outside, I find Mrs Ishtiaque pottering in her garden. The houses in the road are all the same as Mum and Dad's – red-brick, two-storey, council-built in the 1950s – and most of the neighbours don't bother much with their gardens until well into spring. But Mrs Ishtiaque has blooms for all seasons. It's a wash of colour over the low brick wall, and not just the usual daffs and crocuses either. The only other neighbour with flowers at this time of year is that Sheila Dakin across the road, but she's got airs and graces according to Mum, so it's no surprise.

There's nothing stuck up about Mrs Ishtiaque, though. She might wear the most beautiful sarees even when she digs in her borders – pale green with silver threads today – but she's totally down-to-earth and unflappable. She leans over the wall to stroke the twins' heads. 'Emma, I am making mutton curry tonight. Would you like to be having tea with us?'

She's also been my curry connection since I wore plaits to school. Mum did try to spice up our meals, bless her, but her culinary journeys were more to Blackpool than Bangladesh.

'Thank you, I'd love to, but Kell and I have to go cake tasting after work tonight and you know I've got no self-control. I'll be too full for tea and probably a little bit sick.'

'Cake tasting sounds like such hard work,' she says, her face creasing into a smile at her own joke. 'Next time, then. You know where I am living.'

'Thanks, Mrs Ishtiaque. I've got to hurry or I'll be late meeting the lady who's training us to make sandwiches.'

'Training to make what?'

'... Sandwiches.'

She purses her lips but doesn't answer.

I'm probably going overboard getting sandwich training. It's just a bit of bread and some filling. I'd have happily slapped together a few tuna mayo sarnies if it hadn't been for Lou scaring me. She might have been taking the piss when she had Joseph make her complicated coffee order, but who knows what customers might actually want? Their sandwich expectations could be as intricate as their drink orders.

The woman is waiting in front of the café. She's about forty, I'd say. She's swathed in some kind of complicated series of jewel-toned capes, wraps and ponchos, and she's wearing a garland of daisies on her head like kids do when they're off their heads at festivals.

Lou and Joseph are standing across the road leaning against the wrought-iron railings that ring the grassy square, pretending they don't know she's there. As teenagers, they are experts in the fine art of utterly blanking a person.

'Are you Magenta?' I call to the woman as we approach.

'Your aura is glowing!' she calls back in the deepest voice I've ever heard from a woman. 'I could see it from up the road.'

'Thanks, I washed it this morning. New shampoo. Come inside and I'll make introductions.'

'Oh, no introductions necessary,' she says. Inside the café, she squats in front of the pushchair where the twins can get a good look at her. 'I'm very perceptive. These are ... your children!'

It's not exactly a wild assumption. Does she fancy herself

as some kind of psychic too? 'Oscar and Grace, yes. And these are my colleagues—'

'Don't tell me!' She holds her bejewelled hand to her forehead. 'You're Lou and you must be Joseph.'

I'd be impressed if I hadn't mentioned their names in my email. Still, she figured out which was which, so bravo.

I sneak a glance at Lou as she regards the twins. She's hiding her mummy pangs better than I could. I'd probably be sniffing their heads if I were her. As it is, I've been going back to Mum and Dad's every lunchtime just to satisfy my craving. I'm okay first thing in the morning after dropping them off, but then the feelings build until I can't think about anything else. Are they all right? Do they need anything? Are they happy? Of course they're happy. They're with my parents, who happened to do a fine job raising me. So are they as happy with them as they are with me? Happier? What if they prefer them to me? I've got to go check.

Now I've got them to myself all day and they're crowing to be set free. 'If it's okay,' I tell Magenta, 'we'll stay out here so I can keep an eye on the children.'

She spins around twice, sending her layers fanning out around her. 'The vibe is authentic here.' She starts rearranging the tables and chairs. 'You just need better flow.'

'For foot traffic?'

'For positive energy. And I'll need to check wherever you'll usually make the food. You might require a few adjustments. Back there behind the bar?' She goes to explore without waiting for my answer.

'She's checking the kitchen for energy?' says Joseph. He hasn't relaxed his dress code. If anything, his tie is even tighter. 'Maybe she can check your electrics while she's there. You get me? Check the electrics?!'

'She's bare mental,' Lou whispers. Her eyes are wide with alarm. 'Seriously. I've got an auntie who went insane. She used to freeze her lightbulbs so they couldn't spy on her. She still thinks her toaster gives her the Lotto numbers.'

'Your auntie's won the Lotto?' I don't know why this is the question I'm asking about someone who talks to her appliances.

'Nah. It always gives her the wrong numbers. Burns her toast too. She hates that toaster but she won't get rid of it.'

This is the first time that Lou has talked about any family. When I asked her in the interview, all she would say is that she lives in a foster home. The social worker did tell me that she ended up there after her mum died three years ago. I don't know what happened. Maybe it had something to do with the insane auntie. 'Did she …? Is she okay, your auntie?'

Lou shrugs. 'Depends on your crazy scale.' She glances

into the kitchen. 'She's probably better than that one, though.'

'I know, but we need Magenta to show us how to make the kind of sandwiches our customers will want.' Now I'm whispering. 'She'll give us all the recipes and comes highly recommended.' There were all kinds of testimonials on her website about the deliciousness of her sandwiches. 'Plus, she'll do the hygiene certification course we need as part of her fee, and I've got loads of sandwich meat that'll be wasted if we don't practise with it.'

Magenta is back with us a few minutes later. There's a blissful look on her broad ruddy face. 'Your kitchen will be a comfortable space for the sandwiches to thrive.'

'As opposed to the bog, I suppose,' Lou mutters to me.

I have to stifle a snort. 'Thanks for checking, Magenta. That's good to know. Maybe we should get started while the children are occupied?' They're sitting on the play mat on the floor surrounded by every toy I could think to haul here with us.

Magenta clasps her hands together, not exactly in prayer mode like Pablo did, but close enough. What is it with café people? 'I knew I had a gift at an early age,' she begins. 'I've always been able to see food in a special way. I feel *at one* with food, and it feels at one with me.' She stops to make uncomfortably long eye contact with each of us.

'Today I will share some of its secrets with you. These are the ingredients?' Carefully she picks through the bags, examining each package of cheese, putting each jar and pot to her ear.

She's an absolute loon.

'Is none of this is organic?' She points an accusatory carrot at me. 'Don't you love our planet? Why wouldn't you at least get free-range?'

'You didn't tell me to get organic or free-range,' I say. What's a free-range carrot, anyway?

'So much work we have to do,' she says, like a ham-and-cheese Yoda. *So savoury, this sandwich is, hmm.*

A squawk from the play mat stops our progress towards vegetable enlightenment. 'Excuse me, I'm sorry.' Grace has piled all the toys on to Oscar's lap and he's tired of the game. 'Maybe play with the truck instead,' I tell Grace, wheeling the plastic fire truck along to demonstrate.

But my daughter isn't interested in the truck. She hauls herself to her feet. 'Grace, why don't you stay here?' I call after her waddling backside. As if she'll listen to me.

Oscar isn't about to let her have all the fun. He's off too.

Lou deftly kneels down and scoops Grace up. Like she's done it before. 'Come here, little one.'

'Fast reflexes,' I say, grabbing Oscar.

But she's not admitting anything. When Grace starts to

squirm in Lou's arms, Lou bounces her on one hip and babbles in a singsong voice that my daughter finds fascinating. 'Where do you want her?'

I know better than to try to strap them into their pushchair. They can shatter glass with their screams when they want out of that thing.

Lou considers one of the café chairs. 'Pen them in,' she says, flipping it on its side with her free hand, and then another beside it so that the backs make a sort of fence.

'Genius idea,' I say, 'just don't tell Social Services.'

Too late I realise the joke is probably in bad taste, considering the company.

By the end of our training, I still don't believe that Magenta can taste the difference between happy lettuce and sad lettuce, but she's got great recipes for sandwiches that we'll actually be able to make. She'll probably be too busy dancing round maypoles or harvesting her parsley by moonlight to ever come into the café once it's open, so she'll never know if our carrots aren't free-range.

'Have you got any questions?' she asks.

Joseph raises his hand. 'Is your name really Magenta? I mean your given name? What?' he says, catching Lou's expression. 'She asked for questions.'

'My parents named me Julia, but it doesn't suit my aura. Which is magenta, as it happens.' She brushes back her wiry brown hair, causing the daisy crown to slip a bit. 'Magentas are a combination of red, blue and violet. That makes us grounded as well as spiritual and emotional, and we seek joy by focusing our positive energy on worthy causes. Like your café. Does that answer your question?'

'You call yourself a colour on purpose,' he asks, nodding. 'That's aiight. Magenta the Sandwich Whisperer. They call me the Professor.'

Lou rolls her eyes. 'Pssh. Only you call yourself that. I told you. Everyone else calls you a—'

'Okay,' I say over Lou. 'Thank you, Magenta.'

Lou pulls on her hoodie to go as soon as our trainer leaves. But now I know why, so I can't really object. It's obvious that she's not going to admit to the baby when she's pretending we never saw each other the other day. And I'm sure there's some kind of employment law against me asking.

'Lou, be sure to take any sandwiches you'd like, okay? I don't want them to go to waste. Really, take all you like.' I hand her one of the empty carrier bags that the ingredients came in.

She picks out a cheddar and chutney on a seeded bloomer, peering at me with raised eyebrows from beneath her blue fringe.

'Please take more than one. Look at how many there are!'

'If they're going spare.' She snatches another five sandwiches and carefully stacks them in the bag. 'Thanks.'

That girl must really love sandwiches.

Joseph helps me carry everything back to the kitchen from where we were working at the bar. 'You get on okay with Lou, right?' I ask him.

'Yeah, she's aiight,' he says. With a piece of kitchen towel he wipes the egg mayo off a knife before putting it in the drawer.

'You have to wash that, Joseph.'

'But it's clean. You just saw me wipe it. And look.' He holds the blade up to the light. 'Spotless, see? There's nothing on it.'

'It doesn't matter if you can't see it, Joseph. Everything needs to be washed with soap and water. Hot water.'

He holds up his hands. 'Don't be vexed, I got no beef.' Then he straightens his tie. 'I'm not being funny, but it's the end result that matters, boss, not the details.'

'Well, you're not being funny, and the end result could be norovirus if you don't wash things properly.'

He empties about half a bottle of washing-up liquid into the sink, but I don't care. It's cheaper than Food Standards Agency fines.

While Joseph is elbow-deep in Fairy Liquid, I try to find out more about Lou. She's not like any other kid I've met. She's definitely not like I was at seventeen.

113

Joseph gives me a clue when he says one of her foster brothers was also in their year.

'One of them? How many does she have?'

He shrugs. 'There's a bag of youngs, but not always the same ones. Sometimes they go back to their fam or get adopted or something. It's not my job to keep track.'

'Are they good kids?' I ask, and immediately regret my choice of words. I know better than that. 'I mean, have they had any trouble?'

His eyes flick away. Just because he doesn't know Lou doesn't mean he won't protect her.

'I know about ... the problem Lou's been having,' I say.

'Yeah, I heard something.'

'Do you know what it's about? Do you know what she stole?'

I believe him when he shakes his head. 'A lot of people nick stuff, boss.'

Maybe so, but knowing that everyone does it isn't helping me to trust Lou.

My mobile rings just as I get to Kelly's fish van to pick her up for our cake tasting. 'How was your training?' Mum wants to know when I answer the call.

'Like you suspected, the consultant was flakier than a croissant, but we got what we need.'

'I saw Mrs Ishtiaque just now. She says she invited you for curry. Why aren't you going? You always love her curry. What's wrong? Is it Daniel?'

'Nothing's wrong, Mum! I've got to go try cakes tonight, that's all. I'm with Kell now, actually, so I can't really ... What did you tell Mrs Ishtiaque about me?'

'Hmm? Sorry, you cut out there for a sec.'

'Mum, did you tell Mrs Ishtique that something's wrong?'

'I don't know what you mean.'

'Mmm hmm, I've got to go, Mum. Kelly's waiting. Stop talking to people about my personal life, okay?'

Chapter 8

The doorbell goes off the next afternoon just as I'm backing out of the twins' room. I freeze, as if my still figure can absorb the sound ricocheting around the house. It's the first time in weeks that they've gone to sleep at the same time – day or night – and the Jehovah's Witnesses pick *now* to try to convince me I should be paying closer attention to God's good works?

Tiptoe-running down the stairs before the bell sounds again, I've got to weave through the assault course of clothes baskets and toys to get to the front door. I know there'll be a smiley middle-aged man and woman on the step. He'll be neatly dressed in his white shirt, red bow tie and dark suit, clutching a stack of *Watchtower* magazines, and she'll have a blue and green tartan raincoat belted tightly over her round middle. The same two try their luck on the square every few months. They're ever-so friendly and undeterred by my rejection, and I do feel for them. It must be hard dealing with heathens all the time.

But it's not the god-knockers. The bright pink smudge showing through the frosted glass in the door tells me it's Mrs Ishtiaque. 'This is a surprise!' I say, kissing her smooth cheek.

Though it isn't, really. I *knew* Mum said something yesterday. I know she thinks she's helping, but, really, it's bad enough dealing with everything at the moment without having my problems broadcast to the neighbours. Even neighbours that I love.

'There is curry left over that I am bringing you,' Mrs Ishtiaque says, clutching a large pot. 'The girls did not want leftovers.'

I know Mrs Ishtiaque's three grown daughters love her curry as much as I do. Which means they've willingly given up leftovers for me. This is a pity delivery. 'That's kind, thank you! Can you come in? The twins have gone down for their nap. We might even get a cup of tea before they wake.'

Handing me the pot, she crosses both sets of fingers near her ears. It's a gesture we've shared since my school days when I had to sit exams. I hope it works as well for sleeping children.

She follows me through to the dining room, kicking off her sandals in the hallway and adjusting the shawl of her saree. No matter the weather, Mrs Ishtiaque wears sandals.

I glance around the house. I really did mean to clear up after breakfast. The clothes draped over the radiators have gone crispy over the last week. 'Sorry about the mess,' I murmur. 'I just never seem to have time to tidy up.'

'You are only one person doing many person's jobs.' She sits in the dining chair that I clear of bibs and bills for her. It probably says a lot about the state of our family that there's only one usable dining chair at the table. Daniel sits there for breakfast. When we do have tea together, it's off trays balanced on our laps on the sofa.

'I'm glad you're here,' I tell her a few minutes later, setting two steaming tea mugs and a pack of digestives in front of us. 'I'm still stuffed from trying all the cakes last night, but please have a biscuit.'

Cleo's cakes were beyond delicious. She's the baker who owns the Mad Batter, which sounds like the name of a cricketer who does the samba around the stumps before insanely swinging at balls.

She does have some mad cakes, combinations like avocado and chocolate, pistachio and cardamom, and cour-gette and roses. Kell was sceptical about the parsnip cake, but even that was out of this world, and gorgeous too. In case our customers' tastes are more plain vanilla, though, Cleo says we can just come and pick up a few options of whatever she's baked that morning and see how we go. Over time I'll probably get to know the regulars' favourites.

'We'll have the curry for tea,' I say. 'Thank you.'

Mrs Isthiaque nods. 'Every meal that you do not have to cook is a good meal. I know how hard it is for you. I was not working when I married Mr Ishtiaque. One or the other. Not both.'

'But everyone does both these days, Mrs Ishtiaque. At least everyone we know. It's different today.'

I make it sound like Mrs Ishtiaque is ancient when she's only in her fifties. It's her sarees and the way she keeps her black hair swept back into a bun that makes her look so traditional, like she's from the olden days.

'I'm not sure that I'd want to stay home full-time even if we could afford it,' I tell her. 'I like having something else to do, even if it's stressful. How did you do it, Mrs Ishtiaque, with three children?'

She laughs, a sound that matches the silver bangle bracelets that tinkle every time she takes a sip of her tea. 'I was young like you, but I wasn't knowing the ways of the world. I only knew what my mother was telling me, the same thing her mother was telling her. They chose Mr Ishtiaque because he was a good worker, from a good family. He was providing for us and I did everything else.'

'That doesn't sound like such a good deal, Mrs Ishtiaque.'

Her deep brown eyes are direct and searching. 'What is a good deal, Emma? A life where you do some things and your husband does some things? Or a life where you are doing it all? We women are strong, but sometimes I am thinking we are trying to be too strong.'

Her words pierce the fragile membrane holding me together. I don't want to be the happy homemaker while Daniel brings home the pay cheque and puts his feet up at the end of the day. But that's what's happening and I feel like I *am* doing it all.

She's watching me closely. 'Tell me, Emma. What is wrong? Why are you not happy?'

'I'm not unhappy.' But the tears that spring to my eyes tell the truth. 'Is it supposed to be this hard, Mrs Ishtiaque?'

She nods. 'Sometimes it feels impossible, yes? I know. First there's a little bit, and we can do it. Then a little more and a little more. We are strong. Maybe that is why we are being given so much responsibility.'

'Do you mean by God?' We've never talked about religion before. I don't want to be tested by a higher being. I've got enough on my plate with my little beings.

She laughs. 'Goodness, no! I mean by our families. And they are no gods, are they?'

'It's like nothing has changed for Daniel, but my whole world is different now. It's not fair.'

'It is not fair,' Mrs Ishtiaque agrees.

Once I start talking, I can't stop. It all tumbles out – the resentment that keeps bubbling up around Daniel and this feeling that too much is on my shoulders. She listens to me rant and snivel, rage and finally despair.

What *is* wrong with me? Why can't I be happy with two beautiful children and a husband who loves me and my dream business about to open? Women do this every day, and in harder situations than mine. I'm not exactly living on beans and hauling water from a well every morning. So what's wrong with me?

She grasps my hands in her dainty ones. 'Emma, no matter what you think, you are doing a very good job. You must be knowing that. We are all most critical of ourselves.'

But she's being too kind, because I'm not being critical of myself, am I? I'm being critical of Daniel. I'll just add that to my list of reasons to feel guilty.

There's a commotion upstairs. 'They're up,' I say. 'Let me just go get them. They love visitors.'

'No, I must go home. I will see you again soon, yes? Remember what I said.'

Little do I know that curries will turn up on my doorstep nearly every week after that. Each one will be a little pot of love, telling me everything is going to be fine. Maybe if I eat enough jalfrezi, I'll believe it.

I've just folded the crispy clothes and got Oscar and Grace to play quietly on the floor when Philippa rings. 'Yah, darling, hellair! Go look at the café.'

'I can't really right now,' I say. 'I've got the children. Why, what have you done?'

'It's a surprise, but you can see it any time, rahly. Right, let's talk later. Bye, darling!' She hangs up.

Of course, now I've got to see what she's talking about. Shrugging a coat over my stretched-out T-shirt with the bleach stain on it, I wrestle the children into the pushchair. 'Let's go have a look at what Granny Billings has done.'

Because it could be anything. This is the woman who wanted to build the hanging gardens of Babylon for our wedding reception and – with a straight face – suggested a synchronised butterfly release.

As I round the corner and the café comes into view, my hoot of laughter startles the twins. 'It's okay, Mummy's just surprised. Your granny is incredible!'

The whole building has been flower-bombed. A riotous display of blossoms and greenery cascades from boxes on every window ledge on both floors. A man and a woman wearing matching blue jumpsuits emblazoned on the back with Billings Garden Consultancy are hanging the last of half a dozen enormous baskets from supports that they've drilled into the façade.

'Philippa sent you?' I ask the woman, who wipes her soil-smeared hand on herself before extending it. I wonder how soon Mum will get that Sheila Larkin over here for a look. It'll make our neighbour green with envy.

'That's right,' says the woman. 'We'll replant every season, but Philippa said you can change the flowers if you don't like these colours.'

The top of the building is covered in vibrant pinks and reds that transition into deep purple in the middle and finally to pale blues and whites on the ground floor. 'I've never seen anything so pretty!' I say. That sends them beaming into their pots.

But what's all this going to cost us? Philippa knows how much she and Hugh loaned me. I figured we'd get a few bunches of flowers from the market every week to stick into jam jars. I didn't budget for the Garden of Eden on the front of the building.

Philippa answers on the first ring. 'Philippa, the café looks incredible!'

'Oh, I am glad, darling. And I assume they've left room for your sign like I told them to? Right, if there's anything you want to change, just say the word. It's your café, after all. But you do like it?' The insecure wobble in her voice is very unusual. 'It's our gift to you.'

'What do you mean, it's your gift to me?' There must

be hundreds of plants. They've even put boxes all along the top of the roof. I'll need a drone to water them. 'Philippa, you can't pay for all this!'

'Don't be ridiculous, darling. It's my garden consultancy, remember? Flowers cost virtually nothing for us. Now, don't be silly. The team will come weekly to maintain it, watering and so forth, so you won't have to do anything but enjoy them. I know how important this café is to you and I want it to be the most brilliant success too. Right, darling, you will say if you need anything else, won't you? Hugh and I are always here to help.'

I'm feeling pretty weepy as I hang up. Everyone has so much faith in me.

But really, the only potential customers who've shown any interest at all are Carl and Elsie. And they only come in to be nosy. There hasn't been so much as a twitch of a curtain on the square. What if we open and nobody comes? Then this will all be nothing but a big, flower-covered failure.

Chapter 9

Of course the Jehovah's Witnesses would choose today to visit the neighbourhood, just when we're planning to do some door-knocking ourselves. No one will answer their door now. It doesn't matter that we're offering tea and cake instead of everlasting hell for non-believers. A stranger is a stranger when they're standing on your doorstep.

But we've got to do it, even if it means trailing along behind the holy converters. The café opens in three days and so far, our only paying customers will probably be Carl and Elsie, though even they're iffy on a fixed income.

'How's that tea coming along?' I call into the kitchen as I cut little slices of vanilla and chocolate cake into squares and wrap them in blue gingham wax paper.

Joseph pops his head out of the doorway. 'The teabags won't come out of the flask. Do I have to take them out?'

Why would the teabags be *in* the flask? 'Let's see,' I say, looking over his shoulder. He's trying to use the bread knife to fish out the teabags. There's tea splashed all over the worktop.

'I think I got it. Shit.' The burst bag comes out on the end of the serrated knife. 'Just don't drink the last cup. It'll be fine.'

'Why aren't you brewing the tea in pots like normal and then pouring the tea in?'

'Because then you'll make me wash the pots,' he says. 'This saves a step. It's all about efficiency.'

'Except that you've got to get the teabags out in one piece. Come on, Joseph, do it right. We'll go as soon as you're ready. Make one flask white and we'll leave the other black. I've got extra milk in the basket in case we need it.' We've each got one of those old-fashioned wicker baskets like Dorothy had for her little dog in *The Wizard of Oz*. I just hope we don't meet too many wicked witches.

A few minutes later he strolls out with a large flask cradled in each arm. 'Let's roll, boss.'

'Did you taste it?'

He tries to suck his teeth but it comes out as a sort of squeak. 'They should be grateful. It's free.'

'It's our calling card, Joseph. If it's shite tea, then who'll want to come to the café?' I pour some of the steaming liquid into two of the builders' mugs we've been using every day. Pablo insists that the crockery is on its way. I just hope it's not on Italian time.

'It's the best cuppa I've ever had,' Joseph says, smacking his lips after a sip.

'Yeah, I admit it's pretty good. Well done.'

'Does that make me the Tea Barista?'

'Uh, sure. Congratulations on your new title.' I check my phone. 'If Lou's not here in a few minutes, then we'll leave a note. She can catch us up.'

His face goes funny. 'She might not be coming,' he says. 'She got nicked.'

'For what?!'

'For teefin' somfink.'

I hate it when he tries to be street. 'What did she teef? Thieve? Steal, what did she steal?'

'Dunno.'

'Is that a dunno that means you do know?'

'No, honestly, boss, I just heard the po-po went to her house last night and nicked her.'

'Poor Lou. Excuse me a minute, okay?' I go into the kitchen to call the social worker.

She's as tight-lipped as usual, but she does admit that Lou was arrested for theft last night. So that's twice, at least, and I still don't know if she's stealing Smarties from the corner shop or smartphones from tourists.

129

'You won't want to cancel her training contract, will you?' the woman asks. It's more an accusation than a question.

'That's not why I called,' I say. 'I just wanted to make sure she's all right. Could you tell me what happens next? I guess she'll need to go to court at some point.' And maybe prison, if things don't turn out well. Can a seventeen-year-old go to prison?

'Then you'll keep her on?' The relief in the social worker's voice is obvious. 'I can tell you that charges are being pressed, so she will probably need time off for court. My advice is to try to keep things as normal as possible. It's more important than ever for Lou to have continuity now.'

She's not the only one. Even if I did want to get rid of Lou, how would I find a replacement waitress in three days? I need her as much as she needs me.

She's with Joseph when I come out of the kitchen and he's obviously told her that I know. 'Please don't lecture me,' she says when she sees me. 'I've had enough of that already.'

'I'm not going to lecture you. You're almost an adult and can make your own decisions. Besides, I don't know what else is happening in your life.' I shrug. 'You have to take the consequences, that's all.'

'I know,' she says as a strand of blue hair finds its way into her mouth. 'Do you need help with the cakes?'

So she's still not going to tell me anything. I wish I had that much cheek when I was seventeen. If an adult asked me a question or wanted an explanation, I'd have grumbled a bit at first, and definitely stomped around saying it was unfair, but I'd have given it to them. All Mum or Dad had to do was wait, wafting their disappointment at me, and I'd cave.

'Just ... let me know if you need anything, okay?'

'I don't need anything,' she says.

Which is fine, though it'd be useful to know if I'll need to find someone to fill in while Lou does time.

'Did you see the door-knockers when you came in?' I ask her. 'The Jehovah's Witnesses are making their rounds. They went into the house on the corner, the one with all the gnomes out front.'

'Someone actually let them in?' Joseph asks. 'Brave.'

Lonely, I think. It's a man who lives on his own in that corner house. I have tried a friendly wave when I've passed but he blanks me every time. Maybe free tea and cake will warm him up.

The Jehovah's Witnesses have finished with the gnome house and are making their way up one side of the square when we catch up with them.

'Hi, hello!' I call.

The man straightens his tie. It's probably the first time

someone has ever tried to talk to him instead of the other way around.

'We're opening the café just there and we're introducing ourselves to all our neighbours today.'

'I'm Jonah and this is my sister, Martha.'

'Oh, hi, I'm Emma, and this is Lou and Joseph. No, I mean we're introducing ourselves to the people who live in the houses.'

'You're welcome to join us on our rounds, Emma,' says Jonah. 'The more the merrier.'

Now I feel bad about trying to bully him off his turf. 'That's very kind but the thing is, they may not want to come to the door if they think ... well, if they think we're with you. No offence, but do you see what I mean? Maybe you could do your rounds in another neighbourhood today?'

'We're doing God's work,' Martha says.

'Well, we're doing PG Tips' work,' says Lou, holding up her basket. 'Come on, can't you give us a break? Love thy neighbour and all that?'

'You could come back tomorrow and ask everyone how they liked the cakes,' I suggest. 'That'd give you something to talk about.'

'The Lord our Saviour gives us enough to talk about,' says Martha, tightening her raincoat belt.

But Jonah puts his hand on his sister's arm. 'We can come back tomorrow, Emma. We hope your café will be a success. Maybe we'll come by to visit one day.'

'You're more than welcome!' I say. 'And thank you.'

As they walk away, Lou mutters, 'Now look what you've done. You've invited them in. Like vampires. You'll wish you hadn't.'

A few god-botherers are the least of my worries. Even though I know these are my neighbours, my tummy is doing flips as we make our way to the corner house. 'You're going to talk, yeah?' Lou asks me as Joseph rings the bell.

But the man doesn't answer. He must have used up all his hospitality on Jonah and Martha. Nobody answers at the next door or the next one either. That's when I remember about the squeaky gates. It drove me mad when we first moved in, but actually it's quite useful. If I hear the gates squeaking one after the other, it means there's a charity mugger or a Jehovah's Witness on the loose. No wonder nobody is answering. 'Come on,' I say, leading Joseph and Lou to the adjacent road. 'This'll take a bit longer, but I've got an idea.'

We choose a house at random and ring the bell.

A woman of about forty answers, but her look is suspicious.

Seeing us standing there with our wicker baskets probably doesn't help. 'Hi, we wanted to introduce ourselves …'

'Thanks, but I don't want any,' she says, going to close the door.

'Oh, no, I see. We're not selling anything. We're from the—'

'Not interested,' she says as the door clicks shut.

'That went well,' says Lou.

'She didn't even give us a chance,' I say. My face is flaming. 'That's not fair!' In a parallel universe, my seventeen-year-old self is stomping up and down.

'You've gotta hone your story, boss. That was waaaayyy too much waffle.'

'I only said about two words!'

'Maybe they were the wrong two words,' Lou says. 'He's right, we've only got a second to get the point across, and they don't really care who we are. They might care once they know we have free cake. I'd start with that if I were you.'

'All right then,' I say. 'Let's try it. Pick a house away from this one and you can do the talking this time. We'll be right behind you.'

She shrugs like it's no big deal but she pops her hair into her mouth and paces back and forth a few times, murmuring to herself, before picking a house around the corner. This time an older man answers – older than Dad but younger than my grandpa who smells like Pot Noodles.

'Free cake? We're giving delicious free cake and tea to all our neighbours,' Lou tells him. 'Would you like some?'

He frowns. 'Who are you?'

'We've got the new café over on Carlton Square. The cakes are from there. Vanilla cake or chocolate? We've got both.' She holds out one of each.

His expression relaxes. 'I was just about to have a cup of tea.'

'No need to make it yourself, sir,' Joseph says. 'We've got hot tea right here. Would you like it white or black? Sugar?'

I couldn't be prouder of my trainees. Ha, my trainees! They're training me.

We leave the man happy with his tea and cake, and the flyer that Lou remembers to press into his hand at the last minute. Buoyed by the success, Joseph wants to take the next house. 'Back in the square,' I say, leading the charge.

A few doors do slam in our faces, but Lou's and Joseph's approach definitely works better than mine.

Until we meet a woman who wants a fight, that is. She looks like she's been fighting all her life.

'Why would I take fackin' cake from yous?' she demands with her arms crossed and her scowl set deeply into her lined face. 'How do I know it ain't poison?' She's clearly got up on the wrong side of the bed, even though it's three-thirty in the afternoon. An inch of dark roots shows through her bleach-blonde hair, which is standing up on one side and mashed from the pillow on the other.

'But we're opening the café just over there,' Joseph says. 'Why would we poison you?'

'You fackin' lot.'

Lou squares up to the woman. 'Who're you talking about?'

'Lou,' I warn her. We all know who she's talking about. Kids, black kids, blue-haired hoodies, take your pick. Lou and Joseph have probably heard it their whole lives, but it'll take more than arguing to change a bigot's mind. 'The cake's from the Mad Batter,' I say. 'You know, the bakery? They really are yummy if you want a slice. We have tea too.' I wish I hadn't said yummy.

'Gimme, let's see. I can smell poison, you know. I'll 'ave your café if you're fackin' 'avin' me on.'

'*Someone* should poison you,' Lou mutters, but the woman is too busy sniffing the chocolate slice to notice. She takes an exploratory nibble, then stuffs a huge piece into her gob. 'Where's the tea,' she asks, spraying her doorstep with chocolate crumbs.

Joseph pours her a cup. 'And we're having a grand opening on Thursday.'

But when he tries to hand her a flyer, she says, 'Get yer dirty hands off me! I ain't goin' to yer fackin' café. Now get off my property or I'll call the cops.' She takes her paper cup of tea and slams the door shut.

'Another happy customer,' Lou says. 'This job is full of its own rewards.'

I try ringing Pablo, our coffee connoisseur, when we get back to the café, but it goes through to answerphone. 'Hi, Pablo, it's Emma again, just checking about the cups and plates. I know you said not to worry, but we open on Thursday and I really need to have them by then so if you could ring me as soon as you get the message that'd be great. Oh, and the coffee too. Will it come with the cups?'

'Why don't you just get them from somewhere else?' Lou asks when I've hung up.

'Because I already paid him for everything when I signed the contract. We'll use the takeaway cups if we need to, but I really wanted to start out like a proper café. Never mind, I'm sure it'll all be fine.'

'You don't have to do that, you know,' she says. 'Pretend everything is fine when clearly it's not. People are always doing that, like we're too thick to see what's obvious. Just because we're young doesn't mean we're thick.'

'I'm sorry, I know you're not thick, Lou. Far from it. I guess I want it all to be okay so I'm convincing myself as much as everyone else. Actually, I'm shitting myself about the whole thing, if you want the truth. I have no idea if this is going to work. I'm probably not supposed to say that to my trainees, but you asked and there it is. I figure we've got a chance if we can do a good job launching the café and get lots of people coming in regularly. But I have no idea if we can. And even if it's full every day, there are still a million things that can go wrong.'

'Thanks for the honesty.' She's smirking. 'Now I'm shitting myself too.'

'You can always go get another job,' I say. 'This is *everything* to me.'

Lou stares at me from beneath her fringe. 'You really believe I can just go find other work? With what you know about me? You're not the only one who needs the café to work.'

'Wow, that got serious fast,' I say. 'All you did was ask about cups.'

She shrugs. 'It's just real life. Next time I'll pretend to believe you when you say everything's okay.'

Joseph and Lou have gone home and it's just me in the café. I haven't been alone much in here lately. To tell the truth, I'm not used to being alone anywhere. Growing up in the house with Mum and Dad and Gran always around, and then sharing my bedroom with Auntie Rose after Granny died. I moved from there straight into the house on Carlton Square with Daniel, and then the twins came along and I haven't been alone, even in the loo, since.

When I first got the lease, I used to come in here every day just to sit in one of the dusty booths and try to imagine what it would look like. That was only six months ago, and already it's hard to remember what it was like before. Now when I see it, I see my café.

'Knock, knock,' Mrs Delaney calls through the window. 'Am I disturbing you?'

'Not at all, come in.' Mrs Delaney used to own the fabric shop next to the Vespa dealership where I worked. Kelly and I helped her sell the business to two nice dressmakers, giving Mrs Delaney a little something to retire on. After all, she is nearly eighty, though you wouldn't know it to look at her. With her salt-and-pepper pixie cut and trim figure that's always in a dress, she looks more like sixty.

It was Mrs Delaney's fabric sample books that Mum used to make the bunting for my wedding. Mum and I used them for the serviettes too. Mrs Delaney also redesigned Mum's wedding dress for me.

'My,' she says, 'you 'aven't done things by 'alf. This looks nice.'

'And your bunting,' I say, pointing to the ceiling.

'That's your bunting, girl, not mine.' She hands me a carrier bag. 'This is yours too.'

Yards of lace tumble out of the bag. 'I ran up some curtains for the windows.'

'This is from ...'

She nods.

They were the tablecloths from our wedding. Mrs Delaney had bolts of beautiful antique Belgian lace that she let us borrow from her shop. They were all different patterns and looked so romantic draped on the tables in the square.

'It's just taking up space and when I move to Tenerife I won't want to cart around a bunch of old lace, so I thought you may as well 'ave it. And you know I love you, Emma, but you're still shite with a sewing machine, so I figured I'd better run them up for you. There's cord to hang 'em in there. Come on, I'll help.' She kicks off her shoes and climbs into one of the booths. 'What's wrong with you, girl?' She's noticed me staring at her.

'You're amazing!'

'Oh, stop being so emotional. It's just a bit of old lace, not a donated kidney.'

But it feels like a lot more than that.

The house is dark when I get back from Mum's with the twins. She's still tetchy about me taking them to the café the other day, but she's going to have to get used to it. Lou's chair-corral gave me the idea for a sort of holding pen for them at one end of the café. Not that we'll call it a holding pen or, as Lou suggested, a kid cage. Kell's dad proved as handy with a hammer and saw as he is with his fish knife. He built a nice big enclosure for them with toddler-proof walls. It's got foam all around the edges for them to bounce off, soft mats covering the floor and a little bookshelf attached to one side. Now I don't have to worry that they'll get amongst the tables and pull hot teapots down on themselves. They'll still be free-range, though, inside the enclosure. I'm sure Magenta the Sandwich Whisperer would be pleased about that.

The front gate squeaks just as I'm wrestling Oscar into his high chair. 'Just in time!' I call as Daniel opens the front door. 'Catch Grace, will you?'

'Come here, young lady!' He scoops up our daughter to carry her to the dining room. 'Come here, slightly older lady!' He plants a kiss on my cheek.

The smell makes me reel back. 'Where have you been?' It's only six-thirty. 'Have you been drinking?'

He pretends not to hear me. 'What's Mummy got for supper for you two?'

I definitely smell something. Unless Daniel has a new cologne that stinks of drink. *Stinks of Drink, by Calvin Klein.*

'Daniel, you reek.'

'That's harsh, darling. I only had a few drinks after work.'

'This *is* after work, Daniel.'

'Right, we left a bit early today so I could be home at my normal time to help with the children. Will you please stop sniffing me? You're acting like you've caught me cheating. For the record, I am not cheating on you.'

'But you are, Daniel. You're cheating on me with your old life, while I'm here looking after our children.' I should get the chance to think about weekend plans and worry whether the wine is cold enough too. Instead, it's all feedings and faeces in my world.

'Em, I'm here to look after them too.'

Yes, but first he got to be regular old Daniel all day long. It's ugly to admit how envious I am of that.

Chapter 10

Tomorrow morning the Second Chance Café will finally be a reality. It only took five years of university, getting pregnant and rethinking my job prospects, begging a loan from my in-laws, months of renovations, days of interviews with teenagers who sucked their teeth at me or simply ignored me, and a bout of insomnia that I might never get over.

But first there's tonight. I try Pablo one last time even though I know I'll only have to leave a message. He might listen to his coffee speaking, but he never hears his phone ringing. 'You're probably getting sick of me and I'm sorry about that, but we still have no crockery and we open tomorrow. Thanks for your message, but the delivery didn't arrive so I don't know why the driver would say it did. Believe me, I'd notice if there were a hundred cups and plates here, because then I wouldn't be freaking out. So ring me. Please. Thanks. Bye.'

Hopefully people will understand this little glitch. Paper takeaway cups aren't the end of the world.

'Yo, boss, you think we've got enough cake?' Joseph surveys the sea of baked goods laid out on pretty plates and stands along the bar top. He's got his hair gelled straight up off the top of his head in a wavy black wedge, and even has a new tie – purple this time. 'We could feed East London on these, yeah.'

It was impossible to choose between Cleo's cakes when they all looked so delicious. Besides, it's important to be *abundant* when having a party to celebrate the grand opening of your business.

I don't remember if Uncle Colin had a party when he took over the Cock – I would have been too little even if he did. Dad had his own taxi for years, till the MS got too bad, but there wouldn't have been enough room in the back for more than four people to celebrate when he passed The Knowledge. And there definitely wasn't any fanfare when Kelly took over her dad's fish van. She might have got a new fish scaler or something.

Thinking about Kelly puts a little cloud over the night. It doesn't seem like she's thinking in Spanish yet. Every time I ask '*Que pasa?*' she answers 'Shut it' in English, so I don't think she's quite in the Iberian frame of mind. Even so, I'm scared that she's going to move. I couldn't blame her for following her heart, but I don't know what I'll do without her. A year from now she may not be here if I have another party.

'We look like the tossers at the school disco,' Lou says as we're all sat primly on the row of chairs we've pushed against the walls so there'll be room for everyone to stand in the middle. It is quite a big place with the furniture all cleared away. Hopefully not too big to fill.

My heart leaps when my entire family hurtles through the door two minutes before the party's official start. At least there'll be someone to eat that cake, although probably not Auntie Rose. Anything beyond vanilla is too foreign for her.

Uncle Barbara hands me a giant bouquet of yellow tulips. 'Congratulations, me girl!' He glances nervously at his dress. 'It isn't too much, is it?'

'It's perfect.' I grab his hand and drag him over to Lou and Joseph. 'This is my Uncle Barbara.'

'Who?' Joseph asks him as he shakes his hand.

'Barbara.'

'Yo, are you gay or something?'

'Smooth,' Lou says, cuffing the boy on the back of the head. 'I'm Lou. That's Joseph. Ignore him, he's a muppet.'

You can see why Joseph might ask the question. Uncle Barbara has outdone himself on his outfit. The flowery laser-print '50s style dress is definitely new and, paired with his favourite black cardie to cover his hairy shoulders, it goes perfectly with his tall black boots. As far as cross-dressers go, Uncle Barbara is pure class.

I wasn't sure what he'd wear tonight since we don't know everyone here like we do around the pub and my parents' house. He tends to stick close by when he's in a frock. Not that he can't take care of himself. He's six foot three and built exactly like his twin. Dad likes to say there was only so much height and intelligence to go round the family – they had to make do with one or the other – and that's why his brothers are so tall.

'No, I'm not gay,' Uncle Barbara says. He's not fazed by questions like this. People are usually just curious when they first see him. And it throws them that, with his short hair and stubbly beard, he's clearly not trying to look like a woman.

'Cuz it's cool if you are,' Joseph says.

'Thanks, I'm glad you think so, but I'm not.'

Joseph shrugs. 'It's okay. I wear suits and get the piss taken for it all the time. We're cool.'

Lou makes a face. 'You aren't cool, Joseph.'

The café fills up quickly with everyone I know, but I don't have much time to talk because we've got to make all the hot drinks. Every time I look over at Daniel, though, he's smiling at me. *I love you*, he mouths across the room.

We're okay now about the other night. I'm really trying not to resent him for having a drink with his friends like a normal person. It took me a while to calm down, though.

'This is easy,' Lou says, dumping a few more teabags into the last clean pot. I'll have to start using Mum's special ones soon. 'Shame about the cups. Real ones would have been nice.'

If only that was my biggest worry right now. Yes, the café is buzzing with chatter and everyone seems to love the cakes. Auntie Rose even sniffed some of the chocolate Guinness slice on Mum's plate. They're drinking tea as fast as we can make it and seem to be enjoying themselves. The problem is that everyone here is either a friend or family member. And I'm not being all John Lennon, peace and love, 'We Are the World' about it, as in 'Everyone is my friend.' I mean that I literally know everyone in the room.

What happened to all the potential customers? Where are the neighbours we invited, everyone we leafleted?

'Congratulations, you absolute superstar!!' Samantha shouts from behind an enormous bouquet of white lilies. 'These are for you, but I'm afraid they smell of wee. Not because of us. Only because sometimes lilies do. Sorry about that, but they are pretty!' She pulls me into a vice-like hug. 'How are you doing?' she whispers into my ear.

Her eyes search mine when I lie and say everything is great. If I repeat it enough, maybe I'll start believing it.

'For you, to mark the start of your new career,' Garnet says, handing me a little box.

'It's from us both,' says Emerald, as if I wouldn't have known that. 'I wrapped it.'

'You did a beautiful job,' says Garnet. 'I picked it out. Go on, open it.'

Garnet is right, the wrapping job is beautiful. It's intricately folded closed without any tape at all. My friends have a lot more free time than I do if they're learning origami skills.

Inside the box is a delicate silver charm bracelet that tinkles as I pull it from its tissue paper nest. There's a tiny till and a teacup hanging from the silver links.

'For good luck!' Emerald says. 'And you can add charms as you go along.'

'That's so thoughtful, thank you!' I hug them both, equally of course.

'I'm afraid I haven't got a gift,' Melody says, 'but I wish you all the luck in the world. You should be very proud of yourself. And of course we'll be your most loyal customers.'

At this rate, they might be my only customers. I don't even see Carl and Elsie. I thought they'd come for sure, at least for the free tea.

'You'll be most welcome,' I tell my friends. 'You and the children, of course.' Without the children, you probably wouldn't automatically put them together, with Melody in her flowing tunic and scarves of every colour, Garnet and Emerald wearing skinny jeans and sheer jumpers, and Samantha, who also usually wears skinny jeans with sleek tops but tonight is dressed in a wool camel body-con dress and sky-high heels that she swears she can run for the bus in. It really is the children that connect us all.

'Is your family coming tonight?' I ask Lou a bit later. I can't keep the hope from my voice. They don't quite count as customers, but now I'm desperate.

'I don't have family,' she says.

I meant her foster family, but I guess she knows that. 'Joseph, what about your mum and brother?'

'Nah, tea and cake isn't really my brother's thing.'

'Your mum?'

His eyes dart away. 'Nah.'

'I don't understand why nobody else is here,' I say. 'You definitely put the flyers up on the main road too? With lots of tape? It's been windy today.'

I know I'm grasping at straws. What are the chances that the wind blew down all the notices *and* every flyer we put through the letterboxes?

'Darling, hellair!' Philippa booms as she comes through the door. She always comes at you like a category-four hurricane. No matter how much warning you have, all you can do is batten down the hatches and hope for the best. 'We are so excited for your opening! It's gorgeous in here, rahly, you are so clever. And these cakes! Hellair,' she says to Lou and Joseph. 'I'm Philippa, how d'you do?'

They gawp at my mother-in-law. It's not so much what she's wearing – just her usual finely knitted dark jumper, fitted trousers and pearl necklace– as the sheer force she exudes. Philippa is a law unto herself.

When she asks for a cappuccino (only if it's not too much trouble, darlings!), I set Lou on to it. We all listen to the Gaggia build up a head of steam. Joseph carefully grinds the exact amount for the shot and Lou gets the milk ready for frothing. 'I'll bring it to you in just a minute, okay?' I tell Philippa. 'Have you seen my parents? They're over there with the twins and Daniel.'

I think we all feel better without an audience. But despite following Pablo's instructions, the machine is stubbornly refusing to give us any espresso. 'Try it again,' I tell them.

That Gaggia is not a team player.

'One more time, from the very start. We can do this. We did it the other day.'

'Beginner's luck?' Joseph asks.

'Shh, listen,' says Lou, putting her ear to the side of the machine. 'Do you hear that? Is it telling us what's wrong?'

Joseph leans in on the other side. 'It's crying.'

'I cry for the bean,' Lou says.

'We'll all be crying if we can't make coffee,' I remind them. 'Joseph, try getting it to steam the milk. Does that work at least?'

'Yes, boss.'

'And stop calling me boss. Lou, where's that Nescafé?'

A few minutes later I hand Philippa a frothy Nescachino and a slice of cake. We'll have to figure out the machine later.

'Darling, what is this?' She's holding the paper cup like it's a used Kleenex. I explain about the crockery delay, leaving out my panicked voicemails to Pablo. 'Oh, how utterly awful for you!' she exclaims.

Well, in the scheme of world events, it's not exactly a refugee crisis, is it?

Her eyes sweep the room, taking in every detail. 'Do you think you could use some cats in here, darling?'

'Why, do you think we have mice?' Or rats? Has she seen something?

'No, no, I'm sure you don't. It's just that I've heard about the most amahzing café where they have cats. Cats and cakes, isn't that divine? I think it›s near here, actually. Maybe you know them, darling.'

Philippa is convinced that I know everyone east of Liverpool Street. At least once a week she sends me an article from the paper about someone doing something good in East London, always with the same few words scrawled across the top. *How wonderful for your friend!* I suppose that's because of the wedding, when it probably did seem like the entire borough was there. My in-laws expected the champagne-soaked wedding of the century on a beer purse, and we'd never have pulled it off without a lot of help from our friends.

The café door swings open, but it's not a customer. Just Kelly and Calvin. Well, not *just* Kelly, but you know what I mean.

Where are all the customers?

'Congratulations!' Kell shouts in my ear as she squeezes me in a hug so tight I can hardly breathe. 'This is awesome and you did it!'

'There are no real customers, Kell,' I whisper in her ear. I don't have the guts to admit that to anyone except her. 'It's all friends and family. This isn't good.'

'Right then, let's sort that out,' she says. 'I'll be back, Calvin.'

Calvin shrugs and smiles. With his riot of blondy-brown curls and tanned skin he looks like a surfer and he's just as laid-back. He won't mind that his girlfriend is abandoning him two minutes after they get here. He knows us by now.

'Team meeting,' I tell Lou and Joseph, who are doing another round with the teapots. 'In the kitchen.'

After introductions, since Lou and Joseph have heard me talk about Kelly a lot but haven't actually met her, I say, 'I think we should go around to the neighbours and remind them about the party. Nobody's turned up so maybe they forgot, or lost track of time or something.'

Joseph is shifting from foot to foot. 'I don't think that's it.'

'Don't,' Lou says. 'Don't, Joseph, not tonight.'

But he pulls a piece of paper from his jacket pocket. 'This is probably where they all are. We didn't want to show you before, in case it didn't matter,' Joseph says, handing me the folded leaflet.

Kelly and I stare at it.

SICK AND TIRED OF THE GENTRIFICATION OF OUR NEIGHBOURHOOD?
with fancy new cafés coming in charging the world for a simple cup of tea?

Want a good old-fashioned cuppa FOR FREE?
COME TO TOMBOLA NIGHT
6–9 Thursday
Loads of great prizes
at The Other Half Caff

'It's that builder's caff on the main road,' Kell says. 'You know the one, with the yellow front that always looks dirty. Are you saying everyone's there instead of here?'

When Joseph shrugs, the shoulder pads in his suit nearly reach his ears. It's obvious he doesn't like breaking this news to me. 'My mum had the flyer through the door. She would've come here, but she loves tombola.'

'Everybody loves tombola,' I say. I wish I'd thought of it. 'Look at the top. They must have seen our flyer first, otherwise they wouldn't mention new cafés.'

So it's an attack, to keep customers away from us. I lean against the worktop. Why would they do that? Surely there's enough business to go around. We're tucked away off the main road. It's not like we've set up next door.

'What'll you do, boss?'

'Ignore it,' Kell advises. 'At least for tonight. Maybe a few punters will come by after, or they're on their way here now. You can't let it ruin your night. You've worked too hard for this. Tomorrow you can figure out what to do.'

But I can't ignore it, knowing that all my potential customers are around the corner raffling their traitorous little hearts out. 'Let's go see how many people are there,' I say. 'Maybe it's empty. At least then I'll know there's another reason people haven't shown up here. I think that would make me feel better. Are you two okay here for a little while if Kell and I go? Just keep making Nescafé with steamed milk if anyone orders coffee and we'll be back soon.'

Kell and I sneak out the back door and through the gate so I don't have to explain to anyone what's going on.

But she stops me as we get to the main road. 'You definitely can't go in there, you know,' she says. 'And you shouldn't really even go near the place. They might know what you look like. Don't give them the satisfaction of seeing you upset. I'll have a look for you.'

'Thanks, but I need to see for myself,' I say. 'We'll just walk by quickly. It's dark. They can't see out with all the lights on inside.'

The caff glows yellow from the strip lights in the ceiling, illuminating dozens of faces. It's packed, standing room only. Everyone is boisterous, laughing, have a grand time. There's a stocky middle-aged woman with short blonde hair at the tombola. She's shouting at everyone and calling out numbers to raucous laughter.

It's exactly what I imagined our grand opening would look like. Minus the prizes.

'Come on, don't stare,' Kell says. 'We've seen it now.' She loops her arm round my shoulder to lead me away. 'I'm sorry, Em. This sucks, but it's not the end of the world. Just because she got them in for tombola doesn't mean they won't come to the café. You'll see, people will love your place.'

'But why would she do it? That's what I don't get.'

Kell shrugs. 'She probably just saw the opportunity and took it. Think about it. Someone goes to all the effort to let people know there's something on in the neighbourhood. You warmed them up. All she had to do was offer more free stuff and of course people are going to take it. They were probably all ready to go to the party but, sorry to say, the tombola idea trumped it. They're getting prizes with their free tea. I'm sure your cakes are good, but they can't really compete against free bottle openers and Dairy Milks and the market tat that she's probably handing out. Maybe you should give out free fridge magnets with every cuppa. That'd get the punters in.'

When we get back to the café, Mrs Delaney and the vicar, Del, are standing in the doorway. 'Quite the merry turnout,' Del calls when he sees me. 'May we all be the harbingers of glad tidings and manifold successes.'

He always talks like he's on a nineteenth-century stage. You'd never think it to look at him, with his shaved head, crooked nose and all the tattoos covering his arms and neck. The black clergy shirt and dog collar he's wearing do help him look slightly less like a hooligan. 'Ah, I see your lovely offspring and husband are inside. Delightful.' He kisses my cheek and strides off amongst his flock.

His guidance isn't always so much spiritual as it is spirituous. We usually see him in the Cock and Crown, communing with his whiskey.

'How are you doing, girl?' Mrs Delaney asks. 'Happy?' She's dressed up especially tonight and her elfin face is beaming. I recognise the cinch-waisted pale blue 1950s dress from her shop. We put it on one of the mannequins when we were tarting up the place to help her sell it.

'It's great to see everyone here,' I tell her truthfully. Kelly is right. There's nothing I can do about my neighbours not turning up. We'll just have to find a new way to get them in here after the café is open tomorrow.

'Is that your mother-in-law?' She points to where Philippa is talking to my father-in-law, Hugh, and Uncle Colin. 'Has she had work done or something?'

'Who, Philippa? No, she never would!' Most of Philippa's society friends might be on a first-name basis with the cosmetic surgeons on Harley Street, but she hardly ever bothers with make-up, let alone Botox.

Although something about her does look different.

'Hellair, darling, hellair, Mrs Delaney, so lovely to see you again,' she says when we walk over. Philippa never forgets a face, which is handy for keeping all the lords, ladies and heads of state straight in her head for the next drinks party.

'Erm, Philippa, are you feeling okay?' Her face is starting to get puffy.

She puts her hand to her cheek. 'Just a bit flushed, I think, thank you, darling. It's quite warm in here. We were telling Colin about our wine tour in South Africa. It was divine. You really must go, or at least come to supper and we'll open a few of the nice bottles.' She wipes her brow, where beads of sweat are glistening.

'Can I get you some water, Philippa? Or something to eat? Maybe you should sit down.'

'No, thank you, I'b fine. Just a bit warb. Well, baybe sub water would be nice.'

'What's happened to your lips?!' Hugh says.

They're starting to look like someone's used a bicycle pump on them. And her eyes are getting squinty.

'Oh, Phil, what did you eat?' Hugh asks.

'Just some of that divine raspberry cake.'

'It must have had almonds in it,' he says.

He's right. It's made with ground almonds. 'Are you allergic?!'

She starts rubbing at the red blotches on her neck. 'No, darling, don't gib it a thought. It's just a little reaction. I'll be fine in a few hours. Rahly, it's nothing to worry about. If you happen to have an antihistabine I could take one, but otherwise the swelling will go down on its own. So where was I? Oh, yes, South Africa.'

'Does she need the hospital?' I ask Hugh. This is perfect. I've poisoned my mother-in-law.

'Right, no, she'll be fine. She's tough as old boots. It's just swelling. Happens a lot, especially around Christmas. Can't keep her off the marzipan.'

Philippa won't let anyone fuss over her, and she doesn't seem the least bit fazed that she looks like one of those 'after' photos of lip-fillers gone wrong.

Later, Mum finds me leaning against the worktop in the kitchen. 'I'll take Dad and Auntie Rose home, and I think Daniel is ready to go with the twins. What's wrong, love?'

It all comes pouring out: that we can't work the coffee machine, we won't have any crockery when we open tomorrow, that everyone's gone to the tombola and that I could have killed my mother-in-law with a cake.

'These are all just teething problems that you need to work out, that's all,' says Mum. 'In a way that's what tonight is for, really.'

'But Mum, have you seen Philippa? You could use her lips as a bouncy castle.'

She sniggers. 'I saw her. She reminded me of those models of Neanderthals they put on telly sometimes. Look, you'll find a way round all of this. Just be sure to get the ingredients for the cakes and write on cards when there's anything people might want to avoid. Ring your fancy coffee consultant and get him in here for a refresher before you open tomorrow.' She gathers me into a hug. 'I promise these problems are solvable, and it'll all look better in the morning,' she says. 'Especially Philippa's face.'

Chapter 11

Pablo finally answers my voicemails at the crack of dawn the next morning. At first I thought the hysteria in my voice had convinced him that I really did need him, but he just wants the chance to fondle the Gaggia again. He's stroking it with a tea towel, polishing off every fingerprint and watermark from last night's frantic attempts to coax it into doing its job. He keeps murmuring *carina mia*, and I know he's not talking to me.

To look at him, you'd never know I've been leaving him threatening messages for two weeks. His smile is relaxed, blissful almost, and I'd like to strangle him. I can't, though. He's the only person around here who knows how to make coffee. Without him, that Gaggia is just an overpriced hanger for tea towels.

Hopefully I haven't misread my clientele by getting it. Virtually everyone last night wanted tea, not coffee. Even

Philippa seemed happy with the Nescafé, though I'd never admit that to Pablo. And didn't Carl and Elsie reject Rome, one of the most beautiful cities in the world, packed with history and culture, because he couldn't get a decent cup of tea? Maybe all we really need to do is boil water. It would be easier than working that temperamental machine.

Somehow I can't imagine the owner of the Other Half Caff fiddling with one. But then I can't imagine her worrying too much about pleasing her customers at all. She does seem to know what they want, though, judging by how many people were at tombola last night. It's hard not to feel panicky just thinking about it. Lou was being kind to say it wasn't personal. Of course it was. The question is: why?

'Pablo, about the crockery we've ordered.'

'Yes,' he says, not taking his eyes off the steam nozzle that he's wiping. 'I am thinking it has already come and you did not notice. You have been very busy, I think.'

'All right then, if it's been delivered, where is it? Show me, please, because we open in an hour and I have nothing to serve coffee in.'

His movements are so languid that I want to scream. Into the kitchen he wanders, opening the cabinet doors and commenting on everything he finds there. Then he circles the café, peering under tables and into corners.

'I've already checked everywhere. Admit it, Pablo. They're not here.'

'They are not here,' he agrees. 'There may be a problem.'

'Thank you, yes, it seems like there may be a problem. Will you sort the problem?'

'Of course, *carina mia*.'

'Good ... and might that be today?'

'Of course.' He waves the question away. 'And now I will remind you how to ask the espresso to sing. Come, I will show you the magic. We will make the magic.'

But we hardly get started on making the magic when there's a sharp rap at the door. 'Delivery.' A skinny man's handcart is piled with red plastic crates. 'Sign here.' He shoves his scanner at me. 'No pen. Use your finger.' As if anyone in the history of deliveries has ever been able to track down her missing package from a finger signature.

He stacks the crates in the middle of the doorway while I make a point of ignoring Pablo's expression. Nobody likes a smug Italian.

I carry the first heavy box back to the bar. 'That was close, Pablo. We almost had to use the takeaway. Hey, what is this?' I hold up a dainty teacup. They're all the same pattern: white flowers on a bright blue background with gold curlicues and gold rims, and gorgeous colourful roses painted inside. There are scalloped-edge cake plates to match. They are stunning. They are definitely *not* what I ordered from Pablo.

'*Bella*,' he says. 'Very pretty.'

'Very not your delivery, though.' When I glance at the paper the delivery man left on the box, I see that I have a fairy godmother. Or a fairy mother-in-law, at least. 'You still owe me crockery,' I tell Pablo, taking out my phone to ring Philippa. 'These are only temporary.'

'Oh good, darling, I'm glad they've arrived in one piece,' Philippa says when I gush my thanks at her. 'And don't be silly, I'm glad to do it. I'm not using them. We have those lovely big mugs you gave us for Christmas last year, so keep them for as long as you like. I hope forty-eight will be enough. I'm sorry I haven't got more place settings.'

Who, aside from the royal family, has forty-eight place settings in the first place? 'It's going to be hard to go back to normal old cups after these,' I tell her. 'You're spoiling us!'

'Oh, well, darling, I'm happy for you to keep them if you want. They're not heirlooms or anything. Hugh and I got them as wedding gifts and I'm sure they still make the pattern. I can always get replacements for us.'

'But I didn't mean for you to give them to me! I'll get them back to you as soon as the ones I've ordered turn up. I'm sure it'll be sorted out today.' I shoot Pablo a pointed look. 'Thank you.'

I always have to be so careful with compliments around Philippa. She'll literally hand you the shirt off her own back if she thinks you'd like it. This is the woman who sent me a two dozen handmade chocolate bars to taste – big ones, too, not the tiddly little sample sizes – on the off-chance I might like one enough to have at the wedding. I'm just glad I steered her away from her café cat idea or she might have sent live animals instead.

'It's just gone nine,' Lou says. 'I don't suppose everyone's waiting outside.' A slight twitch at the corner of her mouth gives her away.

'You're joking,' I say, because, despite the twitch, I still need to check these things. Lou is as deep and still as Loch Ness.

'Of course. Can't you tell? I'm practically hysterical.'

I stare at the doorway while Joseph and Lou stare at their phones.

It feels exactly like it did a minute ago, before we were officially open. I didn't expect a stampede, but it would be nice if an actual customer turned up today.

The cakes are sitting along the bar – with warnings about the things that might kill a person – and we've all tied and retied our new black aprons a few times. Pablo has left us alone with the Gaggia and a notebook full of instructions. Now we need customers.

'Maybe we should put some flyers up again on the road,' I say. 'Just to remind people we're here.'

'I don't know,' Lou says. 'When was the last time you paid attention to a flyer that wasn't about a lost cat?'

'Shame we don't have a lost cat,' says Joseph. 'Pictures get attention.'

Pursing her lips, Lou starts scanning her phone around the café. 'Then let's give them pictures.' She aims at the row of cakes. 'Joseph, stand up there and pretend you're making a coffee. You make a good blurry background.'

Thoughtfully, she chooses a few of Mum's teapots to add to the shot, then stacks some teacups beside them. As I watch her, I realise that Lou does everything with care. There's never any hurry or faff about her. She's the kind of person you'd want on a desert island. Joseph and I would be flapping around in a panic after writing SOS on the beach, probably below the tide mark at dusk, and she'd quietly be starting a fire and building shelter for the night.

It's hard sometimes to remember that she's only seventeen.

We crowd around Lou's phone as she scrolls through the photos. 'The café looks beautiful!' I say. 'I guess we should print the flyer in colour. I'll just have to get some more ink.'

166

'You are a living fossil,' she says. 'I'll add some filters and bring these to Snappy Snaps. Give me a tenner. They can print us off a bunch in about two minutes. We can just write whatever we want about the café on the back and hand them out along the main road. They'll get more attention than leaflets.'

'Put them on the Instagram account too,' Joseph says.

They see my expression. 'Don't worry, grandma, we can make one for you.'

'I'll do it,' Joseph says. 'And Facebook too. And that makes me the Head of Social Media, yeah?'

'Christ.' Lou rolls her eyes. 'I'll be right back with the photos.'

'Cup of tea?' I offer to Joseph as he's setting something up on my phone.

'Thanks. You can't be second chance café with a number two,' he says, 'but you can be second chance café all spelled out. I'll do that, yeah?'

'Whatever's best.'

'Don't you know about any of this stuff? That's bare weird, boss. How do you talk to your mandems?'

I shrug. It's not like I've never heard of Twitter – despite what they think, I don't live under a rock – but none of my friends bother being online. What would Kell post about? Hashtag fish scales OMG guts LOL? 'When we want to talk we ring each other or I go down the market,' I tell Joseph.

'Bare weird.'

As I watch him deftly create an entire social media platform for the café, I can't help but think again that they're not the only ones getting training around here.

We both look up in surprise when a man walks through the door. He's got chunky black-framed glasses and one of those hipster beards that I tell Daniel I'll leave him over if he ever dares to grow one. He's wearing a blue tweed three-piece suit. I've never been partial to tweed on men under seventy, and the suit should give this guy a Farmer Ted vibe, but he's tall and slim so it looks more Ted Baker.

He doesn't seem to notice us, though. He hurries past the booths along the windows at the front, peering under the benches before choosing a table near the wall at the side.

'Give him a few minutes,' I tell Joseph, 'and then go take his order. I'll try to get the Gaggia going in case he wants a coffee.'

Our first customer! Whatever he orders, I'm going to have the pounds set into a frame for the wall behind the bar. If he pays with a note, maybe I'll even get him to sign it. I feel like naming something after him. The tweedy tea. Beardy bacon butty.

He sets his leather courier bag on the table like he's planning to do some work while he's here. That could mean cake and maybe even a sandwich. At least a tweedy tea.

He takes out his phone and his iPad. Then another phone. That's right, mate, settle in. Out comes his laptop. He should have picked the booth where there's more room. I'm just about to go over to suggest it when he pulls a handful of cables from his bag and carefully attaches them to his devices. Plugging the ends into a six-socket power strip, also from his bag, he plugs the whole thing into the wall.

Finally, he takes out a beard trimmer and his electric toothbrush.

This guy's not a customer. He's a drain on the National Grid.

'Yo bruv, seriously?' Joseph hisses from behind the Gaggia. 'Has he got a Prius outside that needs charging too?'

'Ssh, we need the business.'

'You're not gonna get it from him, boss, you watch.' Before I can warn him not to assault anyone, Joseph strides over to the man. But instead of threatening him, he says calmly, 'Hi, what can I get for you? Tea? Coffee? We have cake too.'

'Maybe later, thanks.' The man crosses his legs, completely at ease about the trail of cables running up my electricity bill.

'Nothing at all now? Not a hot drink? Are you sure?'

He strokes his beard. He's probably contemplating a trim once his shaver is charged. 'I'll just have a pot of hot water, please.'

As Joseph stomps back to the bar, I see the man take a teabag out of his satchel.

'Boss, he's taking the piss.'

I've got to admit a twisted kind of admiration for him. I could never pull that off. I feel guilty getting free Coke refills at Nando's or accepting those cheese samples they do sometimes in the big Tesco. He's probably scrounging three square meals a day. 'I know he is,' I tell Joseph, 'but it does look better when there are people in here. Maybe someone will see him through the window, come in and actually pay for a drink. Take his photo,' I murmur. 'Post it on your social media as our first customer. He owes us at least that much.'

Our takings at the end of the day are exactly four pounds and sixty pence. Two women came in for takeaway cappuccinos and I had to keep myself from kissing them when I gave them their change. Less the electricity the guy used to charge all his household devices, today was a loss.

Even so, I can't stop smiling. It's my café and it's open. Lou and Joseph handed out dozens of photo adverts and put them through everyone's door too. I'm not expecting a stampede first thing tomorrow morning, but people will start to come and things will get better. Looking at the bright side, they can hardly get any worse.

The cakes are all cling-filmed and I'm just about to lock up when I hear the door open. It sends my heart soaring. I'll stay open all night if it's a real live customer. I'll even work the Gaggia.

But it's better than a customer. It's Daniel, who definitely won't make me work the Gaggia.

'Well done on your first day, Em. Are you nearly finished?' he says, scooping me up in a hug. 'Do you need any help? I rahly wanted to be here earlier to see you in action.'

'That's okay. There wasn't very much action to see. I'm glad you're here.'

'I'm glad I'm here too, and I've got a surprise for you. I've got us a reservation for seven at The Enterprise.'

For the second time in a few minutes, my heart flip-flops. I *love* The Enterprise. Whenever I needed to revise for exams during Uni or finish a paper, I'd decamp from my parents' house to stay at Daniel's. Usually he'd cook for us, but sometimes we'd splurge on a meal out around the corner at The Enterprise. It's full of lovely dating memories, when our biggest responsibility was paying the bill at the end of the meal.

Not like now. 'The children,' I say, speaking of respon-sibilities. As far as I remember, the restaurant doesn't have a lot of room for a double pushchair. It probably hasn't got a lot of patience for two lively toddlers either.

Daniel cringes a bit. 'Yah, right, please don't be cross with me, but I've asked your mum and dad to look after them so I can take you out properly. I rahly wanted a way to mark this day for you and have a mini celebration. It's a milestone, Em. You deserve to be spoiled.'

How can I argue with that logic?

When he takes my hand on the walk to the Tube and I tell him about the beardy electricity hoarder, it starts to feel like it did when we were first dating. Like the months and years are rewinding.

I need this reminder about who we were, about who we are. We need this. It's worryingly easy to get lost in family life till, before you know it, you're just two strangers job-sharing nappy duty.

The restaurant is buzzy and the hostess claims to remember us, which is pleasing even if it's a total lie. We should definitely try something similar at the café. Even if it's someone's first time in, they'll like being welcomed like an old friend.

No, stop thinking about work, I warn myself. I'm out properly with my husband for the first time in months. I have to hold on to this romantic feeling as much as I can. Otherwise we may as well be home on the settee watching *Gogglebox*.

But what will we talk about if not work or the children, when that's all I've thought about lately? I've barely read a magazine, let alone a book, since the twins were born, and Daniel watches all the same telly programmes that I do. There's nothing new to report about my parents or Auntie Rose. He's probably not interested that her haemorrhoids have cleared up nicely, though obviously she's pleased about it. I've obsessed enough over Kelly's possible move to Spain, and there's no news there anyway. She nearly gave me a heart attack when she said *Hola!* the other day, but when I questioned her (*Que?*) she claimed she was just practising with Calvin.

Despite having carried on perfectly entertaining conversations with Daniel for the past three years, now I find myself casting about in my mind for something to say. 'Do you know that astronauts aren't allowed to eat beans before going into space?'

It's not the most obvious dinner topic, I grant you. Joseph reeled off a list of 'facts' today while we waited for the customers who mostly never came. 'Something about the expanding gas in space being bad for their spacesuits. Isn't that interesting?'

'Are you planning to go into space?'

'Pah. As if I've ever farted,' I say. 'Me, the mother of your children.' Instantly I regret saying that. Daniel was in the room when the twins were born. It might take a lifetime to forget what went on in there. He doesn't need any reminders.

'Would you go into space if you got the chance?' he asks as the waiter brings our wine. 'I'd do it in a heartbeat.'

But I shake my head. 'No way. What if I couldn't come back? It's not like having a cancelled flight where you get the next one and might have to land at Gatwick instead of Heathrow. You could be stuck out there forever.'

'Like Major Tom,' he says. 'You're right. I wouldn't do it now, obviously, not with you and the children. If I have to stay on earth, I'm glad it's with you.'

But I wonder what else he'd love to do, if it weren't for us. I haven't got the guts to ask him that. 'What's happening at work?' I say instead, steering us on to safer topics. But as he talks about his latest water project in Africa, I wonder again if he sometimes wishes things had gone differently for us. When we first met, he was sure he wanted to go work locally for his charity at some point. Coordinating projects from London is one thing, he always said. Think how much more rewarding it would be to work with the villagers directly and see how their projects improve lives. Personally I'd be happy never to sleep in a mud hut – I don't even see the appeal of glamping at Glastonbury – or have to worry about spiders that might live in the grass roof. But Daniel wouldn't mind. Now he'll never get to do that.

'We're so lucky to live in the UK,' I say. 'Imagine not even having safe water to drink and always worrying about whether your children will fall ill.' Not to mention the spiders.

'Yah, I know. It puts Oscar's sniffles into perspective, doesn't it?'

At first I laugh. 'What do you mean, Oscar's sniffles? What sniffles?'

'Oh, nothing, rahly. He was feeling a bit peaky this afternoon, that's all. Your mum said it's nothing to worry about.'

'Peaky how? What's wrong with him? Is he ill? What about Grace, is she feeling well?' They're up-to-date on their vaccinations, but they haven't had their last diphtheria shot. What if it's that? Does diphtheria cause sniffles? Why don't I know this?! Or polio? Maybe it's polio. Measles, mumps, rubella?

'Emma, darling, relax. It's probably just a little cold, that's all. Your mum wasn't worried.'

And neither is my husband, clearly. He's sitting there sipping his wine while our children could have polio. 'We need to go,' I say.

'Em, don't do this, please. Oscar is fine. Ring your mum if you don't believe me. She'll tell you. Go on, ring her. You'll feel better.'

But he doesn't need to tell me that. My phone is already out. 'He's fine, Emma,' Mum says when she answers. 'He's not got any fever and he's just eaten like a horse. He's playing peekaboo with Dad. If you turn up here before nine o'clock, I won't let you have him, so you may as well enjoy your dinner. I'm sorry, but it's for your own good. Have a glass of wine and order a starter.' She hangs up.

'Feel better?' he asks, pouring more wine.

'My own mother just hung up on me.'

'It's her brand of tough love. Look, Em, we'll go if you really want to. I want you to be happy.'

He's right. Mum's right. Everybody's right. My children probably don't have a deadly disease. 'I am quite hungry,' I tell him. 'Let's share the calamari.' My heart's not into squid or anything else on the menu now, but the least I can do is pretend after Daniel's gone to the trouble.

The twins are asleep in their cots when we get to Mum and Dad's after dinner. 'You can leave them here if you'd like,' Mum whispers as I adjust their blankets and study them for signs of bubonic plague or similar. 'Come get them in the morning before you go to the café. It'll give you and Daniel a night alone.'

But it took all my willpower not to hail a cab from the restaurant to get to Mum's. I'm not leaving them again if I don't have to.

They barely wake when we scoop them into their pushchair. They're used to being manhandled when they're trying to sleep.

'I have a favour to ask,' I say to Daniel as we push them home. 'Would you go into that caff on the main road and spy for me? I'm dying to know what it's like and the owner won't know who you are. You could take the twins and pose as a dishy daddy.'

'I'm not posing,' he says. 'I am a dishy daddy.' He bats his long eyelashes at me. He is quite dishy. Unfortunately for him, I'm also quite tired. On the menu of after-dinner romance, I could probably manage a simple fruit plate or maybe a slice of cheese. Anything more complicated like a soufflé (forty-five minutes to prepare, madam) is out of the question.

I pace through the house the next morning, waiting for them to get back, until finally I hear the front gate squeak.

'Well?'

Daniel's shaking his head and laughing as he wrestles the pushchair inside. 'You won't believe it when I tell you. She actually threw us out of the caff.'

'She knew who you were?!' Of course. Even wearing jeans instead of his usual red or green or yellow chinos, Daniel would have stood out with the twins. There can't be that many sets around here. I knew I should have tried harder to get Joseph to go in with his mum. Even if it would have meant him dying from shame like he'd claimed.

'No, I don't think she had any idea who we were,' says Daniel. 'She came over the minute we got inside. I thought at first she was going to offer to find space for the push-chair, but she was hostile, Em. She said, "No effing kids in here. Go find a Starbucks." Naturally that put me on the defensive. I mean, rahly, she'd just sworn at our children. I asked who she was and she said she's Barb and what's it to me and I should eff off with the children. I'm glad you didn't go in there. She was irate enough with me and I'm a stranger. Who knows what she'd do if she saw you. We thought it best not to push the issue, didn't we, darlings? So we went to Brick Lane and got bagels for Mummy instead.' He hands me a bag and plants a quick kiss on my lips as I take in this bit of news. 'Honestly, Em, you've got nothing to worry about as far as competition goes if she won't even let parents inside. Rahly rude.'

Chapter 12

Daniel's run-in with the caff owner sticks in my gut long after our bagels have digested. The shear nuttiness of swearing at toddlers is one thing, but what kind of business person is so rude to her customers? She's supposed to be serving people who come into her caff. It's not like Daniel turned up at her house asking to sit in her lounge for a cup of tea.

I know it's an opportunity if my rival is snubbing the parents around here, but how dare she treat my children that way? She doesn't even know how annoying they can be.

Grace is wedging playing cards into the DVD player. It's been one of her favourite games since she found them in the cabinet. We've unplugged the machine so she can't electrocute herself, and I probably shouldn't let her do it but she screams whenever I try getting her to kick her card habit. Frankly, I'm picking my battles.

Oscar isn't interested in his sister's game. The poor little thing has a molar coming through. He's flushed and pitiful and feeling very sorry for himself. All he's wanted since waking was for me to hold him, which wasn't easy in the café. My arms are killing me.

There's a chicken roasting that needs checking, but I can't very well lean into a 200°C oven with a toddler in my arms. 'Daniel, can you please check the roast?' He looks up from his laptop. 'It should be ready, but just check. Grace, darling, have you run out of cards already? Then it looks like the game's finally over, isn't it?'

She's pointing to the DVD player as her face crinkles. That gives me about five seconds to distract her before she goes off. 'How about bear? You love bear.' I move the stuffed toy closer with my foot.

Her face is turning puce. 'No, not bear? What about your music box. Ah, look.' But I can't get the leverage to wind the music with one hand. Fat tears appear in Grace's eyes.

'Come here, my love.' Daniel rushes over to scoop her up. 'Let's have a gallop, shall we?' He jiggles her in his arms, round and round the lounge and through the dining room. 'That's better, isn't it? Yes, that's better.' She's giggling like a crazy baby.

Then Daniel's face goes funny. 'Here, you take Grace,' he says. 'I'll just go check on that roast like you asked.'

He shifts her to my free arm and rushes for the kitchen.

'Oh god, Grace! Daniel, what did you shake out of this child?'

'Hmm? Oh, did she?' He sticks his head into the oven, where I'm sure it smells better.

That hand-off was no coincidence. I've been sapootaged.

'Can you please change her?' I ask. 'I can't really let go of Oscar or he'll have a meltdown.'

'I'd love to, but I'm just dealing with dinner,' Daniel calls from the kitchen. 'I'm sure he'll be fine if you put him down for a second.'

He does this all the time, coming across as helpful, parachuting in to save the day when it's easy. Low-hanging fruit, that's what he's been picking. His basket is overflowing. Meanwhile, he leaves me stretching for the upper branches.

I stomp upstairs with our children, one clinging to my neck and the other giggling and stinking to high heaven. This is living the dream.

The next morning when I shove Daniel in the back, I feel a rush of satisfaction knowing he was in a deep sleep. 'The twins are awake,' I say, hauling myself upright. 'Can you get their breakfast started while I change them? I was up till four with Oscar, the poor little thing. That tooth must be killing him. Didn't you hear him?'

'Mmm, no.' He stretches. 'I didn't hear a thing.'

Which really makes me want to shove him in the back again.

He's at his laptop when I finally get them downstairs after cleaning up the aftermath of two overpowered nappies. 'Daniel. Their breakfast?'

'Just checking an email. I'll be two secs.'

'Right,' I mutter. 'Never mind, don't bother. I'll do it.'

'No, Em, I said I would, if you'll just let me deal with this email. I've only come downstairs this minute.'

'So have I! God, Daniel, you know they won't sit in their chairs without food and I'm not going to let them start playing or I won't get them fed and I have to get to the café early this morning. So I'm sorry you'd like a relaxing morning after your good night's sleep!'

I hate the way I sound, but it all just wells up out of me. I've turned into that person who screams at her husband, like some character off *EastEnders* when a fight breaks out at the Queen Vic.

He's on his feet before I can start on Act Two of my tirade (*The Exclaiming of the Shrew*). 'Em, Em, calm down, I'll make breakfast.' He circles us all with his arms. 'I'm sorry. I'm sorry. I do try, you know. I'm always trying.' He kisses the top of my head and I let my cheek rest on his chest. I know he's trying. He's just no good at it.

'Okay, you take them,' I say, 'but don't let them loose. I'll do breakfast. I can do it faster.'

'I said I'd do breakfast and I will,' he says. 'I'll do the email later. This is more important.'

I sigh. 'But you won't do it right and you'll leave a mess and then I'll just have to do it anyway.'

'God damn it, Emma,' he whispers. 'How do you know I'll do it wrong when you never even give me the chance?'

'I don't have time this morning,' I say, passing our children off to him. 'I'll be a minute. It's just easier this way.'

He goes back to the dining room with Grace and Oscar.

The twins love the play area at the café. With the floor covered in bouncy rubber mats and foamy bumpers lining every edge of the low octagon-shaped barrier of their little world, they only hurt themselves when they hurl toys at each other. At least I can get some café work done in between squawks for attention. It's exactly what I imagined when I thought up the café, only with more customers. At the moment, this is really just a very expensive day-care centre.

After not coming to the party because they didn't want to take my free tea (*You've got a business to run, dear*), Carl and Elsie are fixtures in the café now. They turn up just after we open to sit in their booth, sipping tea from

Philippa's beautiful cups before they go off to do their shopping at the market. They do like a rummage around in their memories over a cuppa.

Elsie was no homemaker like I'd assumed. Well, you would assume it, wouldn't you, to look at her. In her eighties and conventional as you like, she's the stereotypical gran who raised her family and had tea on the table every night when her husband got home from work.

Except she's not that person at all. She stayed single and worked for forty years in the Foreign Service as a French translator. She speaks other languages too – though she corrects Carl when he says she's fluent in those – and she's lived in countries in Africa that I've barely heard of. There's a lot going on underneath that beehive hairdo of hers.

Carl loves to brag about her. 'Elsie met George Pompidou, you know,' he tells me. 'She translated for Ted Heath when they met.'

Pompidou, Pompidou. The name rings a bell. 'As in the building in Paris?'

'That's right, dear, the French president,' Elsie says, making my ignorance sound like the right answer. 'The museum was named after him. He was lovely, quiet and very down-to-earth, no airs and graces.'

'What about Ted Heath?' I ask. Mum and Dad weren't fans, but then they are of a different political stripe.

'Curmudgeonly,' she says.

My parents will love that.

Carl and Elsie are the only regulars apart from the guy who uses the café as his personal charging station. He sits there long enough to fossilise, but he hasn't brought his toothbrush in again, so maybe he tops that up in another café. I've got him paying for pots of tea now, but only by charging him for hot water and putting up a sign over his head that says 'No Outside Food or Drinks Please'.

Just as Carl and Elsie start for the door on their way to the market, there's a commotion outside. But they hardly bat an eye at the noisy crowd. Well, they did live through the Blitz. Before I can see what's going on, the café starts filling up, with Lou and Joseph in the lead.

We've been getting a few stragglers from the leafleting runs they do each morning, but nothing like this. There must be at least thirty Chinese men and women crowding between the tables, all chattering to each other. They're mostly older, some in matchy-matchy North Face-type hiking jackets.

The beardy electricity scrounger glares at the interruption. He must think his £2 pots of tea buy him a private room.

'Great, innit, boss?' Joseph says with a grin splitting his face. 'Me and Lou got them from in front of the Tube station. They're stoked to be here.'

They do seem to love the café. Everyone is taking photos like they've never seen a teapot before. Or a child.

I wade through the crowd as they close in around the twins' play area. Oscar and Grace don't seem to mind the attention, but I don't want a bunch of strangers taking pics of my babies. Climbing into the pen, I gather the children to me and turn away from the cameras as subtly as I can. My back seems to be as interesting as my children. I can hear them all snapping away behind me. How strange.

It's also strange that nobody is sitting. They're just wandering around with their phones and iPads held out in front of them, like those tour groups you see in front of Buckingham Palace.

'Lou?' I call over to her. 'Maybe you can get behind the bar and ask if anyone needs a drink. Joseph, why don't you take the glass domes off the cakes.'

Sure enough, people start gathering expectantly in front of the bar when Lou suggests drinks. 'Who's first?' she asks. 'Anyone? How about you, ma'am?' She points at one woman who's aiming her iPad at the Gaggia. 'What would you like?'

'Yes, thank you,' she says with a smile. She's about four feet tall with wrinkles criss-crossing her face, which is partially hidden by her khaki canvas sun hat.

'No, what do you want to drink? Coffee? Tea? We have herbal.'

'Thank you very much.'

Lou glares at Joseph. 'I told you this wouldn't work,' she says. 'Stupid idea.'

Now that the paparazzi flash mob has moved to the bar, I scoot behind it to join Lou and Joseph. That's when I glimpse the leaflet that the woman is clutching.

'Pardon me, may I see that?'

I stare at the photo. 'Would someone like to tell me why it says "RIPPER" across the front of our café?' It's scrawled with big fat black indelible marker.

'Tell her, Captain Shortcut,' Lou says. 'It was your idea.'

'You said to get the punters in, boss, so we did,' he says proudly. 'We took the initiative, just like you've been telling us. They all meet in front of the Tube station. Tourists. We saw the opportunity and adjusted our marketing to meet a need.'

'A need for tea and cake?' I say hopefully, though I think I know where this is heading.

He shakes his head. 'A need for a story, boss. We sold the café as a piece of local history, and they've all come to see it.' He turns to the crowd. 'Hashtag *secondchancecafé* if you're on Instagram.' Then back to his explanation. 'They came up to us as soon as we got there, like they've been waiting for the chance.'

'Yeah, they were waiting for the Jack the Ripper tour,'

Lou adds. 'He told them this is one of the old pubs where the Ripper met his victims. They think they're on the tour.'

I pinch the bridge of my nose to try to stop the headache that's building there. 'So they're not here because it's a café or because they want to buy anything.' That explains all the photos. 'What else are they expecting? Shall I get a knife from the kitchen to show them? Maybe some fish guts from Kell's van to make it look authentic?'

Joseph perks up. 'Could we?'

'No! Joseph, I appreciate your ... ingenuity, but you can't get people here under false pretences. We're trying to build up a regular customer base, not just sell coffee once to people who'll never come back. There are only so many tourists you can lure away from the Tube station. I'm sorry, but we can't keep them. You'll need to take them back so they can do the real tour.' It'll be a shame if they get home at the end of their holiday with nothing but photos of cakes to show their friends.

After the tour group follows Lou and Joseph back to the Tube, it's just me, the twins and the beardy tweed man in the café. After the initial interruption, he went straight back to his laptop, where he types like he's got a grudge against his keyboard. I wonder what he does for work that lets him faff around in the café all day. It must be night work at a bar or something. He looks trendy enough for it.

'Can I ask you something?' I call over from the twins' area.

'I don't need more hot water, thanks,' he says. He's not rude about it, not at all. Just matter-of-fact. He goes back to assaulting his laptop.

'No, I just wondered why you're here every day. Do you work?'

He pushes his thick frames back up on his nose. Now that I've seen him every day, I can see that he's only in his twenties like me. I've never really taken the time to look properly at a hipster. They're all of a certain type, riding their fixie bikes, waiting around the barber shops for a weekly grooming or drinking their soy lattes.

This one is actually quite good-looking. What I can see of his face is tanned and angular and he has long-lashed eyes of a shade other than brown. I haven't looked that closely. But his bushy dark beard makes him look a bit like a Christmas elf. 'I am working,' he says. 'I do marketing. Mostly for companies in the City. It's boring.'

It takes me a second to work out that he has a lovely Welsh lilt.

'I'd go mad if I worked in the flat on my own all day,' he continues. 'It's better to have people around.'

We both stare at the empty tables and chairs. 'We're not exactly Leicester Square in here,' I tell him. 'But I know what you mean. I felt like I was going mad when I first had the twins. Being at home all day, I was desperate to talk to someone. Anyone.' And here I go again, talking to anyone. I laugh to myself. 'You can see why solitary confinement is considered torture,' I say. 'At least you're able to leave your flat. I mean, you haven't got children there who need you. I'm assuming. Does your whole company work from home?'

When he nods I wonder, *Do they go out to cafés to work too?*

As I consider his beard and dorky specs and his tweed suit, I realise I'm incredibly envious of him and his colleagues. They probably get cushy assignments from their boss – even if they are boring – and regular year-end bonuses and they meet for Christmas parties where they get pissed so they can work up the courage to corner their secret crushes for a snog and then get told off in January by HR.

'Some have office shares,' he answers, slicing through my visions of mistletoe and verbal warnings. 'They're pricey, though. It's not worth it just to have somewhere to sit.' At least he looks contrite about camping out in my café all day to save himself office rent.

But it does spark an idea from somewhere inside my sleep-deprived brain. 'What if your colleagues had a cheaper option for working? Do you think they'd go there instead of a shared office?'

'Are you thinking about here? They probably would, at least the ones who live nearby. It's easy to work in here. Nice and quiet.' He grimaces. 'Sorry. I know that's probably not an advantage for you.'

'Well, we have only been open a little while. If you think you know of someone else who might like to come here to work, maybe you could tell them? I'd even do you a deal. What's your name? Leo? Leo, what if we offered you a free sandwich for every colleague you get to come in here during the week? If you got five people to come in and work with you, then that's your weekly lunches paid for.'

That's catching his interest.

And his eyes are green. Golden-green.

'They'd have to get a tea or coffee while they're here, but it's a lot cheaper than renting a desk. What do you think?'

He nods. 'You'd need Wi-Fi, since most of the cafés have it, but I'll take that deal, thanks very much. I am getting a bit hungry.' He sits up straighter in his chair. 'I could ring someone now?'

Maybe the way to my business will be through Leo's stomach. Now I'm glad we got Magenta the Sandwich Whisperer in. I might even look for free-range carrots.

And if it works for the beardy brigade, then why couldn't

191

it work for others? Maybe Elsie and Carl can be bribed to get their friends in here too. It's worth a try since the only people who've come in so far are probably wondering what floral teapots have to do with Jack the Ripper.

Chapter 13

Our friends have always been there for me when I've really needed help. That was never truer than when we had to figure out how to have a huge fancy wedding on a shoestring, thanks to Dad being too proud to let Daniel's parents help with any of the costs. Everyone pitched in with ways to get us champagne and chocolate-dipped strawberries, designer shoes and handmade bridesmaids' dresses, live entertainment and horse-drawn carriages to the reception. At least, that's what my in-laws saw on the day. If they'd looked closely, they'd have realised it wasn't all quite what it seemed.

And before that, when Dad could no longer work because of the MS, it was the vicar who found me the job at the Vespa dealership. That kept some money coming into the house. Auntie Rose's friends turned up at least once a week with 'extra' roast chicken or beef stew that they claimed they couldn't eat, which meant Mum didn't have to do all the cooking while looking after Dad too.

So I shouldn't be surprised that when I threw myself into the bosom of our tribe for help finding customers for the café, they came up trumps.

Not surprised, but so very grateful.

'Joseph, can you please check if Mrs Ishtiaque's table needs more water?' She's waving to me from amidst a sea of colourful sarees.

She was the first to turn up after I asked for help. 'Hello, dear,' she'd called from the café door. 'Do you mind if we're joining you? I've brought you curry leftovers for your tea. My girls weren't wanting any.'

'You don't have to bribe me to come in, Mrs Isthtiaque, you're always welcome here.'

She'd come through the door with a carrier bag in front of her and her friends backing her up. Together they made quite an entrance, though knowing them a bit now, it was probably the last thing they wanted. Huddled together and shyly smiling, their colourful fluttering scarves and flowing sarees made everyone glance over. Which only sent them into a closer huddle.

'Please, come in,' I'd said again. 'How about this table? I think it's got just about enough room for eight if you squeeze. Really, Mrs Ishtiaque, I'm so glad you're here. All of you!' Their thanks danced around the table on a melodious wave.

'It is nice to be out of our homes,' she said, adjusting her deep aqua scarf over her head. 'Your mum said you were needing customers. And we have an ultimate motive too.' Her look darted to her friends, who all nodded their encouragement. 'We are learning better English, Emma. We meet every week in our homes and I am teaching them.' She grinned. 'Because my English is being perfect, of course. Ha ha ha! I am making a joke but without a joke – we wanted to know if it is all right to be practising here?'

'Of course it is,' I told them all, hardly able to keep my gratitude under control.

Only then did she pass me the curry, I noticed. 'We will all be having drinks too. We will not be having free lunchtimes.'

They'd need to work on their idioms, but they were true to their word. They always order tea and a slice of cake each, even though they never eat more than two bites and take the rest home wrapped carefully in a paper napkin.

Their rapid-fire Bengali floats over the café now, rising and falling with the tales they're telling. I'm not sure how much English study gets done and I can't understand a word, but it's easy to see when someone gets to a good bit of gossip based on all the hand-flapping.

'I'm just getting another slice of cake for Leo's table,' Joseph says. 'We're out of the chocolate Guinness and the chocolate avocado cake now, boss. We can probably do with whole cakes next time.'

People can't get enough of the Mad Batter's cakes. They come in looking for their sweet buttery fix, and cocoa powder is their drug of choice.

'I can bring Mrs Ishtiaque more water,' says Lou, wiping her hands on a tea towel and filling one of Mum's teapots. On the way back from their table she stops at the children's area. Grace crows as soon as she sees her. That catches Oscar's attention. Lou blows them raspberries that reduce my children to fits of laughter.

Just remembering how much mistrust I had for Lou when we first met makes me come up all blotchy red. She seems like a different girl now, though it's really my view that's changing. I still don't know what she'll be accused of when she goes to court next month. She always changes the subject when I bring it up. But I don't guard Mum's teapots around her the way I used to.

It's hard to believe the change from a few weeks ago when the only people in here thought they were on a tour of Victorian murder scenes. Leo now gets a steady supply of sandwiches in return for the small band of hipsters who come in every day to work. Their food and drink orders probably offset their energy usage, even when they do bring in their beard trimmers.

'We need milk again,' Lou says.

'We've gone through it all? It was only delivered this morning.'

'There was no delivery today,' she says.

'Isn't it Tuesday? That's weird. I'll ring them later. Take a fiver out of the till, please, and go get some more for now. The mums look ready for another round.'

My friends have turned into a collective noun – the mums. Samantha's here nearly every day, sometimes in the morning between the school run and yoga and sometimes in the afternoon with her son and daughter. Garnet and Emerald try to coordinate visits with Samantha, and since Melody's got no fixed schedule (for anything), she drifts in and out at random with her two girls.

Luckily it's a big café and there are free tables even with my friends here. It hasn't taken long for them to colonise, taking over the spots next to the play area where they can quickly wave us down for more food and drinks. It's ideal, really, since those are also the least appealing tables in my opinion – away from the windows and close to the loos. That leaves all the window-side booths free for customers like Carl and Elsie and Mrs Ishtiaque's friends and the other customers who are starting to come in. I won't say 'regularly', because I wouldn't want to jinx things.

I've bribed Oscar and Grace with colouring books and soft toys and anything else I could think of to distract them from the invasion of toddlers into their fiefdom. They're still too young to play together, but they rub along okay alongside each other. So far Grace and Oscar have been benevolent landlords, but that's probably because Dad and Auntie Rose are here every day to spoil them.

I should have known they wouldn't stand for being away from the twins. They didn't so much ask as tell me they were going to keep an eye on them in the play area. They are such a huge help and they'd work for tea if I let them. Not that I will when Mum and Dad need the cash, so the café is a family business now. Dad and Auntie Rose staff the play area every day, looking after the customers' children too. That probably makes Auntie Rose the oldest trainee in East London.

'Leo wants a ham and cheese croissant today,' Joseph reports back from the freelancers' corner.

'Okay, go ahead. He's earned it. Pretty soon we'll have to get more sockets put in.'

'There's loads of them in here now,' Joseph says. He means the freelancers, rather than the sockets. 'They've all got whack drink orders. Half-caff soya and shit.'

'Good thing you're trained for it. Pablo would be proud. I'm just glad they're bringing their friends,' I say. 'Everyone's welcome.' That seems to be how the café is working anyway. Since we're not on the main road like Barb, that business saboteur, we don't get the foot traffic. Word of mouth is definitely the most important thing for us.

'Could our bluds come here too?' Joseph asks.

I can't hide my surprise. 'Do you think your friends would want to come?'

'Yeah, why not?' he says. 'Lou's too, probably, if she's got any.'

'The difference is that I don't have to pay mine,' Lou shoots back. I didn't realise she'd been listening.

'Well, then, please ask them,' I say to them both. 'I'm sorry, I would have suggested it before, but I didn't think kids would want to hang around a café.'

'You're always making assumptions,' Lou says, but I can't tell if she's accusing or teasing me.

'Emma, why don't you come sit for a minute?' Emerald calls from the table that they've pushed up against the play area fence. 'You're run off your feet.'

Gratefully I pull up a chair. 'You all right in there, Dad?' I ask.

'Right as rain, me love. You chat with your friends.'

'Your dad is great,' Melody says. 'He's a natural with children.'

She should know. Melody is the earthiest earth mother

I've ever met. Well, with a name like Melody, she's never going to be a hard-arse is she? There's not a baby, toddler or teen that she won't pet and coo over if they let her. You should have seen Joseph the first time she stroked his *sweet little teenage arm* (her words). He froze like she'd put a tarantula on his shoulder. Now he makes Lou serve their table whenever they're in.

My fingers find the charm bracelet they gave me. It has become a kind of talisman. I even found a tiny enamelled slice of cake to add to the charms. That can't hurt, right?

'Business is good,' Samantha says.

'Is that your professional opinion or are you just being a nice friend?'

She glances around the café. 'It's my professional opinion, for whatever that's worth these days. You've got a solid business model. A focus on a targeted range of high-quality goods, client diversification, reputational brand-building. That's textbook business building.'

'I wish it was as well planned as you make it sound, but thank you, I'll take your compliments. If I ever expand, I'll hire you to be my consultant.'

'From your lips to God's ears,' she says.

Melody is shaking her head. 'I do admire you both, even though I would hate to have to work. I mean like you do, not like this.' She gestures into the play area where Eva is reading to Joy.

She's not saying that because her husband is loaded or anything. He does some kind of back-office job out in Slough and they live in a small house on a not-very-nice ex-council estate so they can afford to raise a family on one income. 'You did used to work though, didn't you?' I ask her. Though I can't imagine Melody in any high-pressured job. She moves like she's underwater.

'Oh, I was a secretary in the City for years, but it was just a job to pay the rent. The happiest day of my life was when I handed in my notice to go on maternity leave.'

'It sounds like you've always known you wanted to be a mum,' I say.

Samantha snorts. 'Look at her! Could there be a more natural mum on the planet? Mother Nature models herself after Melody.'

'Thank you,' Melody says. 'Some people just know, don't they?'

'Some are born to it, others have it thrust upon them.' Then she winks at me, adding, 'As long as you mentioned thrusting ...'

'We haven't, actually, but don't let that stop you,' I say. And I mean it. Listening to Samantha's attempted seduction stories is like smoking a sneaky fag with mates in the girls' loo: if you get the chance, you're going to do it.

'Tomorrow's Richard's birthday.' She crosses both sets of fingers. 'Here's hoping I haven't wasted another wax appointment.'

'Just don't wear that body stocking again,' Melody says.

Lou is just coming back with the milk when the screeching smoke alarm launches me from my chair. 'Excuse me,' I say as calmly as I can with my heart hammering in my chest. 'I'll find out what's going on,' I call to everyone. 'I'm sure it's nothing.' We only had the thing installed a few weeks ago. The instructions to shut it up are around here somewhere.

'It's under control, boss!' Joseph calls from the kitchen.

I find him bracing himself in some kind of complicated martial arts stance, aiming a fire extinguisher at the toaster.

'Wait, Joseph, no!'

He lets loose a steady stream of spray, like he's one of the Ghostbusters battling a demon. 'Stop! There's no fire.' But he's not listening. I try wrestling the canister from him, but I'm no match for teenage muscles and testosterone. All I manage to do is send the spray in all directions.

I get the alarm turned off, but Joseph's finger keeps squeezing the trigger of the extinguisher even after the last little dribble has left the nozzle.

He seems to emerge from a trance. We both stare at the fluffy white foam that blankets the toaster, the worktop and much of the wall and floor.

It looks like we've had an Ibiza club foam party, only nobody's had any fun.

'You probably could have just flapped a tea towel at the alarm, but well done,' I tell him. 'Fire safety is important. That one's not for electrical fires, though. Just so you know for next time.'

'What the hell?' Lou says from behind us. 'What did you do, Joseph?'

'I was toasting the croissant,' he says. 'The ham must be flammable. Or the cheese. That toaster is dangerous, boss.'

Lou goes to the cabinet where we keep the sandwich maker. 'Why didn't you use this, you muppet? You've killed the toaster.'

'It's dead in the ground,' he agrees. 'But it was plugged in already. It should have worked.'

'You've got to stop taking shortcuts,' I tell him as gently as I can. 'People get ahead through hard graft, not cheats. It might work sometimes, but it's not good in the long run.' We both stare at the foamy toaster. Not good.

Lou touches Joseph's arm. It's an oddly gentle gesture considering her usual gruffness. 'Come on, I'll show you how to use the toastie maker so you don't burn down the café.' She leads him to the fridge to start over on the croissant. Despite the fact that he's just nearly destroyed her workplace, she's patient with him. She talks to him like a friend.

'I'll go let Leo know his lunch is on the way,' I say. And that there's no need for an evacuation.

But once he knows his laptop's not in danger, Leo's usually happy demeanour sours. 'We wouldn't have been able to get out of here with all the prams in the way, you know.' He's had his beard trimmed to a manageable stubble, which suits him better than the facial pelt he had the first time he came in.

'I'm really sorry, but it wasn't a fire. There wasn't any danger.' It's not like he couldn't push a pram or two out of the way if he had to. 'And technically they're pushchairs. Prams are for babies.'

He's not interested in my vocabulary lesson. 'There's still not a lot of room with them in here.'

'Then I guess we shouldn't try running that aerobics class I had planned,' I say. The mums have the pushchairs ringed around their table, which puts all the adjacent tables out of action too.

'This is just a suggestion,' he says, smiling his thanks as Lou brings him his perfectly toasted croissant. 'You don't want people to be turned off the café because there's no space. If you can find a spot for them out of the way, your problem is solved.'

'You mean the pushchairs rather than the mothers, right?'

He laughs. 'I'm not making a case for segregation.'

He is right. The café needs to be comfortable for everyone. 'Let me think about it.'

'Emma?' He grabs my arm as I turn to go. 'I don't mean that as a criticism. I hope you don't take it that way. You've got a really nice place here. We all love it.'

'Thanks, Leo, that's nice to hear. Let me just—'

'You've gone all red. It's cute.'

I'm aware of Lou watching me. 'Let me see what we can do to make more room.'

I follow Lou back to the bar. 'Leo's right,' I tell her, willing my face to stop blushing. 'I think we need to reconfigure things somehow to make room for the pushchairs.'

'He's right about a lot of things,' she says. 'You have gone red.'

'What do you think?'

She shrugs as she looks away. 'It's none of my business.'

What's that supposed to mean? 'I'm talking about the pushchair situation. You must have some ideas.'

'Dunno. Why?' She glares at me. 'Why aren't you asking Joseph?'

'Well, he probably has a different perspective.'

'Why's that? Because he doesn't have ovaries and I do? Sexist, much?'

'No! Because I saw ...' I lower my voice. 'Because I saw you with your baby, remember?' Of course she remembers. She avoids the topic whenever I try to bring it up. Which is ridiculous because I saw her and she knows I did.

Her face is thunderous. 'My baby?' She crosses her arms. 'That's what you thought. You assumed I got knocked up and had a kid. Of course you did, because I'm just another loser in the system. I tick all the boxes, don't I? Foster family, school leaver, arrest record. Why not teenage mother too?'

'Well, I saw you.'

'Maybe you shouldn't always make snap judgements based on what you see. Not that it's any of your business, but that was my foster sister.'

'Then you're not a single mother?' Her look answers me. 'I'm so sorry. I didn't mean to offend you.'

'Thanks for thinking so much of me. I hate to disappoint you, but I haven't quite fucked up my life that much yet.'

'No, Lou, that's not what I meant.' It is, though. It's exactly what I meant, isn't it? I'm supposed to be helping these kids, not buying into all the stereotypes that everyone else does. I'm as bad as the social workers and the teachers and the strangers who cross the road to avoid Lou because she's wearing a hoodie and a prickly attitude.

I ring Kell after the twins are in bed. She's always been the one person I can show my ugly side to and know she'll never tell anyone. Not that she doesn't judge me. She's no saintly Mother Teresa, or even a foul-mouthed one. She just never holds those judgements against me.

'It's natural, though, isn't it?' she says. 'You see a girl who you know has been in trouble, you see her with a baby, you make assumptions.'

'That's the whole point, though. I'm not supposed to be making assumptions. I'm supposed to be helping them.'

'You can't help what conclusions your brain jumps to, Emma. You can only help how you react to it, how you handle it. So you learned something today. Accusing a young girl of being a single mother isn't very clever. Move on.'

See what I mean? Critical of the action, not the person.

'Actually, I'm glad you rang,' she says.

'Because my drama makes you feel better about yourself?'

'Ha, no. Because I've got something to tell you. Me and Calvin are going to try Spain.'

She leaves the statement hanging in the air like a bad smell that needs clearing. 'Wow, big change.'

'Scary change,' she agrees. 'But if you could do it, marrying a posho – totally different world – then I can live somewhere gorgeous for a year or two. What do you think?'

There are not enough free minutes on my mobile to tell her everything I'm thinking. It all boils down to the same thing anyway. 'I don't know what I'll do without you.'

'You're not without me, you divvy. I'll only be a few hours away and we talk more on the phone than we see each other now anyway. You'll hardly know I'm gone.'

We both know that's a lie, but it's one we need to believe. 'What about your dad and the business?'

She laughs. 'It turns out that he doesn't need me as much as he's said he did all these years. He's taking on Faisal's brother.' Faisal's dad has the other fish stall at the market. 'Faisal's got dibs on their dad's business so Dad's agreed to train up his brother to take ours over eventually. It's like an arranged marriage with mackerel.'

'But what if you need to come back?' I say.

'Dooming my relationship already?'

'No, I ... It's just wishful thinking. It's a shame it's not staying in the family, that's all.'

Though it is staying in East London, and I guess that is sort of family. If only Kelly were staying too.

Chapter 14

Daniel's already gone to work when Dad rings our doorbell. 'You're running late,' he says. 'Can we help?'

'Thanks. Could you change Grace, please? I've got to pack their snacks and clothes. Auntie Rose, could you keep Oscar occupied for a few minutes?' I glance at the breakfast dishes on the table. And the dishes from tea in the kitchen. They'll have to wait till after work.

Dad and Auntie Rose have been absolute lifesavers. They're star employees, turning up at the café earlier every day. It's great that they're so keen, but soon Auntie Rose will be getting me out of bed.

I guess I didn't appreciate how they must have felt being at home all these years. It's one thing to have your weekends off from work to sit around the house in your jimjams. And who doesn't love the occasional duvet day or the Christmas period when there's nothing to do but watch telly and plough through boxes of Celebrations? But when you have every day off it must seem less like a holiday and more like a punishment. Getting up each morning only to have to find ways of filling another long day at home, which was exactly like yesterday's long day at home, must get so boring. Not to mention demoralising. No wonder Dad was so eager to look after the twins when I first started dropping them off. Even wiping babies' bums beats watching daytime telly.

Neither Dad nor Auntie Rose have ever liked sitting around anyway. Dad, as you know, was a cabbie, and my aunt spent her working life cutting and colouring hair and generally being the keeper of all the neighbourhood gossip. Though she wasn't as good at keeping secrets as she was at telling them. She was the one who finally broke the news about Doreen's husband to her, which was more of a public service and duty of a friend. There'd been whispers about him for some time, but nothing concrete, so naturally people didn't want to say anything. Auntie Rose knew that forewarned was forearmed and, anyway, if it came to nothing, then it would quell suspicion once and for all.

Sadly for Doreen, smoke did lead to a roaring bonfire. Auntie Rose was the one who raised the alarm and Doreen appreciated it. Her husband disappeared shortly after. Some say he ran off with his girlfriend. Others think it's best not to say anything.

'Are you all right?' Dad asks as I'm struggling to find the arm hole to get my coat on.

'Stupid thing!' I say. 'It never goes on right.'

'Or maybe you're too impatient,' he says, reaching up to wrestle the coat from me. He rights the garment with a deft flick and holds it out for me. 'Sometimes we just need a little help, that's all. That's what I'm here for, okay?'

'Thanks, Dad.'

My heart sinks as my eyes start searching the front of the café when we all round the corner. I'm not going insane. Someone is definitely pinching our milk deliveries. Every other day the nice man from the local dairy drives around in his electric truck before anyone is awake and drops off the litres of milk we'll need. Yet at least once a week, the milk's not there when I go to open up. It's possible that our milkman is lying – though it seems like a trustworthy occupation to me – or else we've got a neighbourhood teef, as Joseph would say.

Which means we've got to buy replacements and lug them back from the main road. Only the organic shop does the soya milk and almond milk the freelancers want, and organic people must be late sleepers because they don't open till ten. So far, the dairy has been really understanding and haven't made us pay for the missing orders, but if it keeps happening, they could blacklist us for deliveries, because how do they know we're not just cadging free milk? This isn't how I wanted to start relations with our suppliers.

More worryingly, these are my neighbours. If they'll steal the café's milk, I have to wonder what else they'll do. That's the most uncomfortable part.

As it is, it's taken a while for me to get used to living on the square. I knew all the neighbours at Mum and Dad's. I knew who to ask for a biscuit after school and which house to avoid because the slightly strange son who still lived at home had earned a reputation for once exposing himself to Sheila Larkin at the bus stop. Now I've got to learn all over again who to say hello to and who to avoid because they'll talk your ear off for an hour when you're really in a rush. It's not nice also to have to consider who might be nicking your milk deliveries.

The usual jolt of pleasure runs through me when I get inside the café, though. The bunting flutters in the morning breeze that whooshes through the door as I prop it open with the old-fashioned cast-iron doorstop I found at one of the nearby charity shops. Its brightly painted flowerpot shape might be whimsical, but it does its job, and you'll break a toe if you stub it. We'll have to wait till Lou gets here with today's cakes to rewrite the blackboard, but I sponge off yesterday's treats in preparation. The daily updates are Joseph's job, not because he has the neatest handwriting, but because he's appointed himself Head of Communications and the blackboard is his main channel so far. Nobody loves a title like Joseph.

Doreen's at the door before we even open, and it's not hard to see what she wants. She's got a cribbage board tucked under her arm. 'When's Rose's break?' she asks. 'And remember I used to be a union rep.'

'I wouldn't dream of going up against the union, Doreen. She can stop whenever she wants to,' I say. 'We don't really have set break times, though we're not officially open yet.'

'Then she's on her own time, not yours. You're not exploiting your workers, I hope. They could have grievances, you know. Remember Grunwick's, me girl.'

She might be joking, but she really is a pit bull about workers' rights. She organised some of the biggest strikes in the area in the seventies. I've heard the stories a million times. I hope I get to hear them a million more. Grunwick's strike started with six people who walked out over the dismissal of a colleague and swelled to two hundred thousand picketers for the next two years. The workers were immigrants from Asia and the Caribbean and nobody had paid much attention to them before. They paid attention after, though.

All that happened before Doreen's husband disappeared

and he was always going on at her about making him look bad. She couldn't give a toss how she made him look. Doreen's always loved an underdog.

'I promise I'm not exploiting my workers, Doreen. Go get Auntie Rose. I assume you want a game of cribbage.'

'And a pot of tea, please. Thanks, love!' She trots off to tell Auntie Rose to down tools.

As usual, Leo's not far behind us. He greets everyone including Grace and Oscar on his mini commute around the café before settling at his usual table. His tweed suit is blue today, which means it's Friday. It's green on Monday and Thursday, blue on Tuesday and Friday and a snazzy mustard yellow on Wednesdays when he meets his friends in the pub after work.

I suppose one has to be quite regimented to work outside a regular office. Leo is here every weekday, takes breaks at the same time and packs up his electronics at exactly 5 p.m.

I can see the appeal. It's comfortable having a rhythm to the days and weeks. I liked that about being at Uni. Even though it was challenging, I always knew what was expected of me. Read the textbooks, go to lectures, *revise revise revise*, sit exams and chew my fingernails till the results were posted. And I thought *those* were the stressful days. Now the only thing I know for sure is that I have to open the café in the morning and close it at night. What happens in between is anyone's guess. Yesterday there was virtually no one in for takeaway, but the day before I had to send Lou into storage for the backup paper cups – the pretty flowered ones we used for our grand opening party. I hate to use them if I don't have to, though I'm not really sure why I'm saving them either. Maybe in case the Queen comes in for takeaway or something.

'Is the tea all right?' I ask Leo as he sips his first chai of the day.

He peers at me through his steamed-up specs. 'Really good, thanks.'

'That's the last of the almond milk till the shop opens at ten,' I warn, in case it's a two-chai morning. 'The milk's been nicked again.'

'Someone stole your milk? And what do you mean *again*?' He's aghast. 'Who would do that?'

This is a typical Leo response. For a grown man he's easily shocked, which is probably because he's not from London. His father is the only police constable in the tiny village in Wales where he grew up. Leo senior also doubles as the local veterinarian, so they can't really have a crime wave during lambing season or the whole place would go to rack and ruin.

'You're the one with law enforcement in your family,' I tell him. 'Maybe you can track down the culprit.'

'Nah, I'd be hopeless at it. I'd only spill the evidence or get the wrong guy or something.'

He downplays himself a lot. He also claims he was a bad student, though he did manage to finish school before moving away from his little village to Cardiff, so he can't be that thick. That's when he got work temping for a marketing company. They really just needed a minder for the company head, someone to fetch the old man cups of tea, type up the occasional email and generally let him feel like the good old-fashioned days hadn't ended. They'd tried a number of women in the job before Leo, but the head had more interest in their bottoms than he did in the bottom line, so they had to change their hiring policy.

Leo's bottom was of no interest to the head, so the arrangement worked fine.

But Leo got bored with his work so, in between cups of tea and emails, he offered help wherever he could. Sometimes that meant more typing or tea, but sometimes he got to be a sounding board, and that's when everyone realised he had a knack for spin. Eventually his colleagues wondered if he might not be more useful on marketing campaigns than he was drafting emails about dress-down Fridays, and he worked his way up from there.

'Are the baby buggies coming today?' he asks as he finishes his tea. 'I only ask because I have to practise for a presentation. I don't mind chuntering away in a corner, but I don't want the mothers to think I'm a loony or anything.'

With those specs and that suit? Nobody could think Leo was anything of the sort. 'Sorry, I'm afraid you might have an audience. You know they like to come every day.'

He shrugs. 'It's understandable. Coming here probably reminds them that they're not just mothers. They're also friends, coffee drinkers and regular people too. It's important to remember that when you're doing something as all-consuming as parenting. I imagine.'

I stop wiping the table beside his. That's exactly why they come. How does he know that? 'Deep thinking,' I quip, though his insight unsettles me for some reason.

'I think, therefore I am,' he says.

'Descartes.'

'One of my favourites,' he says. 'Do you like philosophy?'

I read a bit of it when I was in school, and some more at Uni, but I haven't read an entire book in ages. It feels too indulgent when there's so much that already doesn't get done at home. 'Once upon a time,' I say. 'A lifetime ago.'

His look of concern is unmistakeable. I don't need him feeling sorry for me when I'm perfectly able to do that myself. 'Just flag me down when you're ready for more chai, okay?'

'Miss? Miss! I'm ready for some chai,' Kell says from

behind me. 'But I think it's pronounced "chee". I 'aven't got all day, so snap to it or you're not getting any tip.'

'Excuse me!' Leo protests. 'There's no reason to be rude.'

'Who the fack are you?'

'Kell, this is my customer, Leo. Be nice to my customers. Leo, my best friend Kell. What are you doing here?' She starts work before I leave the house and usually goes straight through till two or three.

'Oh, sorry,' Leo says with a grimace. 'I thought you were just being rude.'

Kell ignores him. 'Can't a girl take a tea break?' she says to me instead. 'Dad's at the van.'

'What's with that guy?' Kell asks me quietly as she follows me back to the counter. 'How come he thinks he's your knight in shining armour?'

'He doesn't think anything. He's just a customer.' I busy myself with the teabags and hot water.

As soon as Kelly leaves, one of Mrs Ishtiaque's friends sidles up to the counter. She's older than the others, with a centre parting and long black hair swept into a loose plait down her back. 'May I help you?' I ask with what I hope is an encouraging smile.

'Is that chocolate gake?' she carefully enunciates.

'It is chocolate k-ake. Would you like a slice?'

'No, thank you. Is that strawberry?' she asks, trilling her Rs. Now I know this is an English lesson, not an order. 'It is strawberry.' I prefer her pronunciation. Mine sounds so boring. 'What is your favourite kind of cake?'

I try to speak as clearly as I can, but she just smiles and hurries back to her table.

I've gone off script and now I've spooked her. But she'll be back to try again. Mrs Ishtiaque makes everyone practise. And they've borrowed some of the books from the play area to read aloud to each other. I could curl up with my head on Mrs Ishtiaque's lap and listen to them all afternoon.

It's just after lunchtime when Lou notices the furtive woman in the pink coat. 'Who's that?' she asks me, pointing with her chin as she plops a teabag into a pot. 'Haven't seen her before, have you?'

I consider the woman, who's just come down from upstairs. That's weird because the only person up there is Leo, practising his presentation so he doesn't look like a crazy person mumbling to himself in public. It's also weird because there's nothing up there but stacks of tables and chairs. It's more of a storeroom than a café.

She's around my mum's age, with neat wavy blonde hair and just enough make-up to show she's made an effort. She's on her own, but lots of people come in by themselves. She's looking around in the same way the kids down the market do just before they're about to snatch something and run. But there's nothing to nick here. The money is all in the till behind the counter and she won't get far with a table or chair.

Suddenly my heart stops. 'The twins.' I'm around the side of the bar and leaping over the barrier into the play area in what seems like a split second. 'Whoah,' Dad says. 'Since when did you become so athletic?'

But the woman doesn't even look up from the table. So she's probably not a child-snatcher either.

'Oh, I just wanted to say hello,' I tell Dad, willing my heartbeat to stop throbbing in my neck. 'How's everything going over here? They're probably nearly ready for a nap if you want to try your luck.' The children usually sleep for an hour or so back at the house. We got the ramp fitted on the front when we first moved in so Dad can easily get in and out.

Keeping my eye on the woman as I exit the play area, I notice that she keeps looking at the cake board and scribbling furiously in her notebook. Taking notes on our cakes?

'Yo, wassup?' Joseph comes over to where Lou and I huddle behind the Gaggia to observe the woman.

'Ssshh!' we both hiss.

'What?'

'Check out that woman,' Lou says just as our mystery

guest takes her phone out and quite clearly starts taking photos.

'Thanks, but she's a little old for me,' he says.

'Not like that, you prat. Watch what she's doing.'

'Lou, go over and see if she wants anything to drink,' I say. We have had some odd people in here since opening. A few of the local drunks have stumbled in thinking it's a pub again. When I said I wanted it to be just like Uncle Colin's, I wasn't thinking of the alcohol fumes wafting off the customers. And one lady keeps turning up with kittens that she tries to sell table-to-table. Every time I gently steer her out, I'm reminded of Philippa's café cat idea.

Before I know what's happening, Lou is standing over the woman's table. 'What are you doing?' she barks. Even I'd be intimidated if she did that to me. And I know her.

'I'm ... nothing!' The woman shrinks into her chair, holding the notebook to her chest. That's when I see she's got a handful of the photos we've been using for leaflets.

'No? You're not doing anything? Then what's with the photos? Why the notebook?' When she grabs for the woman's book, a little tussle ensues.

Uh-oh. That's not exactly good customer service.

Wresting the notebook from Lou's fingers, the woman draws herself up to glare. 'Waddayou mean what's with the photos?! What's with the fackin' assault? There's no sign

221

saying I can't take pictures, is there? It's a public place.'

'Is there a problem?' I call, rushing over.

'No problem,' says Lou.

'There ain't *no* problem. This girl is harassing me for just sitting here.' She's bristling with indignation as she gathers up her bag. 'If this is how you welcome customers, then you're not gonna last very long. You can be sure this'll go on Twitter.'

'Hashtag Second Chance Café!' Joseph shouts as the woman storms out. 'What? All publicity is good publicity, yeah?'

I round on Lou as soon as the woman leaves. 'What were you thinking, Lou? I asked you to go see what she wanted, not to bully her into leaving. Honestly, you need to work on your people skills. We have to deal with customers professionally.'

'But she was—'

'I don't care what she was, Lou. You know the rule. The customer is ...?'

'An arsehole,' she says.

I close my eyes and count slowly. 'Always right, Lou. The customer is always right. I don't want you scaring the customers away. Do you understand?'

She nods. 'Sorry. Just one thing. What do you think she was doing here?'

I sigh. 'I don't know. Maybe she's taking notes for something she's writing. Maybe she collects photos of cafés. Maybe she just wanted a cup of tea. The point is that we don't know, so confronting her like that was wrong.'

Lou nods. 'Did you see what she was writing in her notebook?'

A thought suddenly occurs to me. 'Oh god, it was a review, wasn't it? She's a reviewer and now we're going to get an awful write-up. That's perfect, thanks.' Just when we're starting to get some regular customers, we'll be slammed with a one-star review for harassment. Auntie Rose will read about us in the *Daily Mail*.

Lou shakes her head. 'It was every item off our menu. Every kind of tea and coffee, with the prices, and all the cake flavours. Every single thing. I saw it before I asked her what she was doing. She's no reviewer.'

This takes a minute to sink in. 'Was she a *spy*?'

'Yeah, she was a spy. I didn't want her to get what she came for. Sorry for defending your business.'

I really have to learn to stop jumping to conclusions with Lou. 'No, I'm sorry, Lou. I misjudged you. Again. She was really writing everything down?'

Lou nods. 'You've got a problem.'

I don't know if she means the spy or my attitude. Either way, her words ring in my ears all afternoon.

So I'm probably a little tetchy when I get home to Daniel later. At least, that's what I tell myself later as we're lying with our backs to each other in bed. Not that we've got a serious problem, because I don't know if I can handle another one right now.

Unusually, he was home by the time I got in with the children. Closing the café seems to take longer every day. All the administration slips further down my to-do list as more customers turn up looking for their half-caff no-foam fixes. Besides, all work and no play makes Emma a dull girl. I love finally having all-day access to people who can speak in full sentences and don't need nappy changing. Between the mums and the freelancers, I might even be getting something close to a social life, even if I have to serve them coffee to do it.

Daniel cuddled the twins as soon as they were out of their pushchair. When they toddled towards him squealing their delight, I was hit with love for them and jealousy of Daniel in a nicely aimed one-two punch. I didn't understand it. Babies were supposed to be closest to the person who looked after them most, right? Didn't our twins get the memo?

I had to fight this feeling, though. I knew it wasn't right. Emerald and Garnet were always complaining that their children didn't let them out of their sight. Of course they fought over which of them had it worse. I should have been happy that Daniel could share the responsibility.

But maybe sharing was the problem.

'Daniel, could you please do the washing up so I can get tea started? I didn't have time this morning with Dad and Auntie Rose turning up early.'

'Give me five minutes?' he said. 'I've just got in.'

'I know you have, but so have I. Look, I'm sorry, but we have to be on the same side here. I can't fight the twins and you.'

We stared at each other over the children's heads.

'Does it have to be done right this second?'

'Otherwise I can't start tea.' The sink was piled with dishes, pots and pans. I really didn't want to be the harpy. I wanted to be lovely Emma, the woman Daniel married. The one who didn't constantly worry about nappies and laundry, dirty dishes and mealtimes.

No, I wanted a lot more than that. I wanted to be myself again, the woman I'd always liked – not the Moaner-in-Chief who constantly squeezed the fun out of everything. I was so tired of playing the bad cop, but if I didn't, nothing got done. Daniel just didn't seem to grasp that life with our children was about more than being their favourite entertainment. All the boring stuff was important too.

'Fine,' he said, pulling Grace and Oscar on to his lap and making them giggle like mad. 'Sorry, darlings, Mummy wants me to do chores. You'll have to play on your own.'

Two little pairs of arms reached for him when he got up. Oscar's lip started wobbling. Perfect. I was making everyone unhappy.

As I cleared some of the laundry and paperwork from the dining table, Daniel took out his frustration on our dishes. Cutlery clattered into the holder. He banged the pot that I burned the porridge in on the bottom of the sink. I knew without looking that it was scratching the enamel. By the time the bowls went crashing onto the drying rack, one atop the other, crack, crack, crack, I couldn't take it anymore. 'Daniel! I'm sorry you're miserable, but could you not break our dishes?'

Off went the water. He came out drying his hands. 'What do you want? You want me to help, so I'm helping.'

I had a pair of his pants clutched to my chest, mid-fold. 'Only under duress. I want you to *want* to help. It's different.'

He looked at the twins. 'Mummy wants me to whistle while I work.' A few seconds later, the theme tune from *Snow White and the Seven Dwarfs* floated back from the kitchen.

'And stop calling me Mummy!!'

You can just call me Grumpy these days.

Chapter 15

Word about the spy in the café yesterday has spread faster than news of a new 1D concert tour. Everyone has a story about where they were when it happened, but the prize goes to Leo for the weirdest. The woman just sat on one of the chairs to watch him practise his presentation upstairs. Then she went around the room like she was measuring its size and tried opening all the windows.

'Maybe she was having a hot flush,' he says, sipping the last of his morning chai. 'My mum used to get those. She had to put her head in the fridge.'

But I don't think the menopause was behind this. It was the Other Half Caff Barb. It would be too big a coincidence to have *two* enemies in the space of a month. And didn't the woman say something about us not lasting very long? That smacks of Barb's vile leaflet.

Leo pulls a book from his satchel. 'I went through my

shelves last night and thought you might like this. If you haven't read it yet.'

I flip the slim, well-thumbed volume over to read the back. 'Thank you. I've been thinking about the philosophers since you mentioned them. It'll be nice to get familiar with them again.' I make it sound like we were once best friends, when what I actually mean is that it'll be a welcome change to read something other than picture books or the instructions on a ready meal.

'It's just a potted version of the main players,' he says. 'It makes me feel smart to read it.' His smile is infectious. 'If you ever want to talk about them, I'm all ears. Without wanting to sound too wankery about it, philosophy is best shared ...' He blows out his cheeks. 'No, I definitely sound wankery, but I mean it. I'm sure you'll have an interesting perspective.'

It's not till I go back to the counter that I realise it's been a long time since I've felt interesting.

'This officially makes you regulars now that I can start on your order the second you walk in,' I say later to our vicar, Del, and Mrs Delaney as I drop off their pot of tea and slice of chocolate Guinness cake. I've known them both for years and I still think they make an odd pair of friends, at least on the surface. Even setting aside the thirty-year age difference, he's as large and rough with his tattoos and shaved head as she is small and delicate in her frocks and pumps. She hates football and I'm sure he's got little interest in dressmaking, yet they've always got something to say to each other.

'You've got a plethora of regulars now,' Del says. 'Long may it last.' He raises his icing-smeared fork to me. 'Your success is down to foresight more than fortune, my girl. I hope you know that.'

'And some friends in high places to pull strings,' I remind him. It was the vicar who convinced the councillor to give me the lease on the pub in the first place. Our councillor is not the most dynamic public servant. He needs pushing and wants an easy life. So he does usually give in to persuasion if it means getting to drink his pint in peace in Uncle Colin's pub.

'I'll miss these cakes when I go,' Mrs Delaney says, scooping a huge bite into her mouth.

'Mrs Delaney has set a date,' the vicar explains while his friend savours her slice. 'It's Tenerife or bust by the end of the year.'

Well, isn't that perfect. Why doesn't everyone I know just bugger off to Spain? *Bueno tripo*, or whatever they say. 'Maybe you and Kelly can share moving companies.' I manage to keep the snipe out of my voice. I can't really be angry with eighty-something Mrs Delaney for wanting to retire in the sun.

'Is Kelly moving?' the vicar asks.

'Not officially yet, but she will. Boyfriend.' I try not to roll my eyes.

'I'm sorry,' Mrs Delaney says, reaching for my hand. 'You'll miss her.'

Even more than Mrs Delaney will miss those cakes.

I know it shouldn't make a big difference whether Kelly is here or in Spain. She was right. We talk on the phone more than we set eyes on each other. It used to be a given that we'd go out together every weekend. She could count on me stopping by the fish van every day since I worked so close, even though we'd probably only seen each other the night before. And she was such a fixture at Mum and Dad's house that she had her own key.

Those pre-Daniel days seem a lifetime away now. In some ways they are. Her life is as wrapped up with Calvin as mine is with Daniel and the children. Kell got really ratty about that before the wedding, as I remember. She was convinced I'd leave her for a new life.

Only now she's the one doing it to me.

Doreen's on her third pot of tea. She's here a lot now that she knows she can get Auntie Rose to play cribbage any time she wants. Sometimes she sits with Mrs Delaney and the vicar, who don't play cribbage but like to share a pot of tea and a slice of cake (especially if it's chocolate). Sometimes she reads one of the daily papers that we keep on a little table by the door. Sometimes she knits. And sometimes she goes into the kitchen to make herself a sandwich. She probably shouldn't be back there, but she does clean up after herself and it saves one of us making it for her. Besides, she's scrupulous about paying what she thinks they're worth. Which is never the full price but she usually covers the cost.

Lou seems like her normal self when she arrives after her meeting with the duty solicitor who'll be representing her in court, so I hope she's forgiven me for yesterday. It was an honest mistake that any normal person would make. I didn't see what the spy was writing down. I only saw Lou accost her, and you can only go by what you see. At least that's what I tell myself.

Everyone knows now to report any suspicious behaviour, so I can't blame Auntie Rose for snitching on Carl when she sees him.

After all, he is under the table again.

'Carl? Everything okay? Where's Elsie?'

When he crawls back into the booth I can see that his knees are bothering him. 'Oh, thank you, yes, Elsie's at home. She's not feeling very well.'

'Nothing serious, I hope?'

'Nothing unexpected, thank you for asking. I was just feeling nostalgic.' He points under the table. 'That reminds me of the old days.'

The café is filling up, but I take a seat beside him. 'Do you want a cup of tea? We can have a nice chat.' Sometimes the business is as much about listening as anything else.

'That would be grand,' he says. 'I do miss her when she's not with me, but there's nought I can do at home. She kicked me out for a bit.'

I can imagine. When Dad first had to stop driving his taxi, Mum nearly went mad with him underfoot. You get used to doing things a certain way, she'd said. There's a routine – time in the bathroom, sitting for a cup of tea in a certain spot, making whatever you want for breakfast without having to worry about another person. Mum managed about a month before sending Dad to the Cock and Crown each morning to help my uncles set up for the day. He didn't do much apart from dry a few pint glasses, but everyone was pleased to help save their marriage.

Elsie is usually the one who carries the conversations, so it's nice to talk with Carl for a change. And for once he's in the mood to talk, at least about the past. When he gets going there's no stopping him.

'Elsie only had one sister, called Hettie,' he tells me. They were very close. Especially with only a three-year age difference. Their parents became best friends with Carl's in the war, when everyone went to the pub during the all-clears. It was better than sitting in the house worrying about dying. Carl would have been ten then, three years older than Elsie and around Hettie's age. But Elsie was the one for him, as proven by the graffiti carved in my table, so the families always assumed they'd marry.

Carl assumed it too. 'Then there was some trouble with Hettie,' he says, shaking his head. 'Terrible time. Elsie was beside 'erself. At one point we didn't know if Hettie'd make it.'

'Was she ill?' I ask. Who knows what kind of everyday diseases people died from in those days – chilblains and scurvy and such. Weren't women always getting attacks of the vapours? Or maybe that was earlier.

'Not ill,' he says. 'She found herself in a family way.'

'That wouldn't have gone down well with her parents, I imagine. When would this have been?'

'Nineteen fifty, so no, it wasn't a good situation. There were single mothers, of course, but they had a hard time. Sometimes even their families turned from them.' He shakes his head. 'Terrible time.'

'What happened, if you don't mind my asking?' He'd better not clam up now or I'll have to go round to Elsie's, pass her a Kleenex, fluff her pillows and get the rest of the story.

But I'm not prepared when he tells me that she was interfered with. That's olden day speak for rape, isn't it? 'How old was she?'

'Nineteen. The other party would have been pressurised to step up and do the right thing in those days but, you see, she couldn't marry the man in those circumstances.'

'Did nobody know who he was?'

Carl smiles. 'She never even mentioned the incident until she couldn't hide the pregnancy. Then she wouldn't tell anyone but Elsie. She had no reason to feel ashamed, as she wasn't at fault, but she did. She never even told me. Those were the times.'

With Hettie's tummy growing and her situation becoming more desperate, Elsie had a conversation with Carl. 'We were waiting until Elsie was eighteen to marry,' he explains. 'But we ended up waiting another forty-five years before we even kissed.'

You'd expect some sadness in his voice but there isn't any. Stiff upper lip, maybe.

There was really only one solution for poor Hettie. She needed to find someone to marry, and fast. Elsie couldn't let her only sister's entire life be ruined by one terrible event, especially when she had the power to do something about it.

'At first I couldn't believe what Elsie was suggesting,' says Carl. 'I was dead against the idea. Well, as you'd imagine. I'd loved Elsie since we were children. Of course I loved Hettie as well. We'd grown up together. And she was beside herself. Elsie too, I guess. She told me flatly that she could never be happy if Hettie was miserable. That pretty much put paid to my marriage plans with Elsie. It surprised our parents when Hettie and I announced our engagement, but by then they'd started to suspect the reason. So, you see, it was the sensible thing to do. Everyone got to be a little bit happy. Emma, dear, don't look so shocked. People do what they need to for the people they love.'

Of course I'm shocked! Kelly's as close to me as any sister could be, but I'm not sure I could have given up Daniel for her. And I know I couldn't stand seeing them together, knowing she had the life I wanted. 'I admire you, Carl. I couldn't have done that. I guess I'm too selfish.'

'But don't you see? Elsie couldn't have been happy married to me if it meant her sister being unhappy. And we're together now, that's what matters.' He looks at his watch. 'I should get back. Elsie'll be wanting her dinner.'

He unfolds himself from the booth. 'Thank you, Emma. It's nice to see friendly faces in here again.'

His eyes are a bit wet when he puts his hat on and turns to go back to his wife, who he waited forty-five years to kiss.

I'm just getting more coffee beans to feed the Gaggia when Joseph hurries in. 'Boss, we have a problem.'

'Shh, keep your voice down! You're the one always going on about how there are no problems, remember? Only opportunities.' He likes to google inspirational quotes when he's on the bus. 'Where are the cakes?'

'That's the opportunity, boss. There are no cakes. She's sold out.'

'What, *all* of them?' Cleo at the Mad Batter must make seven or eight cakes at the crack of dawn every morning. Personally, I couldn't do it. At 5 a.m. I wouldn't know my butter from my bicarb. 'I'd better go see her.' This might be serious.

Cleo's tiny cake shop isn't really much more than a kitchen with a few tables crammed in. People queue up, though, for her daily offerings and she does a roaring business. Too roaring, maybe. It sounds like we're victims of her success.

She's just pulling a tin from the oven when I see her. 'Let

me just get this cooling,' she says, deftly sliding the hot tin on to a rack. 'I'm running a little behind this morning.'

Wiping her hands on her flour-covered apron, she tucks a lock of wavy blonde hair back up into her hairband. She looks exactly as homely as a baker should. She wears jeans and T-shirts instead of pinnies and circle skirts, but she'd be at home in any illustrated cookery book from the 1950s.

'That smells delicious,' I say. My mouth is watering.

'Thanks, and I'm really sorry about not having cakes for you today. I just got a huge order.' She looks back at the tiny kitchen. 'I can't really make any more than I do now. I'm stretched as it is.'

'That's okay. You're only one woman and we still have a bit of the chocolate and the plum left over from yesterday. Can I put in an order for tomorrow?' That was our mistake. We've been turning up to buy them instead of ordering ahead.

But she shakes her head. 'I'm sorry, Emma. I'm going to be tied up for at least a month with this new order. I could probably let you have a few slices each day from the ones I do for the eat-in crowd, though I wouldn't want to run out for my walk-in business. My main advertising is word-of-mouth so I can't let that dry up. I'm really sorry.'

I'm struggling to make sense of this. What about the little enamel cake I've just put on my charm bracelet? Does that mean *nothing* to you, Universe?! 'So you won't have any cakes for us for at least a month?' Then a terrible thought occurs to me. But I'm just being paranoid, like one of those conspiracy theorists who believe the US government is hiding spaceships in Hangar 18. 'Who made the order, if you don't mind me asking?'

When she tells me it's a new customer on the main road, I don't need to hear any more to know it's Barb from the Other Half Caff.

Maybe I shouldn't be so quick to dismiss the idea of aliens in Hangar 18 either.

'I'm sorry, but she's made the order in advance,' says Cleo. 'Nobody ever does that. I'm sure you understand that I had to take the business. I wish I could do more, but I'm really at the limit.'

I can't put pressure on a fellow entrepreneur when I know exactly how it feels to be stretched flat out. 'No, no, of course I understand. We'll have to find another supplier. It's just that your cakes are the best. I'm going to miss them. Especially the chocolate.'

She smiles. Then she cuts a huge wodge of gooey dark chocolate Guinness cake, puts it into a box and hands it to me. 'I am really sorry.'

When I return to the café with one measly slice of Guinness cake, which I'm not sharing, by the way, I break the news to Lou and Joseph. 'Barb's holding our cakes hostage.'

'Will her customers even eat them?' Lou wonders. 'They don't look like flourless organic types.'

'I'm sure they'll love them, beetroot or not,' I say. 'Who wouldn't? Even Auntie Rose has tried a few and she never eats anything that's not from Mister Kipling. Anyway, it doesn't matter if Barb's customers eat them or not, because we still have no cake. We'll need another supplier.'

This is a blow to Joseph, who likes picking up the cakes because Cleo smells of vanilla. 'Couldn't we bake them ourselves?' he asks.

'Can you bake?'

'Pssh, no, but you must be able to. Or Lou.'

'Why's that?' Lou asks, sweet as you please.

He shrugs. Can't the boy see he's walking face-first into a proverbial cricket bat? 'Because you're girls. You bake.'

'Oh, will you piss off back to nineteen fifty?!'

I put a steadying hand on Lou's arm. 'Forgive him, for he knows not what he says,' I warn. 'Joseph. Just because we're girls, doesn't mean we can bake, any more than you'd know how to do DIY just because you're a boy. They're skills that people learn, not innate abilities. You've got as much chance of being a baker as Lou or me.'

'All right, then let me have a go. I'll bake our cakes.'

'You?' Lou says, which does undermine her original point a bit.

'Yes, why not?' I say. 'Look up a recipe, Joseph, and you can try. I'd suggest something easy to start with. Let me ring Mum. She's got the tins and stuff we'll need and you can take some cash from the till for the ingredients. Remember to get the receipt. I won't be much help, though, just so you know. I definitely can't bake.' Visions of Kell and my disastrous wedding cake experiment pop into my head. Joseph can't do any worse, and for the cost of a sack of flour and a bit of butter, it's worth a try.

These are temporary setbacks, I tell myself. All new businesses have trouble with suppliers, so we just need to pick ourselves up and find a solution. You never know, maybe Joseph will turn out to be Star Baker. At least we can work the Gaggia now, and we've got a steady stream of customers coming in every day. I still haven't seen many of our neighbours in here, but Lou and Joseph are learning skills they'll be able to take with them, and I'm really quite proud of that. That was the reason I opened the café in the first place.

While Joseph tries to work the oven and Lou looks after the takeaway counter, I bring Mrs Ishtique some more tea. 'How is Daniel?' she asks.

I haven't got the heart to tell her that her curries don't

seem to be the miracle cure she hoped they'd be. So I say the usual. 'He's fine, thank you.'

She holds my gaze, nodding slowly and squeezing my arm. 'I was once fine with Mr Ishtiaque, a few years after we were married. When my mother-in-law was asking how I was, I was fine. My mother too, was always asking and always hearing I am fine. Even Mr Ishtiaque was asking sometimes and went away with fine. I was fine. Fine as this saree, Emma. I was fine like this saree.' She holds the end of her flimsy scarf in front of her eyes and looks at me through it. 'You could see through me. Nobody looked at me, but I am looking at you, Emma.'

'Can you take a break?' Samantha calls over a little later. She's alone at the mums' table.

'For a minute,' I say. 'Everyone's just topped up on drinks. How are you?'

She juts her chin at the play area where her daughter is studying a picture book upside down. 'Her highness is waking every two hours again.'

'You get up with her?' I mean instead of her husband.

'Of course. He needs his sleep. More than I do, apparently.' She rolls her eyes.

I'd like to give her a solidarity eye roll, but Daniel does get up with the twins nearly as much as I do, or at least he did until lately. He still will, as long as I remind him with a knee to the back. 'Things any better on the bedroom front?' I ask instead of keeping to the mummy track. Sometimes I like to remind myself that the world doesn't revolve around children, and that's definitely something the old Emma would have asked.

She gathers her chestnut hair into a loose bun on top of her head. Then she pulls a small vial from her bag. 'I'm going to try this. Supposedly a few drops and he won't be able to keep his hands off me. Yeah, well, we'll see. I might need the extra-strength dose.'

I know that sexual attraction isn't just about looks, but Samantha's husband can't be completely immune to hers. She's got the kind of tall slender figure that looks perfect in designer clothes – skinny jeans and sleek silk tops and beautifully soft-looking asymmetric jumpers with zips and buckles and things that would make me look as if I'm wearing seconds – which is what she usually wears when she's not on her way to or from yoga.

The vial she hands me has a handwritten label that says *Guarantee pleesure*. 'What is this? Is it safe?'

She shrugs. 'The women in the forum I'm on swear by it, and it hasn't killed any of their husbands yet.'

'It there a forum for ...?'

'Women who can't get men to have sex with them?

Dozens.' She sighs. 'Don't uncork it. It smells of yak wee. I'll have to hide it in pungent food.'

'How do you know it's not yak wee?'

'I'll try anything at this point just to get some kind of normal life back. Though I can hardly even remember what a normal life is. You might not be having sex, but at least you get to exercise your brain every day.'

I shouldn't laugh because she means it as a compliment. And I'm definitely not going to mention the quickie I ordered off the Express Menu after dinner at The Enterprise. It'll only make her feel bad. Besides, it only half counts. 'Samantha, I make coffee and tea all day.'

'Don't put yourself down. You're running your own business.' She leans in. 'Tell me what it feels like. Go on. Let me live vicariously through you. Don't leave anything out.'

'Let's see. I go home stressed every night and worry about everything that's going wrong. I've got Barb, who hates me for some reason, trying to shut me down, and half the time I have no idea what I'm doing here. I'm supposed to be training Joseph and Lou, but I don't know if I'm doing that right either. In a few months they'll leave and I'll have to find two new kids to replace them, and believe me, finding those two wasn't easy in the first place.'

'You lucky cow,' she says. 'It sounds wonderful.'

'I'm not finished. That's just the business side. Then

there's the constant worry that working is taking time away from the children and I'm missing something with them because I'm too busy or stressed or tired. You saw Grace take her own shirt off yesterday, right? Well, I didn't because I was bringing the freelancers their cappuccinos. I missed my child's milestone thanks to a few cups of hot foam.'

'Cheer up. I bet you'll be there when she gets her nappy off. That kid's got stripper written all over her.'

'You didn't just call my child a stripper.'

'Do you really think it's a big deal in the scheme of things that you missed one bloody milestone? You get to see her nearly all the time, every day. If you hadn't been serving hipster coffees, you could have been in the loo at home. Are you going to avoid the toilet in case you miss something?'

She's right. I sound ridiculous, at least about Grace's shirt. I do mean the rest of it, though. 'You really miss work?' I ask.

'You know I do.'

'Then why not go back? You must have made enough as a consultant to hire a childminder for Dougie. And Amanda is old enough to be left with someone now.' I say this even though just thinking about putting Oscar and Grace with a stranger makes me go cold. I've been so lucky with Mum and Dad and Auntie Rose. And the café. Samantha is right.

'Ah, but you've answered your own question,' she says. 'What if I miss Amanda taking her shirt off for the first time?' She sips her tepid tea. 'Dougie's a trooper, but he needs a lot of help. How can I trust anyone else? It's hard enough to let him go to school. It's the guilt, the GUILT. It gets us all in the end. If I stay home, I'm miserable. If I go to work, I'm selfish. Which is easier to live with? Damned if I know.'

We both hear the plea for help from the play area. 'Call of duty,' she says. 'Coming, Dougie. Hang on.' In one graceful motion she sweeps through the gate, plucks her daughter from the mat and deposits her on her son's lap. 'Thanks, Jack, ta, Rose, hope they weren't any trouble.'

Auntie Rose beams. 'No, they were lovely as always. Bye, Dougie, bye, Amanda. See you tomorrow?'

Samantha's son, Dougie, waves happily. 'Thank you, Mr Liddell, Auntie Rose. See you tomorrow!'

'Definitely see you tomorrow,' Samantha says to me as she wheels her son's chair through the play area gate. 'Let's get you changed before we go, okay?' she says to him. 'You've got tennis in an hour.' Then to me, 'Could you give me a hand with those?' She nods at the pushchairs in front of the loo door. 'Sorry to ask.'

'Don't be sorry! We really need to figure out a better system.' It's one thing to joke about Leo being able to push them out of the way in case of fire, but Samantha has to navigate Dougie's wheelchair. That's no laughing matter.

I still cringe when I remember how I scoffed at her whinging about having to stay home from work just because she'd had a baby. Like nobody in the history of motherhood has ever had to juggle work and childcare. This was before I knew the real situation and before I had the twins, when my prejudices were as intact as my peritoneum. I hadn't the faintest clue what it was like to look after a child, let alone one with the kind of health problems Dougie has.

He was born with spinal muscular atrophy so he can't stand or walk and needs round-the-clock care. Luckily he hasn't got the breathing problems that some kids with the condition do. Well, I say luckily. It's still pretty unlucky for poor Dougie, if you ask me, though he doesn't let his wheelchair get in the way of being a seven-year-old boy. His social schedule is more packed than mine.

It takes Joseph most of the day to bake something that looks like a cake, proving how deceiving looks can be. 'Nice effort,' I tell him, trying to swallow the oversweet, under-mixed brick of flour on my fork. 'I couldn't eat another bite.'

'Not without vomming, we couldn't,' says Lou as I dig

her in the ribs with my elbow. She flashes me a smile. 'Sorry to tell you this, Joseph, but you're no Mary Berry.'

'I do appreciate you trying,' I tell him, 'but I think we'll need another plan for the cakes.'

'Go round to the caff and steal them?' Lou suggests when Joseph goes out front to wait on a customer.

'Another plan, Lou. I was thinking more along the lines of having someone else make them.'

It's a long shot, but I might know someone. Zane and I used to work together at the Vespa dealership, where he spent most of his time either complaining about our boss's son, who never turned up for work, or reading paperbacks. Then, out of the blue, he quit to go to catering college and he did manage to come up with a wedding cake for us from his baking course. It was actually a gay pride rainbow cake with a huge wedge cut out of the back from when his tutor taste-tested it, but Kell fed some story to Daniel's family about the missing piece being an East London tradition at weddings. We've lost touch over the last year, but he's worth a try.

'Since you mentioned stealing ...' I say to Lou, in possibly the most awkward attempt to introduce a topic in the history of conversation.

'It was a joke. I wouldn't really do it,' she says. 'You know that, right?'

There's no challenge in her question. Its uncertainty breaks my heart. 'Lou, of course I know that. You're not going to do anything to hurt me or the business. I'd trust you with ... anything ... the business, even my children. That's why I've been wondering if it would be helpful to have a character witness for your court appearance. You know, someone who'll tell them that you're a good worker and a good person.'

The more time I spend with Lou, the more I feel like she needs that. Presumably her mum would have stood up for her, but then she died. As if being an orphan isn't hard enough. Lou's got no one to fight her corner. 'I'd be happy to do it.'

To my surprise, she doesn't flare up. She just shrugs. 'It's Youth Court. I can't stop you if you want to be there, though you'll need to get permission.'

That's about as close to a thank you as I'm probably going to get, because she quickly changes the subject. She won't be happy that she's let her defences down, even briefly.

'Are you gonna use all the meat and cheese in the fridge before it goes off, do you think? The use-by date's tomorrow.' She asks this casually as she rotates the contents of the fridge like the Sandwich Whisperer taught us.

'Probably not. The sandwiches aren't selling nearly as well as the cakes.'

'If it's just gonna go off, would it be okay to take some?'

I smile. 'Midnight snacks?' I tease.

'It's for the kids.'

'Sure, it's okay. Just leave a few slices for tomorrow in case we need it. What kids?'

'The kids at home.' Something about the way she says it warns me against asking anything more. Am I ever going to learn to stop asking so many questions? She never answers them.

Only Leo is left when it's time to lock up. 'You're later than usual today,' I say, setting the chairs upside down on the tables so I can sweep the floor. 'Do you have a lot of work on?'

'Tons,' he says. 'And the presentation was this morning, so I'm behind on everything else.'

'That's right, I'm sorry I forgot!' I shake my head. 'I was busy with CakeGate this morning. I hope the presentation went well.'

He nods. 'We got the account. I heard about the cakes. Sorry.'

'We're also missing our coffee delivery. I don't want to sound paranoid and blame Barb, but given everything else ...' Pablo isn't answering his phone again, so I don't know if it's an admin error or something more sinister. At least we can get coffee from the market if we need to. Cleo's cakes are harder to replace.

'You probably haven't had time to start reading that book?' Leo asks. His eyes are slightly too big from the strong prescription in his glasses. That, coupled with the way his hairy chin juts out, makes him look really keen to know the answer.

'Actually, I did start it last night. For about five minutes before I fell asleep.'

'That would probably make the author sad to hear,' he points out. 'But you must be dead on your feet by the time you go to bed. Running a business and a house and looking after your children. Most people complain about one job. You've got three. Somehow women find incredible energy reserves, not just for everything you have to do, but everything you have to think.'

'I think, therefore I am exhausted,' I say.

'Said Descartes' wife,' quips Leo.

How different he is now that I know him. I hardly even see the tweedy hipster who stole my electricity. Leo is a very nice person. I look forward to seeing him every morning. 'It does seem like an interesting book,' I tell him. 'It's just a lot of information to take in. I used to be able to juggle more than one class, even working full-time. Now I can't seem to remember a shopping list. My brain's turned to porridge since having the twins. What I need is an idiot's guide to philosophy.'

'One idiot, at your service.' He does a formal bow in his chair, making me laugh. 'Sometimes remembering one key thing about each philosopher helps trigger the rest of their ideas. Take Socrates, for example. Or Socrates with a question mark, as I think of him, because he wanted people to question their problems and views and come up with their own solutions.'

'So he didn't actually have any answers himself? *I* could do that. In fact, I'll probably try it on the twins when they start asking *why* about everything.'

'They'll be students of Socrates and not even know it,' he says.

'Socrates, question mark. Got it. Go on, give me another.'

I should be getting home to start the tea. I check my phone, mentally sifting through the freezer for a quick meal to throw together for Daniel and me.

Leo notices. 'Sorry, am I holding you up?'

'No, not at all.' But it's sweet of him to notice. 'The children are happy enough here and they don't need feeding for another hour. Their meal is easy to fix. It's just steamed veg and some chicken.' And fish fingers for the grown-ups. That'll do for us.

I've got no idea how much of what Leo tells me will

stick in my brain, but it turns out to be the nicest chat I've had in a long time. Though I do have to push away the little niggle of guilt about enjoying myself.

'You should be a teacher, you know,' I tell him. 'You're really good at this.'

He shrugs. 'I just really enjoy talking to someone who's smart and engaging.'

'You probably need to go meet your friends.' It's yellow tweed Wednesday.

His smile is really quite fetching. 'I see them all the time. Getting to hit it off so naturally with a person is rare.'

I know what he means. It's about as rare as feeling like someone actually understands me.

Chapter 16

'Late day at the café?' Daniel asks when I get home. He's clearly pleased with his rhyme.

'Long day,' I tell him. Leo did eventually go meet his friends who, he said, love their craft beer too much to ever leave the pub early. Part of me wished he'd asked me along, though it would probably be irresponsible to drag my toddlers into a bar with strangers just so mummy could keep talking to the nice bloke.

Again, there's that pang of guilt. Why, though? Why shouldn't I make a new friend when we enjoy each other's company and have things in common? Just because he happens to be a man? It's the twenty-first century.

'I'm making supper,' Daniel says. 'It should be ready in a few minutes and I didn't use any spice, so the children can eat it too. Saves us a step.'

I gaze at Daniel with my mouth open, like he's just found

the solution for world hunger. 'What have I done?' he asks.

'Nothing. I mean, everything. You've thought of every-thing, thank you.' I stand on my tiptoes to kiss him. Daniel used to do all the cooking when we were first together. That was because we always had dinner at his house – it was more romantic than trying to crowd around the kitchen table at Mum and Dad's. But he's also much better at it than me. I can follow a recipe, but Daniel actually makes up dishes from leftovers, like my very own home edition of the MasterChef invention test. My mouth starts to water.

'The wine's in the fridge,' he adds. 'I'll have a glass too if you're pouring.'

If we barricade the children into the dining room with the safety gates, we can keep an eye on them from the kitchen. That's not to say they can't still get into mischief, just that we've got a chance to catch them before they do too much damage.

I pour two ice-cold glasses of wine. Those glasses were a gift from Cressida for our wedding. She was Daniel's friend originally, but we used to hang around together a lot. She was even one of my bridesmaids, so I really should have kept in touch more than I have. I think I last talked to her just before Daniel's birthday party, and that was late last summer. That long. How did that happen? 'I haven't talked to Cressida in ages,' I tell Daniel as he checks whatever's in the oven. I watch him as he potters around the kitchen, my heart quickening like it always used to. He's adorable.

How nice it is to have those familiar feelings! Just because the man makes my tea. I'm such a cheap date, but still, I'm absolutely going to savour this moment while it lasts.

'She's doing well,' he says. 'I saw her for drinks a few weeks ago.' Then he looks guilty because he knows he didn't tell me this before. 'We just had one drink quickly after work. It wasn't worth mentioning.'

My annoyance wrestles with all the lovely feelings I had seconds before. It must be nice to be so casual about having a social life while I'm rationing my time like it's the last of the chocolate on Christmas Eve just after all the shops have closed.

'She asked about you,' he says. 'Why don't you give her a ring?'

'Tea's in a few minutes,' I say, my voice tight.

'It can wait, darling. Ring her. You'll feel better.'

I feel just bloody fine, thank you very much. 'Any other social events I should know about?'

His hesitation speaks volumes. 'Actually, yah, now that you mention it.'

I cross my arms. He wouldn't have told me if I hadn't asked.

'There's a charity do in two weeks that we've been organising, and I'd love to take you. It's a dinner and dancing thing. You can dress up …' He sees my face '… or not. You're beautiful in whatever you wear. I thought it would be a nice night out for us.'

Dinner, wine, romantic propositions. Leave it to him to be kind and thoughtful just when I'm trying to be angry that he sneaked off, again, for a rendezvous with his old life.

I suppose I could ring Cressida, but I feel as if I've lost that privilege after missing the call-back window. You know the one, after a friend leaves a message, or two or three, when it's still okay to say you've been busy/out of town/ ill. Once the window closes, though, it's a lot harder to sound like you really did mean to ring back. And you can't very well string together excuses – I was just going to ring when my phone died and it took a week to get a new battery and then it was Mum's birthday, which is where I must have picked up the stomach bug that knocked me out so we had to reschedule the holiday till I felt better, but then coming back into work after so long off was crazy. Phew, sorry it's been six months.

Everyone's window is different, depending on the

temperament of the friend involved. Some people are fine not hearing from you for a month. Others get sniffy if a week goes by. Cressida isn't the sniffy type, but there's also the relationship to consider. She's more Daniel's friend than mine. It doesn't make sense to ring out of the blue after six months to whinge about him. That would only be awkward for us both.

So I call Emerald instead. 'Give me ten minutes to convince Anthony to mind the baby,' she says when I suggest a drink.

'No, no, Emerald, I don't mean for you to drop everything right now. It was only an idea if you weren't busy. Daniel is making tea now so I couldn't meet till after.'

'After, then,' she says.

'I'm going to meet Emerald after we eat,' I tell Daniel back in the kitchen. 'I can get the children ready for bed if you'll put them down and read to them. I won't be out long.'

He hesitates before answering. 'Of course, darling. We'll have a nice time together. You go out and meet your friend.'

I wish I didn't feel guilty when he says this. I'm not exactly abandoning my family, am I? 'I won't be gone long.'

'Go as long as you want. Enjoy yourself. Really, Emma. You need to get out and have fun sometimes.'

He's probably trying to be nice, but that just feels like a judgement.

I turn up to the pub that Emerald suggests to find Garnet, Samantha and Melody already clutching wine glasses. 'Wow, did I sound that desperate?' I ask, taking up the fifth chair at the table.

'Solidarity,' Samantha says, and they all raise their glasses as they hand me mine. 'We know what it can be like.'

I feel silly now. I was just a bit fed up with Daniel, that's all. Nothing catastrophic or life-threatening. Married people go through these ups and downs all the time. It probably just means we're out of the honeymoon phase. Perfectly normal, in other words.

But my friends aren't letting me brush the whole thing off. 'You can talk to us,' Melody says. 'Trust me – whatever it is, we've all been there.'

'I don't think anything unusual is happening with us,' I tell them. 'I guess it's just taking a while to adjust to the children. These things take time, right?'

'Of course they do,' Garnet says. 'It's the biggest adjustment you'll make in your marriage because it involves every part of your life.'

Emerald finishes her sister's thought. 'Your relationship

and the way you relate to each other, not to mention your home life and your interactions with the children. Our counsellor explained that. We went to her to learn the coping tools.'

Garnet reaches over to hug her sister, who pats and squeezes her hand in return. 'We've been to counselling too,' Garnet tells me.

Emerald's hand squeezes Garnet's again, a little tighter because Garnet flinches. 'I suggested it to you after we started going, didn't I?' Emerald says. 'It's so important to take care of these things before they become big problems. I've always said that.'

'Mmm hmm,' Garnet agrees. 'There's a plaque in our kitchen. "Tend your relationship as though it were a garden."'

'That's right. I got it for you for Christmas that year.'

I'm not sure who won that round. I don't know if they know either.

'Is your sex life okay?' Melody wants to know.

'Shouldn't we have a bit more to drink first?'

Samantha tops me up. 'So?'

'It's ... there. Sometimes.' I glare at the women. 'You aren't about to tell me that I should be looking after my man, are you?'

'God, no!' Samantha says. 'This isn't the nineteen fifties.

259

Think of sex like a barometer for the relationship. It can tell you whether it's stormy or fine.'

'Or changeable,' Emerald says hopefully.

I put my chin in my hand. 'We're in a drought at the moment. With very occasional scattered showers.'

'Do you want to try some of my love potion?' Samantha offers.

'Does it actually work?!' Garnet wants to know.

'It works. It made him randy, but he got tired halfway through. I need one with added caffeine.'

Melody shakes her head. 'Count yourself lucky,' she tells me. 'Who's got the energy for those marathon sessions anymore?'

'We do!' the sisters say at once. Then, just as Garnet is about to speak, Emerald adds, 'We probably do it three times a week.'

'Us too,' Garnet says. 'At least that often, but it's the quality that counts.'

Emerald nods. 'And also the quantity.'

Samantha just rolls her eyes at me. 'At this point I'd take either.'

We're two bottles into the evening when Melody stands up. 'Well, I've got to get home to make more biscuits for Poppy.'

'Melody, your brain is going soft from all that macrobiotic shit you eat,' Samantha scolds. 'Your girls are called Eva and Joy.'

'And your brain is getting squeezed from all the yoga because you know very well that Poppy is our schnauzer. See you tomorrow!'

Our little group breaks up not long after Melody leaves to bake for her dog.

'Ring me if you need anything,' Garnet says, hugging me.

'Or me. Any time at all,' adds Emerald.

'Day or night, I'm here,' Garnet says.

We've only been together an hour, yet I do feel better having talked to them. It proves that I'm not the only one who's struggling to hold on to whatever tiny bit of me that I can, as meagre as it might be right now.

Watching our clientele build up over the weeks that follow our opening does help me keep some perspective on everything else. If I'm managing to make the café work, then maybe things in the rest of my life are working better than I think.

My friends haven't invited any other mums to the café, but there are a lot more in here now. Just seeing them inside seems to be enough to attract others, like ants to a picnic. As soon as they realise there's a play area, they can't wheel their Bugaboos in here fast enough. The whole ground floor is nearly full of them.

When Dad and Auntie Rose first started in the play area they were really just there to get out of the house, but now they're surrounded by under-fives. Auntie Rose does a reading corner and you should see the children's faces when she acts out the scenes and does all the voices. Not to be outdone, Dad's concocted a whole parallel universe where the kids brew tea and coffee in the mini kitchen and serve cake to waiting customers at the tiny tables dotted around the play mats.

Mrs Ishtiaque loops her arm through mine as I watch my children playing with the toy kitchen. 'They are loving it here, Emma. We are all loving it. You should be very proud.'

'I am. All the hard work is worth it when I see everyone enjoying the café.' I watch Carl sitting with Doreen and Auntie Rose. Elsie did come in after her last bout of illness, but she's in bed again today, and Carl looks worried.

If the café wasn't here, then where would he go for a friendly chat on days like today when Elsie isn't well? And what about the others? Auntie Rose would be stuck in the house all day long with Dad, doing her crossword puzzles and binging on daytime telly. Where else would the mums snatch cups of tea in between tantrums and nappy duty?

'People really do seem to love it, don't they?' I say, almost to myself.

'We are loving it because it is full of love,' Mrs Ishtiaque says. 'You are making a community.'

'Thanks, I guess I am. We are, all of us together.'

Having said that, the mums do grumble about Joseph's friends who come in being loud and lairy and generally teenagers. The freelancers aren't always crazy about the mums blocking the aisles, and the teens don't want anyone near them.

So I shouldn't be surprised when a tiny row starts over one of the freelancers spilling a bit of his coffee as he tries to manoeuvre around a pushchair. Unfortunately, the splash goes close to one of the new mums, who happens to be breastfeeding. 'You nearly burned my baby!' she cries.

'Sorry, sorry,' he says. 'I couldn't get past this bloody chair.'

'I'll thank you to watch your language too,' her friend says. 'There are children here.'

'As if I hadn't noticed,' he mumbles. 'And I didn't spill any coffee on your baby, so just relax.'

'You relax! You should be more careful. You people are always shoving things around and trailing cables all over the place. You could hurt someone.'

One of the other freelancers speaks up at that. 'If you

didn't always hog all the space, then we wouldn't need to rearrange the furniture to get by!'

Before I know it, it's all kicked off. The mums are shouting at the freelancers. The freelancers are shouting at the mums. And the teenagers are mocking everyone and cheering whenever someone scores a really snarky point.

'Oi, will you shut it!' Lou eventually shouts. Her voice booms across the din, shocking everyone into silence. 'Look, we can't have everyone rowing in here or there isn't going to be a café. Then where do you think you're going to go, have you thought of that? To Starbucks in the City with their four quid coffees? You really think they're going to let you bring your power strips and your beard trimmers in there to charge? And you mums, you can go to Barb's, where you'll be about as welcome as piles.' The teens air snap and hoot at the mums. 'What are you lot so happy about? You'll be back hanging out with the junkies in front of the Tube station if we close, so we'd better figure out how to get along or we're all out on the street.'

She's right, although we need more than a peace treaty. Even if the freelancers did manage to get along with the mums, they'd still have to wear earphones to block out all the children's noise. It's not really a good long-term solution if they want to keep working here.

'Look, you might want to have a café that's entirely

devoted to mums and babies, and that's okay,' Leo tells me quietly after everyone's calmed down. 'Lord knows there's probably a huge demand for more space where they can feel comfortable. Mothers and babies, I mean.'

As usual, he's said exactly what I've been thinking. I did once try taking the twins to one of those play centres. They loved it, but I was left standing just outside the play gate for two hours, barred from entering but ready to alert one of the staff if they got into difficulty. Far from the pleasant all-round entertainment I imagined, I spilled tepid take-away tea down my front and came home feeling more stressed than before I went.

The thing the mums like about the café is that they can sit like normal people and have a hot drink or a sandwich and still watch their children.

But I don't want the entire café to be about mums, any more than I'd want it to exclude them the way the Other Half Caff does. Otherwise I'm no better than Barb.

'I know that a café full of children isn't the best work environment,' I tell Leo. 'Maybe there's another option. I really don't want to sound like I'm banishing you, but I've been thinking about using the upstairs. We could clean it up and make it nice. I'd ask the mums but the stairs are a problem with the buggies.'

It's not ideal from a service point of view – I'm not crazy

about traipsing up and down those stairs all day – but we need to do something.

Leo strokes his beard as he thinks. He's let it go bushy again, but it's not as off-putting as it was before I knew him. 'You mean setting it up as an actual work space, like a proper office café? There used to be one of those nearby, you know, but it closed down. I'm sure if you did something similar it would be just as popular.'

'So popular it closed down?'

He laughs. 'Nothing gets by you. They took the whole block down to build flats. It wasn't the café's fault. I could tell you everything I liked about the old place and you can use the good ideas to set yourself up. Just off the top of my head, you'd want to arrange the tables so everyone's got the right space and maybe have some music. And pitchers of water. I did mean to mention that to you anyway. Maybe with some cucumber in. It's very refreshing.'

'It won't be a private space, though,' I warn. I can tell Leo is already decorating 'his' office. 'The whole café is open to everyone. We just want to make all our customers as comfortable as possible. I imagine people who don't want to be around babies will join you upstairs ... the teenagers will probably like it up there too.'

'Yes, of course, I understand. It's still a great idea.' He

gazes at me. 'You're very good at all this, you know. I hope everyone is giving you the credit you deserve.'

The other freelancers have been ignoring our conversation. Insulated in giant puffy earphones, they're oblivious to everything but the tracks they're listening to. Leo waves his hands in front of their screens to get their attention. 'Emma has an idea for us,' he says.

They listen politely as I start talking about all the features they might want – speakers and a docking station for music and an old-timey *Upstairs-Downstairs* bell system so that we know when someone on the first floor needs another drink. Before I can stop myself, I'm offering extra electric sockets and a printer. If I don't calm down, next I'll be promising them a gym and sauna and free Massage Fridays.

'Or walkie-talkies instead of a bell?' Leo wonders. 'Then we could give you our orders and save you trips upstairs to take them. Just a thought.'

The freelancers are nodding along with all our ideas.

'Let's take a temperature,' Leo says. 'Emma is proposing to open the upstairs so that we have a quieter place to work, though it won't be solely for our use. Anyone is welcome, whether they're working or not.'

All their hands shoot up in the air and their fingers start to wriggle.

'Leo, what's happening here?'

'Twinkles, great,' he says.

'Which means?'

'Everyone's in agreement.'

'Then why don't you just say so?'

'We did. We'd like to use your office café, thank you.' He turns again to the freelancers. 'Should we help Emma put it together?'

Their hands twinkle again.

Shyly I do the jazz hands back. That's one problem down, only several dozen to go.

Chapter 17

Zane arrives at the café like a vanilla-scented guardian angel, trailing flour wherever he goes. His dreadlocks are tied up neatly on top of his head and everything, from his walk to the way he greets me, radiates a confidence he never had when we worked together at the Vespa dealership.

I probably never gave him enough credit then. His street slang and teeth-sucking and the fact that we'd been in school together nearly our whole lives bred familiarity. And while familiarity didn't breed contempt, it didn't exactly breed respect either.

'Hiya,' he calls from in front of the café. 'Aiight?'

'Yes, not bad for the middle of the night,' I say, unlocking the door.

'Yeah, sorry about that, but classes start at ten.'

Zane's in his last year of catering college, and now that he's perfected his white sauce and learned a hundred and

269

one uses for a rolling pin, he's branching out. The rest of his classmates might be jobbing as kitchen help. Zane's come up with another plan.

Which is lucky for us, though I'm not asking too many questions about the details. When he told me that he and some of the other students could use our kitchen to bake them, I said yes. When he offered to charge less than the Mad Batter, I said yes please. When he said he was skimming students from the catering college, undercutting their class fees to run his own bootleg cake-making courses, I asked him not to tell me anything else.

The important thing is that we've got our own source for cakes.

'I bought all the things you asked for, and you can let me know what else you need as you go along.' I set the keys on the kitchen worktop. 'Take them. You can let yourself in.'

He flashes his megawatt smile. 'You trust me?'

'What are you going to do, steal the bunting? I don't want to get up at five o'clock every day, thank you very much. Just be sure to lock up when you leave.'

He sticks his head inside the big fridge. 'You need more milk,' he says. 'I'll use up most of what's there for the cakes.'

'Go ahead and use it. There's more being delivered.' If it's not there when I come back to open up, then I'm going to the Other Half Caff to find out why. I have had it with things going missing around here, and I *know* Barb is behind it. Pablo finally rang back about our coffee order. He claims I rang the distributor to cancel it. Someone cancelled it, but it wasn't me. They reinstated the order without any trouble and now they'll ring my mobile whenever there's an order change, just to make sure it's not a mistake.

Mistake. That's what we're calling it. It sounds better than sabotage.

I don't expect the milk to be there when I get back to open the café later, so I'm not disappointed. Just royally pissed off. It's such a childish thing to do, stealing our milk. Barb is at least my mum's age. Old enough to know better.

Lou arrives a few minutes after me. 'Want me to go buy some?' she offers when I tell her the delivery's gone missing again.

'No, thanks, I'll go.'

She grins. 'Gonna kick some heads in?'

'No head-kicking. I'm just going to talk to her. This has to stop.'

But I start to lose my nerve before I even get off the square. I've never been great about confrontation. Example: faking an entire society wedding instead of just telling my mother-in-law we didn't have enough money. Kelly's the one who isn't afraid to stand up to people. I'm the coward who urges her on from safely behind her back.

I've got to pull on my big girl pants now, because the café is too important. They might be small setbacks that we can overcome, but small setbacks can chip away at a business. I can't let them fester and grow. That's what I keep telling myself as I walk to the Other Half Caff.

It's full. They're mostly tradesmen in work boots and spattered clothes, with a few businessmen dotted around the tables too. Barb is busy at the till behind the counter and as I get inside, I realise how small the caff is. I'm going to have to do this in front of a closely-packed live audience.

She catches my eye while I'm still in the doorway. Instead of looking embarrassed or sorry in any way, she squares her shoulders. She's washed out and rough-looking under the fluorescent lighting. You just know she was the girl at school who'd pin weaklings to the ground and steal their tuck shop money.

'I'm Emma from the Second Chance Café,' I say over the counter. My voice doesn't sound nearly as shaky as it should, given that I'm cacking myself.

'I know who you are.' Her hard blue eyes narrow.

'Then would you like to explain why you're stealing my milk and cancelling my coffee orders?'

Her clientele isn't about to miss a second of this. Chairs scrape as they position for the best view.

'I'm not doing nothing,' Barb says. 'If you ain't doing well, it's nothing to do with me. Now I suggest you leave my caff and go back where you came from.'

At first I think she means the café, but then I don't think so. 'What's that supposed to mean? I'm from here just like you are.'

She snorts. 'You're nothing like me, with your fancy cakes and your chai tea.'

Both our glances fall on her display case. 'Whose fancy cakes are those, then?' I'd recognise the Mad Batter's icing swirls anywhere.

She smirks. 'A little bird told me about a good baker, is all. They were right. I can't keep them in stock. The brickies have a huge sweet tooth.'

'Well, enjoy them. We've got our own in-house bakery now, so we don't need them.'

That throws her for a split second. 'It don't matter. You'll be out of business by the end of the year.'

That's what the spy said too. 'What is wrong with you? Why do you want to see the café fail? You can't be that mean.'

She shrugs. 'I ain't mean. I'm the caff owner around here. Now I think you should get out.'

I'd love to slay her with a witty comeback right there, but nothing comes to mind so, instead, I turn and stride

273

from the caff like it was my idea to go anyway. What a spiteful, petty, thieving woman she is.

I can't hire security to watch my milk, can I? Unless I get there to take it in before she gets there to steal it, there's not much I can do except cancel the milkman. Which would mean going to the shop for milk and lugging it back. I know it wouldn't be the end of the world. We're not exactly having to milk the cows ourselves. But it's just one more thing to have to worry about.

The bigger question is: why is she doing it in the first place? I've got no answer for that.

By the time I've stopped at the shop for the milk and waited for the organic one to open for the freelancers' almond milk, my hands have unclenched a bit. If Barb wants a fight, she's going to get one.

The café is in full swing for the day when I get back. Its warm cosiness and the lovely scent of freshly baked cakes only makes Barb's determination to hurt it more poignant. It's like when your boyfriend looks extra hot and loveable as he's about to ask you to delete his number.

I do a double-take when my eyes naturally go to the freelancers' table and see strangers there instead. Right. They're upstairs charging their laptops in peace and quiet before the teens get here.

There's no peace or quiet downstairs. As nice as it is to

put loads of children together, it does guarantee that at least two will be crying at any time. That's making everyone else have to talk louder to be heard, and it sounds like a madhouse.

'Everything under control?' I ask Lou as I scoot behind the bar to help.

'It's all good,' she says, pointing to the cake stands where there are already slices missing. 'The new cakes are popular.'

Zane's students have made a pineapple upside-down cake, all gooey and dripping with caramelised brown sugar. It makes my mouth water just looking at it. And a lemon cake topped with fresh lavender, judging by the yellow icing and little purple bits on top. There's also a Victoria sponge that's a bit crooked, but I'm sure it tastes delicious.

'Did they leave a mess in the kitchen?'

'No, it's all wiped down and the bowls and pans are washed. That was a good call, getting them in. Ditto putting the freelancers upstairs.' Her silvery-blue hair shimmers when she nods her approval.

Maybe I feel so proud because Lou is as careful with her praise as she is with everything else. Well, why not? We have come a long way from a disused pub and no idea how to use the espresso machine. Lou can run the café on her own now. I can't say the same about Joseph and probably wouldn't put him in charge, though he did ask the other day if he could be the Chief Closer. As long as that just means turning the key in the door when we all leave for the night, I'm fine with his new job description.

'But you've got to do something about those prams,' Lou continues. 'It's out of hand. We need NCP parking for pushchairs out there.'

That is our biggest problem right now. More customers would fit on the tables if the prams weren't blocking all the aisles. 'Let me check again out front.'

It's while I'm wondering if we could get the council to suspend the parking spaces in front of the café (not likely) that I notice the window boxes.

Philippa's flowers! The foliage is as wilted as the bagged lettuce in my fridge and nearly all the blooms are droopy. Yet I'm sure her company has been coming to water them. I've definitely seen the truck with the long watering hose they use. Sure enough, when I stick my finger into the soil, it's damp. I'm afraid my gardening skills end at chucking some water into the pot and hoping for the best, so I have no idea what's wrong.

Somehow I'm managing to kill an entire wall of flowers without even touching them.

I ring Philippa to confess. Maybe it's not too late for her to save them. 'I'm really sorry to tell you this ...'

'What is it, darling, is it the children? You? Is something wrong with Daniel? Your parents?'

'No, no, it's nothing like that! It's your flowers. In front of the café.' I feel a bit silly now. Nobody should ever start a conversation sounding so doomy. 'They don't look very good. I'm afraid I might have killed them somehow.'

Philippa laughs. 'Oh, darling, I won't let you give it a thought. I'll send someone around for a look later. I'm sure they're fine, rahly. As long as Daniel and you and the children are all right. We can always plant new flowers. You're irreplaceable!'

My mother-in-law's attitude is a relief. Hopefully she won't mind too much either about the two teacups I've broken. She insisted we keep them (*I wouldn't dream of using them, darling, when we've got those lovely photo mugs you gave us for Christmas!*). Of course, we haven't broken any of the cheap ones we got off eBay. Sod's Law.

Philippa must be as worried about the flowers as I am because she sends her gardeners round in the afternoon. 'Right, we've tested the soil in the boxes,' the gardener tells me. She's the same one who installed them in the first place. She probably left here that day assuming she could trust me with her plants. 'Has anyone been using mop water or anything like that to feed the plants?'

'No, we always put that water down the grate in the road just there.'

She nods. 'It was a long shot anyway.' When she wipes

277

her hands down the front of her blue jumpsuit, she leaves a streak of soil behind. 'The chlorine levels in the compost are too high for that, really. That's what's killing the plants. We've tested the water in our truck and it's not coming from there. Also, it's only on ground level. The flowers on the first floor and above seem fine.'

'So you're saying the flowers have been ... poisoned?' That's bloomicide.

She nods. 'In a way, yes. The chlorine is killing them. Whether it's an accidental contamination or intentional, we'll have to change over the compost and put new plants in. We can come back tomorrow, if that's all right.'

'Yes, but ... Do you have any plants that are immune to chlorine? In case this happens again?'

'No, sorry.'

'Then maybe it's best to leave the ground floor window ledges bare for now.' Otherwise I might be condemning hundreds of flowers to their deaths. I don't want that on my conscience.

If Barb is behind this, then it's no mere business rivalry. This is starting to get dangerous. What kind of monster poisons innocent begonias?

'Emma, Emma, come in, over.' Back inside the walkie-talkie squawks and crackles on the bar.

'Yes, Leo, can I help you?' The freelancers just love this new mode of communication.

'Come upstairs, please. Over and out.' The handset goes dead. They haven't got the hang of the time-saving element, though.

Glancing at the play area, I catch Dad's eye. Oscar is asleep on his lap and Grace is stuffing the play oven with books. He nods when I jerk my thumb to the ceiling.

'You know that the whole point of the walkie-talkie is to tell me what you need while I'm downstairs to save me a trip,' I tell Leo as he grins at me.

'This is definitely a better setup,' he says, 'but we miss seeing you.'

The other freelancers do twinkles. They think it's hysterical that I didn't know what that was. So sorry to disappoint them, but I was busy working full-time and going to school and looking after Dad and Auntie Rose while they occupied St Paul's chanting 'We are the 99%' and having consensus meetings about what to cook for dinner.

'Did you call me up here to tell me that?'

'Everyone likes to feel appreciated,' he says.

I try my best to look annoyed at the interruption of my otherwise very important day, but I can't help smiling when I go back downstairs.

Chapter 18

It's a Tale of Two Cafés around here. On the ground floor a messy stew of motherhood bubbles away. People come and go throughout the day, working around school runs and errands, nap times and meals. At any given point someone's in tears – and it's not always a child.

Upstairs there's a thick layer of East London life, slightly quieter, less chaotic and with fewer tears, where hipster freelancers rub along with most of the neighbourhood's teenage population. Despite inhabiting the same space, though, they don't seem to be in the same world. Everyone is focussed on some kind of electronic device – the freelancers peering into their laptop screens and the kids on their phones 'talking to each other' on Snapchat. The things they all have in common is a taste for coffee, an obsession with electronics and an aversion to the mothers and children below them.

That seems to suit the customers on the ground floor just fine.

Elsie is back, but she doesn't look fully recovered. Her face is drawn and pale and she's not moving as steadily as usual. She looks happy to be out of the house, though, as she and Carl sit in their usual booth holding hands, talking between sips of tea. Now that Carl's told me some of their story, of course I want to know more. Well, who wouldn't?

When she mentions that it's their ten-year anniversary next week, I grab my chance with both hands. 'That's worth celebrating, especially since Carl mentioned that you two had a … delay in your relationship.'

She laughs. 'Forty-five years. I'll say it was a delay!' She goes on to tell me the same story that Carl did and I pretend I'm hearing it for the first time, even though I've just told her I already know. Auntie Rose tells the same stories over and over too. The pleasure is in the telling, and I never mind humouring her.

'I can't imagine what it's like to give up the love of your life,' I say when Elsie's finished. 'I mean, it's not as simple as handing over a favourite pair of shoes, is it?' Though I'd probably resent that too.

Elsie smiles. 'It was the hardest thing I've ever done, and Carl didn't help matters.'

'What did you expect?' he says. By the way he's smiling,

I know that this is a well-worn exchange, the kind of gentle argument that comes from a deep understanding. Whether in-laws or lovers, their connection must have always been there. 'It was a complete about-face, me girl. One minute I'm planning our wedding and the next you're asking me to spend the rest of my life with your sister.'

She pats his gnarly hand. 'I know, dear, it wasn't easy for any of us, but it was the right thing to do. Today we wouldn't dream of it. People are surprised when you have a baby *in* wedlock, but times were different then. It was the most sensible thing.' But she doesn't look sad when she says this.

'What I don't understand, Carl, is how you were able to transfer your love to Elsie's sister.' I hope he doesn't mind me saying that, but think how hard it must have been. 'Love isn't something you can turn on and off just because circumstances say so.'

He laughs. 'I didn't transfer my love. I still loved Elsie. I loved Hettie too, just not in quite the same way. She was a great girl, though. She had the same sense of humour as Elsie, but she was the live wire. You have to look harder to see it with Elsie, but if you know where to look, it's there.' They smile at each other. 'I did love Hettie very much, though, and her daughter – our daughter – so don't feel sorry for me, love. It's really Elsie who suffered.'

'Now, Carl, it was my decision and I never regretted it.'

'You didn't marry anyone else,' I say. When she shakes her head I wonder, 'Did you two carry on, then? I mean, if Carl and Hettie were married in name only, and Hettie knew how you felt for each other.'

But Elsie says no. Somehow I knew she would. I've only known her a few months, but already I can see how strong she is. 'We made a decision. Once you do that you have to carry through. It wasn't a sham marriage, just a convenient one.'

'And she died ten years ago?' I ask. 'I'm sorry. That must have been hard for you both.'

Elsie nods. 'It wasn't a nice time. Hettie got ovarian cancer, you see, like our mother. It wasn't very far advanced, but she died in treatment.' Carl squeezes her hand. 'I'm lucky. Hettie wasn't yet eighty when she got hers.'

It takes me a second to understand what she's saying. 'Elsie, have you got cancer?'

'Yes, dear. They say I've got plenty of time left, though, so mustn't fret!'

She's acting like Tesco's have run out of her favourite biscuits, like it's a bit of a bother, but she'll live. Except she won't.

'But aren't you getting treatment?' If I found out something like that, I'd be trying everything I could to beat it. Just hearing about Auntie Rose's strokes was enough to send me straight to our GP, Helen, to find out what could be done to help her. The answer wasn't what I'd hoped for, but at least I'd tried.

'Oh, no, I'm not interested in all that,' Elsie says. 'Hettie could have had years more if it wasn't for the treatment. For all I know, I'd drop dead in the middle of it like she did. And who wants to be so ill when the end is the same anyway? No, I'll take what God gives me and count myself lucky to have whatever time I get.'

Auntie Rose isn't too fussed about her strokes either, and she's definitely not interested in any poking and prodding, as she calls it. Maybe what I think of as resignation is really just the practicality we get when we're older.

That explains why she wasn't with Carl the other day. The poor woman was in bed with *cancer*. 'I'm sorry, I should have sent around some cake or something. I'll do it next time, I promise.' She's become completely devoted to our cakes. It was buttercream love at first sight.

'Aren't you angry about the cancer?' I ask. 'I'd be mad at God or Fate or someone.' It's just so unfair, after waiting forty-five years to finally be with Carl.

She takes a last sip of her tea. 'Where's the good in that, dear, when it won't change anything? Be grateful for what you've got, not resentful about what you 'aven't.'

As I'm thinking about this, another group of teens blusters through the door. They go to the takeaway part of the bar to get their drinks, even though they'll sit upstairs to drink them. They seem to love the idea of the café – if nothing else, it gives them somewhere warm and dry to hang out – but they're not interested in having anything to do with the rest of us. Typical teens, in other words.

'Do you mind having all the kids in here now?' I ask Carl and Elsie. 'I mean the teens, not the babies.'

'Oh, no, it's lovely seeing so many young people,' says Elsie. 'Both teens and babies.'

'Don't let the wrinkles fool you – we weren't always ancient, you know,' Carl adds.

Carl and Elsie might not mind all the under-eighteens in here, but the babies are still causing parking problems downstairs. There must be a dozen prams and pushchairs wedged between tables and people have to twist and turn to get around them.

'What about out back?' Lou wonders as we gaze out over a sea of nappy chariots.

Joseph sucks his teeth. 'Nah, man, how're they supposed to get the prams out there?'

He's always shooting down Lou's ideas. Then he makes virtually the same suggestion and acts like it was his all along. He's going to make a great CEO one day.

'If only there was a way for prams to move,' Lou says

with her finger to her temple. 'I don't know, wheels or something ... I mean, they have to get them all the way through the café.' She glares at him. 'Duh.'

'I *mean*, there's no room, Einstein,' he shoots back. 'They need a straight run from the front door.'

'Then we'll make one,' I say. It only takes a few minutes and a few apologies to shift people off their tables, but we end up with a nice clear path from the front door to the back. It looks a little M4-ish, but it's more practical.

'You could stick up some of that bunting you like so much out back with a few VIP parking signs,' Lou says. 'They'll love thinking they're special.'

'Come on, then, let's do it.'

We go together out the back door, where the reality of our solution becomes clear. It isn't a pretty walled garden. It's a run-down weed-covered courtyard that doesn't get any sun thanks to the buildings that crowd up around it. The brick walls are filthy and crumbling, the paving stones cracked and buckling. 'It's not exactly the Chelsea Flower Show out here, is it?' says Lou.

'But people don't have to sit out here, and it won't be so bad for parking. We can paint the walls if we use some of that stuff that seals bricks first. I can't remember what it's called, but my mum knows. Go grab us some bin bags and let's at least clean it up for now.'

A few decades of paper and plastic bags have blown over the walls, and there's a tangle of bindweed underfoot.

'You could get a cheap awning to cover it over in case it rains,' Lou says as we're carefully peeling up all the decomposing lumps of paper. 'The mums won't want their pushchairs getting wet. Some of those things in there cost a fortune.'

'You should know,' I say, adding when I see her expression, 'I mean because of your foster sister. Stop being so tetchy. I'm not accusing you of anything.'

'I'm not tetchy. And she hasn't got a pushchair.' She answers my surprise. 'I put her on my front when we go out. You saw.'

'But what about your foster mother? It's a lot easier running errands with the chair. I can stuff a whole weekly shop in with the twins.'

'It's even easier never taking her out in the first place,' Lou snaps. 'Which is what she does. Or doesn't do.' Then she starts yanking up more weeds.

'Lou, is everything all right at home?'

She glares at me. 'What do you think? I live with six other foster kids because my mum is dead.'

I can't believe I've just asked an orphan if everything is all right at home. She probably doesn't even think of where she lives *as* home. I wouldn't if I'd lost my mum at fourteen.

'I'm sorry, but I don't know, do I? Maybe if you told me I could help.'

'You can't help,' she says as she pulls a blue strand of hair into her mouth. 'Believe me, don't bother. Nobody can help.'

'Lou, you should know me by now. I'm just going to keep asking, so you may as well save yourself the trouble of having to ignore me every time. And you might be wrong.'

'Yeah, everyone says that and then nothing happens.'

I cross my arms. 'I'm not going away, Lou.'

She blows out her cheeks, but she can see that I mean it. 'Put it this way. We're a business for our foster parents. We're the income-generating assets. It's in their best interest to invest as little as possible to get the highest margin. Don't look so surprised, Emma. I did pay attention in school. If my foster parents can still get those cheques without actually having to take care of us, they will.' Now she crosses her arms. 'You're going to tell me to go to my social worker. I have. A lot. It's their word against mine. Guess who they believe?'

It's no use pointing out that they might have believed Lou if she hadn't been nicked, twice, for stealing. 'Does this happen to have anything to do with your court case? You may as well tell me because I'll hear all about it when I go. I might be able to help more if I know beforehand.'

She takes a minute to weigh up the question. 'I stole cases of Nurishment, okay? It was stupid and I got caught trying to get them all out of the shop.'

'You mean that stuff that old people drink? What were you going to do, have a party for OAPs?'

Her laugh has no mirth in it. 'For my sister. The baby. She needs it.'

Alarm bells start ringing in my head. 'But that's for undernourished people. Lou, why would the baby need it? Aren't your foster parents feeding her?'

'I told you. We're just a business to them. They do the bare minimum to collect the cheques.'

'That's why you've asked for the leftover sandwiches and fillings.'

'The lady gets a prize,' she says.

'You've got to tell your social worker!'

'I told you, I have. She won't listen.'

'Fine, then, let's see if she listens to me. You can look after the café while I'm gone, right?'

'You're going right now?'

'Right now, Lou.'

I'm shaking as I ring the social worker. Miraculously she finds time for me when I say I want to talk about one of the children in her charge as a possible abuse case.

I'm not naïve about the way the kids around here are

treated. Suspect first, ask questions later. Or never bother to ask, simply accuse. But it's harder to make broad-stroke assumptions when you know the person first-hand. And the social worker knows Lou. She should know that she's not a liar. Obviously she needs reminding of that.

She looks exasperated already as she reluctantly leads me to her cubicle, and I haven't said anything except hello. 'Mrs Billings. I'm very busy today, so I'm afraid I can't spare more than a minute or two.'

Her name is Mrs Boggis-Stanton, or Mrs Bog-Standard, as I'm starting to think of her. The name fits. Everything about her is middle-of-the-road, from her slightly pale forty-something face and her mousy brown tied-back hair to the shapeless grey jumper she's wearing.

'I'm sorry to bother you, but it's about Lou, my trainee. She's just told me that her youngest foster sister isn't getting enough to eat. I thought you should know.'

Mrs Bog-Standard nods. 'We've looked into that allegation. We're satisfied that there are no violations in the foster arrangement.'

I'm trying to be reasonable, I really am. Screeching at someone I need to help me won't get me far, even though it'll feel good. And besides, it's not fair. I know how much pressure the woman is under already. Isn't that why I wanted to work in the charity sector in the first place, to support the social care system and help these people? But, honestly, hearing her brush off Lou's concerns with that kind of by-the-book admin-speak isn't helping me to like her.

'If that's true,' I say, 'then why did Lou have to steal cases of Nurishment?'

She fixes me with a tired look. 'That's a very good question for which we don't have a very good answer.'

'But Lou's given you the answer. She took them for her sister. Are you saying you don't believe her? Have you even gone to the house to see what's happening?'

'Mrs Billings, despite what you might think, we take our jobs very seriously around here. We've gone to the house. We've talked to the foster parents and to the children, and we're satisfied that there are no violations. Please try to understand. I've been doing my job for over twenty years.' She looks sad. 'I know you want to believe Lou, but I hear similar stories a hundred times over. It's never their fault, they say. Unfortunately, a lot of them are lying. Do you really expect me to believe them all on the off-chance that one person isn't?'

'I don't expect it,' I say. 'But I hoped you'd believe Lou because she's *not* lying.'

'Maybe I would have if this was the first time, but she's been caught before. And when I talked to the foster mother she told me that Lou has taken cases of Nurishment from the house to sell as well. Lou is lucky they didn't officially report the home theft. It's a pricey item. So she probably robbed the shop to sell them again. They go for over a pound per tin.'

'Right,' I sneer. 'Because there's such a thriving black market in nutritional supplement drinks. Did you ask yourself why the foster parents need to have it in the first place if they're feeding the children properly?'

'Mrs Billings, I'm sure you've got better things to do than play amateur sleuth, when there's no mystery to solve.'

'I do have better things to do, Mrs Bog-Stanton. I have to prepare to be a character witness at Lou's court case. Because I do believe her.'

'It's Boggis-Stanton.'

'I know your name.'

When Lou asks me later what happened, it's my turn to be vague. It won't make her feel any better to know that her social worker – the one person in the system who might be able to help her – thinks she's a liar.

Chapter 19

At first I don't think anything of the man who comes into the café, even though he doesn't fit in with our normal clientele. Not that our clientele is always normal. The lady who wears the tinfoil hat doesn't come in much now, and we haven't seen the lady selling kittens lately, but the Jehovah's Witnesses still like to hand out their *Watchtowers* if I don't stop them at the doorway with a polite reminder about soliciting.

With his white work shirt and nondescript chinos and cleanly shaven face, this man looks like a civil servant, not a hipster. He's got no children with him, so he's not one of the occasional dads that we get. And he's at least two decades too old to join the Instagram teens upstairs.

He doesn't leave me in suspense for long, though. Maybe the notebook should have clued me in. 'Health and safety inspection,' he says. 'You've got a crèche?'

'No, no, it's definitely not a crèche,' I say. I did enough googling to know that if we call it a crèche, there'll be all sorts of red tape. 'It's just a play area for our customers to use with their children.'

We both look at where seven or eight toddlers are having the time of their lives with Auntie Rose and Dad. 'The parents aren't always inside the gate,' I explain. 'Sometimes they, erm, play from the sidelines.' Play, gossip, eat, drink.

'Are those relatives of the children?' The man points his pen at my family.

My heart starts racing. Is it perjury to lie to a health and safety officer? 'They're friends. Is there a problem? You did the inspection when we first opened. Well, not you, but your colleague did.'

Instead of answering he says, 'Is it all right if I look around?'

Dad's already spotted the man and wheels over. 'Emma, me love, is everything all right?'

'Yes, fine,' I say brightly. 'It's just an inspection. Perfectly normal. Would you like something to drink?' I ask the man.

'No, thank you.'

No, right. That's probably bribery.

Everyone's pretending not to notice the man, in the same

way you'd pretend not to see an uncle getting royally pissed at a wedding. If we all pretend everything's okay, then maybe he'll go sleep it off.

But he's no drunk uncle and he's not going to sleep this one off. He's scribbling furiously in his notebook as he peers at every single bit of the play area. When he taps Dad's wheelchair, I know he won't have good news.

'Right,' he says. 'There are a few issues. When was the last time the play mats were disinfected?'

He can tell by my expression that the answer is never. 'We sweep them every night.'

'Mmm hmm.' He writes something down. 'Some of the children aren't wearing socks. That can spread infection.'

Clearly he's never tried keeping socks on a toddler. Besides, Oscar licked the bus stop seat the other day. Bare feet are small beer.

'And I saw several dummies inside the play area. Again, that can spread infection, especially if the children drop them on those mats.'

I don't like that implication one bit. 'My mats are not dirty,' I snap.

'Then you do disinfect them after each use?' His pen is poised above his notebook while I stay silent. 'Right, so your original answer was correct. Do you disinfect the toys?'

'We wipe them down!' As if I don't feel bad enough

about my house being a tip. Now I'm being criticised at the café too.

'What cloths and cleaning solutions do you use on them?' he asks. To give him credit, he doesn't look like he's enjoying this any more than I am. Just doing his job, I bet he'd say.

'The ones from the kitchen.'

'Are those the same ones you use to clean up food?'

We both know he's got me bang to rights. 'Yes, sir.'

'The final issue is that man's wheelchair. I can see that his spokes are covered over, but there are other parts that could be a problem for small fingers. Just as no prams or pushchairs should be inside the play area, there shouldn't be a wheelchair in there either.'

I'm tempted to snap that maybe my dad could just crawl in there on his elbows, but I know that's being dramatic, and Dad would hate being called helpless when he's clearly not. He's perfectly capable of using his crutches to walk.

I'm not really surprised when the inspector writes up the citation and tells me the café has to stay closed until all the violations are corrected. So, for the record, they're not tears of surprise I'm having to fight back.

'You'll have to close right away,' he tells me. His voice is a bit gentler now. 'People can use takeaway cups if they want to finish their drinks.'

'Right now? This very minute? You're telling me I have to kick everyone out?'

'I'm afraid so.' He sticks a menacing, humiliating notice on the outside of the front door. 'I am sorry, but as soon as you've cleaned everything and posted notices about the socks and dummies and pushchairs, you can open again.'

He stands beside the doorway and watches me tell everyone they have to leave my café. 'It's not that it's dirty!' I try telling the mums as they gather up their children.

'Of course it's not,' Melody assures me, shooting a filthy look in the man's direction. 'He'd close down any of our houses if he saw the state they were in. Please try not to worry too much about this, okay? We'll be back tomorrow or the next day, whenever you're open again.' She hugs me.

'I bet my house would pass a health inspection,' I hear Garnet murmur. 'Our cleaner is amazing.'

'She is, Garnet, you could almost eat off your floors!' Emerald says. 'It's just a shame she can't come three times a week like ours does.'

Upstairs, they don't take the news as well. 'Yo, how come we have to go just because the little'uns do?' one teen asks as the others back him up with air snaps and teeth-sucking. 'It's not our problem.'

I'm a little surprised to hear the kids giving me aggro because they're generally very polite. Ever since Lou stood up that day and shouted at everyone, they know we're all in this together, all for one and one for all, like Musketeers in hoodies and trainers.

Leo steps in to back me up. 'The whole café has to close,' he tells them. He shuts down his laptop and starts unplugging his charging cables. 'We can come back tomorrow.' Then he says to me, 'Are you okay? This must feel like a huge setback and I hope you're not too upset. You'll see, it's not a big deal in terms of your business. Everyone will just come back when you're open. Don't let it dent your confidence. This is just a hiccup.'

'Thanks,' I say gratefully.

'We could go get a drink or something if you think it'll cheer you up.'

That is *such* an appealing offer, but a little voice whispers that it wouldn't be the smart thing to do. 'Thanks, but I'd just end up crying into my wine. I should probably take the children home.'

The sound of scraping chairs and raised voices fills the room as the teens prepare to leave.

'I'm sorry! I'm really sorry about this! Come back when we're open again and I'll have free cake for everyone!'

The teens are still outside when I lock up. They've taken up residence in the square, lolling against the railings and trying to out-boast each other. I wave as I pass but most ignore me. What happens in the café stays in the café, clearly.

Leo is right, I tell myself as I wheel the twins back to the house. Of course there'll be setbacks and everyone who runs a business like mine has health and safety to deal with. We can scrub the whole place down tomorrow and it might not even take the whole day. We could be open again by lunchtime.

I just wonder why the inspector turned up in the first place, when we'd had a thorough going-over the week we opened.

When Daniel gets home from work, I'm on the sofa with a large glass of wine. The children are happily flinging every toy they can reach at the velvet-covered footstool. I don't know what the stool did to provoke them, but it's going to have to fend for itself. I'm too tired. At least the toys aren't being fed into the DVD player. That game is so last week.

He throws himself down beside me and plants a kiss on my temple. 'Tough day at the office?'

'The office is closed,' I say.

'Cheers to that. I'll get a glass too.'

'No, I mean the office is *closed*. Health and safety shut us down today.'

'What?! Darling, what happened? Why didn't you ring me?'

That's a good point. Why didn't I ring him? 'It all happened so fast that I didn't have a chance. There's nothing you could have done anyway.' His brow starts to furrow when I tell him about the inspector's objections. 'That doesn't sound like something you should be closed down for, though. It's not as though they found rats in the kitchen. Even then you'd get several warnings first. Don't you remember that restaurant near my old flat?'

We'd renamed it after they finally shut it down. 'The Curry and Mice,' we say at the same time. 'I remember. Well, having dummies in the play area is obviously a very serious offense, because he didn't even let me wait till closing. He made everyone leave as soon as he gave me the citation. He taped a notice to the front door, like it was a plague house or something. It was humiliating.' My face flushes just thinking about it.

'That sounds over the top, Em. Surely you could have just picked up the dummies.'

'He didn't like that some of the children weren't wearing socks either.'

Daniel shrugs. 'Ask the parents to put their socks back on?'

I don't need Daniel to tell me that Dad could have easily

corrected his citation by wheeling out of the play area. 'He shouldn't have made me close early,' I finally say. This has Barb's fingerprints all over it. Of course, I'll never be able to prove it. She'll only deny the whole thing. And probably throw me out of her caff again.

Daniel envelops me in his arms. 'I'm sorry, darling. But you'll get everything put right tomorrow and be back in business.'

True, except that I've got a nemesis who's trying everything she can think of to shut me down. My plants are dead. My café is closed. What's next?

The sun's not even up yet when I drag myself out of bed. I'm achy from all the cleaning yesterday and I have to meet Zane at the café to make sure his little baking elves are happy to increase their cake production. We're selling out every day.

I stare at myself in our bathroom mirror as Daniel snores away in bed. Even with the make-up I've dashed on, I look like death warmed up. I look like death warmed up with slap dashed on. I'd laugh if I wasn't so tired.

I can tell myself a million times that the health inspector was a one-off, or that his citations were nitpicky enough to excite one of those compulsive cleaners from the telly. I can be thankful that it only took a day to put everything right and we'll open as usual today. None of that matters because they're red herrings anyway. If it's not bare-foot babies or death-by-dummies, it'll be Joseph's soap aversion (his love affair with the Fairy Liquid was short-lived). Or the fact that by the time the mums leave the café for the day, the bins in the loo have enough dirty nappies in them to be declared a Hazardous Waste Zone. Thank goodness the inspector didn't go in there, but what about next time or the time after that? The point is that a person will always find something if he wants to look hard enough.

And if it's not the health inspector, what will it be next? I may have stuffed fake flowers into all the window boxes so they can't be poisoned and secured an in-house supply of cake that can't be cancelled, but there'll always be another way for Barb to tamper with our business.

As I unlock the café door, I stick up two fingers. They still feel dried out and wrinkly from being elbow-deep in Dettol. 'Eff off, Barb, you can't stop us!' I say into the empty room. Then I feel stupid in case Zane heard me.

He's alone in the kitchen and all the worktops are gleaming as usual. He runs a tight ship with his students. 'Where is everyone?'

'They've got exams so I gave them the rest of the week off. It's nice to have the kitchen to myself. Everything takes twice as long with them here. Come see what I've made.'

Carefully he smooths the icing on his cake. 'Well, you can't see now because it's iced. You'll have to wait till you cut it.'

Zane looks like a natural in his white apron. Even though his dreadlocks are as crazy as ever and his tattoos as vivid, the apron gives him an air of professionalism that suits him.

'At least tell me what it is, Zane.'

'Pssh, impatient. I've been playing with a new recipe idea for cakes. You know how certain flavours go well together – strawberries and cream, chocolate and orange, that kind of thing? I want to try it in cake.'

'You already do that. Your chocolate coffee cake is delicious.'

He shakes his head. 'Nah, I don't mean flavour combinations. I want different flavours in each sponge. And not normal sponge with filling, either. Just putting strawberries and cream between the layers is cheating. I want to make a sponge that tastes of cream and another that tastes of strawberries.' He grabs a knife. 'Here.' Carefully he cuts a sliver from the cake he's just taken all that time to ice. 'Taste.'

The sponges are slightly different colours, which should tell me they're different flavours, but even without that clue, the aroma of pear and caramel is unmistakeable. My mouth starts to water as I raise the fork to my mouth. 'That's delicious!'

His grin is bashful and proud all at once. 'I'll still make the bestsellers, but maybe you could feature one new one a week and see how people like it. Next week I'll start the students on pastries and patisserie. That okay?'

That's not exactly a hard question to answer. Sticky sweet delicious morning pastries and delicate petit fours for the afternoon? Yes, I'd say that's okay.

Melody, Samantha and the sisters turn up together as if they'd never been chucked out by the health inspector, but there's no sign of most of the other mums. I wish I could blame them, but I'm not sure I'd rush back to a café that had been closed down either. Especially when they're bringing their children. Even though I was only trying to accommodate them by having a play area in the first place. And it was their children's infectious feet and dirty dummies causing all the trouble. Actually, you know what? I *can* blame them.

There is one long-term effect of the health inspector's visit that I didn't think about at the time. If my dad can't take his wheelchair into the play area, then neither can Samantha's son. 'I'm so sorry,' I tell her. 'They should make allowances for disability, don't you think?'

She just smiles. 'It's okay. Dougie's a resilient kid and he's used to it.'

Even so, I hated watching Samantha have to carry her son into the play area like that. He looked so little and vulnerable out of his chair. He can only sit in one place on the floor, which can't be as much fun as zinging around with the others. 'You do seem to be taking it well,' I tell him across the table later while he's having lunch.

He takes another bite of his cheese sandwich, then realises he can't answer. 'I'm used to it,' he says after he's swallowed.

'Yeah, he's a happy lad, aren't you, Dougie? Please don't worry about us.' Samantha fiddles with her teacup, tapping a manicured finger on the saucer as she shoots a glance at Melody. 'Are you almost done there?'

Melody smiles. 'Are we almost done?' she asks her daughters.

Neither child unclamps from their mum's breast. 'Mmm mmm,' her five-year-old says.

'Seriously, Melody, how long are you going to do that?'

Emerald puts her coffee cup down. Garnet's fork stops midway to her mouth as we all wait for Melody's answer. Nobody's dared to challenge her directly like this before.

'As long as we all want it,' she says. 'How long did you all breastfeed yours?'

'I did six months,' Garnet announces. 'It was too painful.'

'Seven months and two weeks,' counters Emerald. '*Way* too painful.'

'I didn't, and you know that,' Samantha murmurs.

Melody shifts her toddler to cover one breast with her button-down shirt. 'Did anyone judge you for that?'

Samantha nods. 'Only everyone, all the time.'

'I bet that didn't feel nice,' says Melody. The smile is still on her face but her voice is steely. 'See what I mean? There's enough judgement out there. Let's not do it to each other.'

'I'm sorry,' Samantha says.

Melody smiles her forgiveness. When Eva has finished, she buttons her shirt back up. I doubt anyone will mention it again.

'Dougie, tell everyone what you want to be when you grow up,' Samantha says. Then to us, 'They were asked about it in school yesterday.'

'I want to be an Olympian,' Dougie says. 'For our wheelchair basketball team. Mum might let me start playing next year. I'll have to be really strong, but I think I can do it.' He throws an imaginary ball from his chair. I'm no expert but it looks like a good shot to me.

Samantha beams. 'And why shouldn't you?'

'If you were in the Olympics, I'd definitely come watch you,' I say. 'I might even make a big banner to cheer you on.' Melody's daughter, Eva, is sitting forward on her mum's lap, dying to be included in the conversation. 'What about you, Eva? What would you like to be when you grow up?'

'Either the foreign minister or a sausage dog,' she says right away. Her pale freckled face beams at the idea of such a bright future.

'Why the foreign minister or a sausage dog, honey?' Samantha asks with a perfectly straight face.

'Nice poker face,' I whisper. All those years pretending she doesn't care about her husband's lack of libido is paying off.

Eva says, 'If I was the foreign minister, I'd get to travel to different countries, like being paid to go on holiday. But if I was a sausage dog, I'd get treats for being good and everyone would stroke me.'

'I'd pick the sausage dog if I were you,' I say. 'It sounds like a lot more fun.'

Chapter 20

Carl stops in a few days later. 'Elsie's not well, me girl, and I don't like to ask but could you possibly make me a sandwich?'

'Of course I can, and I'm sorry to hear about Elsie. Is there anything I can do? Does Elsie want one too?'

'No, no, she can't eat a thing, but thank you.'

Poor Elsie! 'What kind of sandwich would you like?'

'Oh, anything you have to hand is fine. I'm ever-so grateful to have it made for me. I never got the hang of anything more complicated than beans on toast.' Sheepishly he hands me a flyer. 'I hate to be the bearer of bad news, but these are taped up all over the square. It's better coming from a friend.'

Don't have a baby?

**Don't even think about going to the Second Chance Café on Carlton Square!
It's only for mothers and delinquent teens**

If you haven't Bred or Done Time, You're <u>Not Welcome</u> there!

If they're up on the square, they're probably all over the main road too. They weren't there when I came in this morning, so Barb must have put them up while we've been in here. I don't like the idea of her creeping around out there, but at least she can't kill the plastic flowers.

'Don't give the haters a chance,' Joseph says, reading over my shoulder. 'Your fear gives them the oxygen they need. Starve them of their oxygen.' He adjusts his tie at this pearl of wisdom.

'I'm not afraid, I'm pissed off. What does that do to their oxygen?'

'Doesn't matter, it's still wasted energy if you're not gonna use it,' says Lou.

'When did you get so smart?' She's right, of course. It does none of us any good to whinge about it. The fact is that I can't stop Barb from doing these things.

'This woman's really got a beef with you,' Joseph says,

leaning his elbows on the bar. 'What'd you do to her?'

'I didn't do anything!'

'She's obviously unhinged,' says Lou.

'Anyway, she seems to like leafleting.'

Joseph nods. 'Right. Should we go take them all down as usual?'

I'm about to say yes when I get a better idea. What is it they say about judo? Use your opponent's momentum against them. 'No, they should all stay up.' I dig around under the bar where we keep our 'office supplies'. Joseph made us start referring to the cardboard box like this when he appointed himself Stationery Guru. 'Here, I'll show you.' They lean in to see what I'm carefully writing across the front of the leaflet Carl gave me.

Don't have a baby?

Don't even think about going to the Second Chance Café on Carlton Square!
It's only for mothers and delinquent teens

If you haven't Bred or Done Time, You're <u>Not Welcome</u> there!

EVERYONE IS VERY WELCOME!!
BRING IN THIS LEAFLET FOR A <u>FREE SAMPLE OF CAKE!</u>

I hand each of them a bright blue sharpie. 'Make sure you write the same thing on every single one you find, nice and big like this,' I remind them. 'Underline our name. Let's make those flyers work for us. If Barb doesn't like it, then she can bloody well take them all down herself. But hopefully new customers will do the work for us if they know there's free cake on offer.'

Lou glances at Joseph, who glances back at her. It's done in a split second, but I know they've communicated in their secret teen language. 'Boss, that's genius,' he says. 'Truly inspired.'

'I've got to admit, that is good,' Lou adds, and I feel proud enough to burst. Who knows? Barb may actually have done us a favour. She's going to hate that.

It's quiet in the café while they're gone. Barb's little health inspector stunt did hurt business. At least for now. 'Leo, Leo, come in,' I say into the walkie-talkie. 'If you guys want anything, you'll need to come downstairs for it. I'm on my own till Lou and Joseph get back, okay?'

'Roger that,' Leo says. Even over the crackling reception I can hear the smile in his voice. 'Over and out.'

He's downstairs five minutes later. I kind of hoped he would be. He leans against the bar. 'Having a good day?'

'No, actually, not really, but we may be turning it around.' He registers his usual surprise when I fill him in on the nasty leaflets. But when I admit Barb has killed all the plants in our window boxes, his expression darkens. 'Emma, she actually sounds dangerous. You should watch yourself.'

I laugh off his concern. 'Nothing's going to happen to me here, Leo. There are too many people around. Dad's here, and Lou and Joseph. You lot are right upstairs.'

'But everyone leaves before you close up,' he says. 'If she'll poison innocent plants, what could she do to you? Really, you shouldn't be walking around on your own. Especially at night. Especially with the children.'

A cold shiver runs through me. What kind of mother am I, putting the twins at risk! 'You don't really think she'd do anything, do you?'

'Who can tell with a madwoman? Do you want to take the chance?'

Of course not. I am not a jumpy person, but the mention of my children has me spooked.

'Let me walk you home,' Leo offers. 'I'm usually the last one here anyway.'

'Isn't that a little drastic?' I think of what Joseph said. Fear is her oxygen, or something like that. 'I only live across the square.'

'Emma.' He fixes me with his golden-green stare. 'Let me walk you and the children home. It's only about five minutes out of my way and it will make me feel better. You and your parents too, I imagine. Besides, it's in my best interest. I don't have any idea how to work the steamer on the espresso machine so I couldn't replace you if anything happened.'

'Thank you,' I say. 'I'll really try to leave right on time so I don't hold you up.'

'I don't mind if you do. I'm happy to help.'

That night, as I potter around the kitchen getting the kids' tea ready, I realise it's the first time in weeks that I've been home before Daniel. Though I'm hardly in danger of becoming a workaholic, pedalling cakes into the wee hours or escaping to the café on weekends to practise my espresso pulls. I don't really even need to be there full-time these days with Lou there.

She's been such a surprise. Sure, she can be prickly and she doesn't suffer fools, but I appreciate her honesty (mostly) and she's very clever. This is a drawback to my business plan that I didn't anticipate. I know the whole point is to train young people to go on to better things, but I don't want to lose Joseph or Lou. Especially Lou. That's why I've been thinking about making her a full-time proposition. We're doing well enough, assuming that health inspection stunt doesn't dent the business, and who better to help train young people than someone who's been through the training herself? I'm going to ask her after her court appearance tomorrow. No matter what the judge says about her, I value Lou very much. That's exactly what I plan to stand up and say in court.

'I'm worried,' I tell Daniel when he comes home.

Without a word he strides across the floor to fold me into his arms. 'About what, darling?'

My anger flares up at the question. I've only been talking about Lou's court date for the last two weeks. Sometime he just doesn't listen.

'Has Barb done something else?' he asks. 'You didn't see her, did you? Are Zane's new cake ideas all right? I hope he's not trying weird combinations like hazelnuts and kale. Is it the children? Tell me and let me help.'

Or maybe he does listen. I didn't realise how many things I *have* been worrying about. 'It's Lou's court date tomorrow.' I pull back from him. 'I've got butterflies just thinking about it. I've never been in court before. Officially, I mean.' This is exactly what I wanted to avoid, actually, by opening the café. But that's naïve. The kids who need help usually need it because they're in trouble. There could be a lot of court visits in my future. It's a depressing thought.

'You'll do fine,' he says, letting me go. 'You'll speak from the heart like you always do and that's the best that Lou can hope for. What time do you need to be there? I could look at leaving work to join you, if you'd like some moral support?'

'That's very sweet but no, thanks, I'll be okay. It's youth

court anyway, so it's not open to everyone like regular court. Even if it was, if I were Lou I'd want as few people gawping at me as possible. Not that you're a gawper. You know what I mean. This isn't exactly her shining moment, is it, being called up in front of the magistrate.'

Daniel picks up Grace, who's making grabby hands from the floor. 'Yah, I couldn't blame her. I don't see why the case should go to court in the first place. Weren't they just a few tins of supplements?'

I sigh. 'I thought so too. Lou is extremely thorough. She took the shop's entire supply. There were cases and cases of the stuff. The social worker told me that if it's worth over two hundred quid it needs to go to court. Besides, this is her second offence. She got off with a caution last time.' I gather Oscar up into my arms so the whole family can be at eye level. 'To make things worse, she won't plead guilty. Even though she was caught carrying the evidence. I'm sure it's not nice to admit to something like that, but she did do it.'

'Has she said why she's not pleading?'

'No, I got all my information from the social worker. Lou isn't talking.'

'Well, she must have a good reason. You said she was smart.'

'I hope so.'

It's so frustrating seeing someone do something stupid and not being able to do anything to stop it. Especially when it's someone that you care about. And I do care about Lou. She needs all the people like me she can get right now.

'Why don't you let me feed them?' Daniel says. 'Go have a bath and relax.'

A bath! With actual hot water fresh from the tap and a door that stays closed and no toddlers looking over the side of the tub. But Daniel makes a sour lemon face when he sees me hesitate. 'What is it?' he snaps.

'Don't get me wrong,' I say. 'I really appreciate the offer, but it's easier if I just do their tea.'

He sets Grace down and crosses his arms. Daniel hardly ever crosses his arms. 'Because I don't do it right?'

'Well ... yes.'

'Emma. I don't know what you want from me. I might not do everything the way you do, but I can do it, if you'll only let me. You say you're tired and you want help and then you won't let me help. Which do you rahly want, Emma? Because I'm confused. Should I be helping or not?'

'Yes, of course I want you to help.'

'Then will you please stop making it so ...' He glances at Grace who's busily emptying the laundry basket. '... So

319

bloody hard. I get that you're perfect and I'm far from it, but how am I supposed to learn how to take care of our children when you never let me try?'

I frown. 'Oh my god, I am not perfect!'

'Well, you look perfect to me. You always know exactly what you're doing and yes, I have no idea most of the time, but I want to do it. I *can* learn, you know.'

I stare at Daniel. This lovely deluded man actually thinks I have a clue about what I'm doing. That I'm not making it up as I go along and in a constant state of anxiety that it's all wrong and I'm doing irreparable harm to our children. 'Daniel, I'm really sorry to tell you this, but I have no idea what I'm doing! It's nice that you think I do, but I'm as clueless as you are. I'm totally faking everything. We should face it. If we needed a licence for parenting, we'd be in front of the magistrate like Lou.'

'That is such a relief to hear,' he says. 'I know it shouldn't be, since it probably means we're both ill-equipped to look after our children, but all this time I've felt like an utter failure.'

And I'm the one who's made him feel that way. What an arse I've been. 'You're not doing everything wrong. You're their father and you're a good one. I shouldn't be judging you.' Didn't Melody just say the same thing? 'I'm sorry,' I say again. I have the feeling I'll be saying that a lot. 'You're right. I haven't been fair. I'm glad we're in this together.'

When he smiles at me, I feel closer to him than I have in a long time. I remember how much I love knowing that we've got each other's back, feeling like the two of us together can get through anything life throws our way. It won't be slick or pretty or without wrong turns, but we can get through anything together. 'I will have a bath,' I say. 'Thanks for taking over. You'll do just fine.' I tip my head up to kiss his lips. 'I love you.'

'I love you too, Em. Have a nice bath. I won't disturb you unless we need the Emergency Services.'

Everyone's jumpy at the café the next day before Lou's court appointment, even Joseph, and he's got no reason to be. He's been avoiding me and hasn't taken the piss out of Lou once.

But I'm wrong. It's not Lou's court appearance that's got him spooked.

'I hate to tell you this, boss, but our social media campaign is whack,' he finally says just as Lou and I are about to leave.

'This isn't great timing, Joseph,' says Lou. 'Couldn't you wait till after we get back?'

'I'm really sorry, but it's getting critical. Don't worry, we can go over it when you're back.'

Not if it's getting critical, we can't! 'What's wrong?'
Lou huffs.

'Lou's right,' says Joseph, and now I know something's really wrong, because he never admits that. 'I just need to know if you want me to answer the reviews or not? Sometimes offence is the best defence, but then again, silence can be golden.'

'Will you stop with the stupid clichés?' Lou snaps. 'God, you had to do this right now.' She turns to me. 'We're getting malicious posts online. As *Head of Communications*, Captain Bad Timing here should probably do something about them.'

'It's not a problem with Facebook because I can delete the posts from our page and block the poster,' Joseph says. 'The review sites aren't so easy. We've got almost all one-star reviews.'

'Where are these reviews? Can I see?' My heart sinks with every single star as he scrolls through one of the sites on his phone. 'It's all the same stuff she's putting on her leaflets,' I say. I should have guessed that Barb would do something like this, though I figured she was as clueless about social media as I am. She must have someone helping her. Then I see a comment that leaves my blood running cold. 'We do not have rats! Or cockroaches! That's not why health and safety closed us. Those are total lies.'

'They're all lies, boss. What do you want me to do?'

'Can't you have them taken down? Explain to the people who run the sites that they're not true.'

He nods. 'I've already flagged them up on the sites that let me, but I haven't heard anything back ... we could respond to each review.'

'And say what?' Lou says. 'That we were shut down by health and safety for having a dirty play area? That doesn't sound much better. I say leave it. Nobody pays attention to those sites anyway. Not for cafés. It's not exactly a Michelin-star restaurant, is it?'

But this is *my* business they're talking about. It feels like I'm being attacked personally. I want to respond. I very much want to respond.

Lou is probably right, though. The extenuating circumstances don't sound that much better than the lies. 'Leave it,' I tell Joseph. 'Take the posts off Facebook when they come up, but otherwise ignore it. Sticks and stones may break our bones.'

'What are you on about, boss?'

'Never mind. It's just an old expression my parents used to say to me. Lou and I really need to go now. Text if you need anything before we're back, okay?'

'Good luck, Lou,' he says as we leave.

* * *

Walking into the blocky Portland stone and brick magistrate's court is exactly as intimidating as it's meant to be, and I haven't even done anything wrong. I can't imagine how Lou must be feeling.

As if to answer, she pops a lock of hair into her mouth as we go up the steps together.

'You'll be okay, Lou. I'm going to do my best to make sure.'

I've only ever been to the regular magistrate's court, back when I did my criminology course. We had to go there a few times to observe, but I don't know what to expect here at the youth court. Not that I can tell Lou what an amateur I am. It'll make her even more nervous. My swagger is meant to convey confidence, but it probably just looks like my pants have bunched up.

Mrs Bog-Standard is waiting outside with a middle-aged couple who are wreathed in smoke from the cigarettes they're clutching. The woman's face breaks into a smile as we get close. 'There's me girl!' she says, chucking her fag on the ground and throwing her arms wide. 'Didn't I say we'd be here for you?'

'Great,' says Lou, sidestepping her foster mother's arms. 'Why are you here?' she asks Mrs Bog-Standard.

'It's my job,' she says. 'How are you, Lou?'

'Just fantastic. Best day of my life. I'm going in.'

I have to rush to catch up as she sprints up the steps. 'It's good that your social worker is here,' I say.

'Yeah, because she's been such a help so far. This is all just a sideshow for the magistrate. My foster parents are only here to make sure they keep those cheques coming. And like Boggis-Stanton said: it's her job. She doesn't give a shit.'

I can't sit still in my plastic chair as we wait in the echoing corridor for Lou's case to be called. Introducing myself to Lou's foster parents seems like the right thing to do, or at least making some small talk to fill the tense silence, but it also feels disloyal. So we all just sit there avoiding eye contact until finally someone calls for us.

I'm surprised when the magistrate, a grey-haired man with a kindly face, calls Lou by her first name. Louise. She'll hate that. I guess this is the gentler face of law enforcement these days. Lou sits with the duty solicitor in the front row. Mrs Bog-Standard, her foster parents and me sit behind. When I reach over the bench to squeeze Lou's shoulder, she turns slightly to see whose hand it is. Then her head nods just a bit.

Lou's foster parents seem to be expecting a riveting courtroom drama, not the boring procedural details that take up the next few minutes. They're fidgeting in their seats, throwing glances at the wall clock and looking like they wished they were outside smoking. Lou is right. They're just here to protect their interest. 'Do you mind?' I finally hiss when the woman's shoulder bashes into mine for about the tenth time. 'If you have somewhere better to be.'

They settle down when the prosecuting council gets her first crack at Lou in the witness box. I'll find out soon what it feels like to be up there. I just hope I'll be as composed as Lou.

Since Lou pleaded not guilty, despite being caught with the cases of Nurishment in her arms, there are a lot of questions about what she was doing on the night in question. The prosecutor doesn't pace up and down, though, or make expansive hand gestures when she scores her points, like every courtroom drama I've ever watched on telly. It's more of a friendly Q&A.

'So you were at the shop when it was broken into, is that right, Louise?'

'Yes, but I'm not guilty.'

The prosecutor's forehead wrinkles in confusion, which must be an act, since it was Lou's not-guilty plea that brought us here in the first place. At least Lou's foster parents are getting a bit of a show.

'Yet you did say you were there at the time of the robbery and that you were alone. Did you also take the items in question?'

'Yes, but I'm not guilty.'

'So you keep saying. Did you break into the shop? I'll rephrase. Did you force entry into the shop?'

'Yes, but I'm not guilty.'

'Did you take the items in question?' She consults her sheets of paper. 'Five cases of Nurishment from the shop?'

The prosecutor doesn't seem quite so friendly now.

Lou's foster mother makes a WTF? face.

'Yes, but I'm not guilty.'

'You keep saying that, Louise. Yet you were at the shop at the time it was broken into. You forced entry into the shop and you took five cases of Nurishment. As you were carrying the cases you were observed and apprehended by police. And this isn't the first offence, is it, Louise?' She turns to the magistrate to detail Lou's previous caution. She took six cases last time. I wonder if she's cross about her decline in performance. 'I don't think I have any more questions.'

Lou's duty solicitor has slumped further into his chair with each admission and I can't really blame him. He only rouses himself when it's his turn to ask Lou some more questions. But all he seems to be doing is confirming what the prosecutor has already asked. How's that supposed to help her?

With every repeated question, my anger goes up a gear

until, finally, I can't take it anymore. 'Ask her why she did it! God, do your job, counsellor!'

Everyone stares at me. Then the magistrate says, calm as you please, 'It's the duty solicitor's turn now, Mrs Billings. We'll ask for your input shortly.'

But that seems to have jarred the counsellor out of his stupor. 'Why did you need the Nurishment, Louise?' Then he turns to me. 'It was my next question, actually.'

I can't tell from Lou's expression whether she's grateful or angry about my outburst. 'My foster sister needed it,' she says. 'My job at the café hadn't started so I didn't have any money or any way to get money. Well, I could have stolen some, I guess, but that would have been even worse. I took it for my foster sister. Because my foster parents won't feed her enough. I didn't have a choice. I couldn't wait any longer. I'd been looking for a job for months, but nobody hired me.'

'Has this been brought up with your social worker?' the magistrate asks. Mrs Bog-Standard nods, telling him the same thing she told me.

Lou turns to the magistrate. 'What I'm telling you is true. Look, use your common sense. Why else would I steal that stuff? Twice. If I wanted money, would I really nick cases of supplement drinks? I've just told you why I did it.'

'But if you admit to the crime, then you're wasting the

court's time by pleading not guilty,' the magistrate points out.

'How else am I supposed to get anyone to listen to me? Those people are not taking care of the children.' She points at her foster parents, who have the nerve to look affronted. 'I've told my social worker. She hasn't done anything about it. Those kids need help. I did what I thought was right. It might not be what the law says is right, but it's what *I* thought was right.'

The magistrate *has* to see sense. I know Lou is telling the truth, and by the time I get my turn in the witness box to say so, I think the magistrate knows it too.

Once everyone is finished, we all wait while he gathers his thoughts. 'Louise, I wish you hadn't wasted the court's time when there are other ways you could have handled this. However, I understand why you did it. You clearly care about and have concerns for the children in your foster home, and don't feel as though those concerns have been adequately addressed. I'm not sure that they have either, so I'll ask that they be looked into again as a matter of urgency.' He waits for Mrs Bog-Standard to nod her agreement. 'As to the charge of theft, since you admit you were there and broke into the shop and took the goods in question, a guilty verdict seems reasonable.'

I catch Lou's foster mother hiss 'Yes' under her breath.

'However, I think there are mitigating factors in this case that need to be considered as well. Motivation has to be taken into account for any alleged crime. For that reason, Louise, I'm returning a verdict of not guilty due to mitigating factors. There will be no sentencing and your record will show your acquittal. Is that all right with you?' For the first time, he smiles. 'I want this looked into thoroughly,' he tells Mrs Bog-Standard again. 'And if there is a case to answer,' he says to Lou's foster parents, 'you *will* be made to answer it.'

Lou won't even look at her foster parents, who do briefly try talking to her before giving up. Mrs Bog-Standard and I hurry after her as she stalks away from the court.

'Lou, will you please stop for a moment?' Mrs Bog-Standard says. 'I'll file the paperwork to reopen the case tomorrow. But this is likely to take time. You know that nothing happens fast in Social Services. Can you be patient?'

'Will you honestly do your best?' Lou asks her.

'I promise I will. And Lou? I'm sorry I didn't believe you last time. If it makes any difference, I should have trusted you.'

Chapter 21

'Get in!' Auntie Rose shouts, nearly upending the Scrabble board in her excitement. 'That's triple points for the Q and a double-word score.'

'Well done,' says Elsie politely. 'Although I don't think sequitur is a word on its own.'

Those are fighting words to Auntie Rose. 'Non sequitur is the word,' Elsie continues. In fairness to her, it's the first time she's played Scrabble with Auntie Rose. She doesn't know what a bad loser my auntie can be.

It's so good to see Elsie back and looking well. I'm sure every time she becomes ill Carl worries whether this might be the end, but she seems to have nine lives. I hope she's got ninety.

'Isn't that Latin anyway?' Carl asks.

'*Audere est facere*,' the vicar says with a broad sweep of his arm that almost takes out Mrs Delaney. 'It's worth a try.' The vicar always comes last when they play Scrabble, but he doesn't seem to mind. He says it gets him away from the church for a few hours where there's too much blah blah blah from his flock. Given the choice, God would probably rather have him shirking over a board game than shirking over a pint.

'You two, stop ganging up on Rose!' Doreen says. 'Though they're right, Rose. Sorry, it's not a word. You can't have it, but I'm sure you'll think of something else with a Q and two Us.' She can't keep the smile off her face. Doreen loves winning as much as Auntie Rose.

So does Elsie. Her old-fashioned frilly blouse and skirt and white spun sugar beehive might look genteel, but she's got the heart of a mercenary when it comes to board games.

'Well, *I'm* sorry, Doreen,' Auntie Rose shoots back. She's not taking the disqualification lying down. 'Just because I'm winning, you take their side. Emma, me girl, come 'ere! We need an adjudication.'

Why can't they just use a dictionary like everyone else? 'Give me a sec.' I scroll through the answers on my phone. 'Well, it is in the *Oxford Dictionary*.' As they'd have seen for themselves if they'd bothered using one. 'But the phrase is non sequitur. I'm sorry, Auntie Rose.'

'Hmph. After I practically raised you and all,' she says.

'I'm not going to cheat for you!'

'She does enough of that herself,' Doreen murmurs. 'Next time, we're playing cribbage.'

'Excuse me, Emma,' says one of Mrs Ishtiaque's friends, pulling the scarf of her mustard-yellow saree around herself. 'Is your cake being made fresh, please?'

'It's made right in the back there by an excellent baker,' I tell her. 'Would you like a slice?'

Her lips purse. 'No, thank you. How am I knowing its freshness?'

'Well, you'll know when you take a bite if it's still moist.'

'Is it fresh tomorrow too?'

'It should be if we seal it tonight.'

'It is not the freshest tomorrow, though?'

I shake my head. 'Not as fresh as today, no. Is fresh your word for the day, by chance?'

'Yes, am I using it rightly?'

'Perfect, well done.'

Mrs Ishtiaque gives me the thumbs up when her student returns to their table to report her success. Then the whole table erupts in clapping. They seem like different women now than when they first came in huddled behind Mrs Ishtiaque. Now they happily chat to everyone. Dougie and Melody's daughter, Eva the future sausage dog, are learning words in Urdu, though they were disappointed to hear that 'poop' is the same in both languages.

'What's happening now?' Lou is carrying a huge tray down from the first floor. I don't know how she does that without going arse over teacup. I still don't even use the small trays unless I have to.

'English practice again,' I tell her. 'Variations of "fresh" this time.'

'Mrs Ishtiaque must have had them on restaurant vocabulary the other day. They all came up to ask about vegetarian options, one after the other. I had to repeat them about six times.'

As she loads the dishwasher out the back, I realise that it's the first time we've been alone together since her court appearance. Now's my chance to offer her permanent work. 'Lou? I wanted to ask you something.'

But my moment is ruined when Joseph sticks his head into the kitchen. 'Boss, the po-po are here.'

'Now what?' I wipe my hands on the tea towel.

Two constables are standing in the middle of the café. They've both got stab vests on and one is speaking into the radio clipped near his shoulder. They don't look like they're after a caffeine fix. 'Hi, can I help you?' Try as I might, my voice is wobbling even though I haven't done anything wrong. I wonder who has?

'We're checking into a report we've had about the café. Are you the manager?'

'I'm Emma Billings.' I peer at the name tag sewn into the man's vest. Constable Peters.

'There's been a report of public indecency.' Constable Peters looks around with an expression on his face like he's missed something.

Of course, as soon as the mums hear this, they hurry into the play area to snatch up their children. I don't blame them. If Dad wasn't already with the twins, I'd grab them myself. Imagine some perv exposing himself in here in front of the children! 'Did someone see something?' I ask the blond constable – Constable Wojciechowski. 'What did they see?'

His spotty face reddens. Joseph and Lou don't look like the only ones young enough to be on work training around here. 'Is this always a café?' he asks. 'There's no other purpose?'

My mind flies upstairs where the freelancers are working. Am I supposed to have another licence for them to bring in their laptops? No, that can't be what this is about. Unless they're only pretending to work and are really up there watching porn. They don't really seem the type, though, with their jazz hands and chai tea lattes. 'No, it's just a café,' I tell Constable Wojciechowski.

'What time are you open until?' he asks.

'Five.' Joseph and Lou are standing beside me now.

'And there's no entertainment of any kind?'

'There's music upstairs on Spotify,' Lou offers. 'The customers play what they like. We don't control it.'

'Has there been a crime against bad taste in music?' I shouldn't joke, but I feel better now that we don't have a pervert on the loose in here. 'What exactly did the report say?'

Now Constable Peters says, 'There's been a complaint about topless women on the premises. I have to say it doesn't seem to be the case right now.'

We all look around at Mrs Ishtiaque's saree-clad friends, Elsie, Auntie Rose, the mums with their children. Carl and my dad aren't exactly demanding lap dances.

I shrug.

'You don't mean because some of the mums breastfeed?' Lou asks. 'There's nothing indecent about that.'

Both men shake their heads. 'No, no, we're not interested in breastfeeding mums,' says Constable Wojciechowski. Then he blushes furiously. 'No offence. I'm sure you're all very attractive.'

Now the women probably think he's imagining them topless. Constable Peters grabs his colleague by the arm to stop him digging any deeper. 'Do you mind if we have a look upstairs? Just so we can close out the complaint. Sorry to have bothered you.'

But before they can take two steps there's a commotion at the top of the stairs. There's shouting, harsh and aggressive, loud and panicky. The hairs on the back of my neck stand up. Even though I know it's just the same teenagers who drink their tea and coffee from delicately handled china cups and often save half the cake or sandwich they've ordered for a brother or sister to have as a treat later. The constables hurry up the stairs.

The teens are on their feet as soon as they see them. They move fast, like a really badly coordinated flash mob. They pull their hoods down as low over their faces as they'll go, jam their hands deep into their pockets and, without a word, make their way to the stairs, jostling empty chairs out of the way as they go.

But they can't get past the constables without pushing them over. 'What's the rush, ladies and gentlemen?' Constable Peters asks. He and Constable Wojciechowski are both twitching. Of course they want to stop them – they're kids and their faces are covered – they must have done something wrong.

'Emma, are you okay?' Leo asks from his table. The freelancers have all closed their laptops in case it all kicks off.

'Everything is fine. I would like to know, though, why the constables are keeping my customers from leaving my café.' I can hear my voice shaking. 'Is there some legal reason for that?'

'Come here a lot, do they?' asks Constable Peters.

'Yes, every day in fact. They're some of my ... most loyal customers.' I almost said my best customers, but they do like to buy one cup of tea and then sit up here for hours. 'Now, if there's no problem, would you like a hot drink before you go?'

I can't believe I'm being so ballsy! But really, what right have the constables got to bother my customers just because they don't like the look of them? Everyone is welcome here, whether they happen to wear a hoodie or not.

'If you don't mind, we might stop by again,' Constable Peters says loudly. 'Just to keep an eye on things. All right lads?'

Nobody answers him.

'That was whack,' Joseph says after they've left. The kids have gone too. Nobody wants to hang around in case the constables come back today. Thanks for that, Barb.

Now she's getting the police involved in her twisted schemes. 'It was whack,' I agree. 'But as long as we're not doing anything wrong, there won't be a problem. So just make sure we're not doing anything wrong.'

'We can use the walkie-talkies!' Joseph says. 'I'll radio up to warn my bluds if the po-po come back.'

Lou puts her hand on his shoulder. 'Nice work, Captain Loudhailer, and while you're keeping lookout I can show you how the ordering process works. If you want to be CEO one day, you'd better learn how to do admin.'

'Yo, I'll have people for that.'

'Joseph, you *are* people for that,' she says. 'Come on.'

'Lou? Can I just talk to you quickly before you show Joseph?'

We go out the back amongst the pushchairs. With the brick walls painted white, it doesn't look as dim, and Lou was right. The mums love the bunting and the VIP (Very Important Pram) Parking signs we had made up.

'Relax, it's nothing bad,' I tell her. 'I wanted to talk about the business and your employment. The thing is, we're doing well and I've run the figures and I can afford to take on someone full-time.'

'I'm full-time now,' she says.

'Sorry, I mean permanently, not just for six months. I know the training hasn't been very ... formal, shall we say, and I'd like to work on that. But with managing everything day-to-day, I need another full-time person. I wondered if you'd like to be that person?'

'You want me? Even with what's happened and court and all that?'

'Yes, Lou, I want *you*. You've done a really good job here

and I'd be happy to have you working with me permanently.'

But she shakes her head. 'It's not fair to take the training spot from someone else. Thanks, but I'm benefitting from this job and someone else should get to when I finish.'

'You don't understand. I'll still hire two new trainees in a few months. It's just that I'm run off my feet and I could use a partner. You've got a job here as long as you want it, though I suspect you'll go on to better things quickly.'

'No, I won't,' she says.

I remember being told the same thing a few years ago. I didn't believe anyone when they said it either. 'You should. One day, when you're ready.'

'You're seriously offering me a job? Seriously, really?' She looks as surprised by her excitement as I am. She recovers quickly. 'I'll take it. We'll have to talk more money, though.'

When I stick out my hand, I remember the first time I did that.

She's not wary this time when she takes it.

Leo is unusually quiet as he walks me back across the square after we close. It's getting lighter now in the evenings, so he doesn't really need to anymore. If Barb jumped out from behind a bush, I'd see her coming. 'Are you okay?' I finally ask. 'You know, I only noticed now because you haven't asked about me. Talk about a selfish friend, the way I'm always prattling on at you.'

He hip-checks me as we walk along the stone path through the middle of the square where Daniel and I had our wedding marquee.

'You're far from selfish, Emma. I've got something on my mind, that's all. Nothing to worry about. I hope.'

'That sounds ominous.'

'Sorry, it's the Welsh in me. We are a dramatic people. I'm fine, really. You're the one who had to outrun the law today. I should be asking about you.'

'Call me Ronnie Cray,' I say. The silence envelops us again.

As we approach my front door, Leo's walk slows until I have to turn around to say, 'Really, is everything all right?'

He strides up to me so fast that I've got no time to register that his lips are closing in on mine. One second I'm being walked to my house and the next I'm getting kissed.

There's just a split second when I don't do anything. Later, when I replay the scene over and over, I'll put this down to shock. Otherwise it's ... something else. 'What are you doing? Leo, I'm married.' I shove him away but his mouth is still uncomfortably close to mine.

'Happily?' he asks.

'Yes, happily!' Why didn't I include that description in the first place? And why aren't I backing away from him?

'Then I've really misinterpreted the situation,' he says, finally putting some distance between us. 'Sorry. Just checking, though. You're definitely happily married?'

'Definitely,' I say, with more confidence. 'Good night, Leo.' With my arms crossed in front of me, I am the very picture of disapproval.

He smiles his usual smile, as if those lips had never touched mine. 'Sure, see you tomorrow, Emma. Have a good night.'

I go into the house, close the door and bolt it. The snort that escapes my lips (my recently kissed lips – stop it!) startles the twins. What was that? *What the hell was that?!* The last time I was surprise-kissed I was about sixteen years old. I don't claim to be an expert in relationships, but I do know the difference between a friend and a potential lover, and Leo and I have absolutely definitely only been the first. I've had lots of bloke friends in my life and not once has one wanted to kiss me. Which means I know how to do platonic.

Leo actually had to lean over the pushchair to kiss me – over the heads of my children! Thank god they're too young to talk. Their first words had better not be 'Leo kissed Mama'.

Not that it's a secret. I will tell Daniel. Of course I will, I've got nothing to hide. Leo is the one who should be embarrassed. He's the one who misinterpreted the situation. I'm just the innocent kissee.

Yet he didn't seem overly mortified by my rebuff, and I'm the one who's got butterflies in my tummy as I wait for Daniel to come home. My mind plays over the last few months with Leo – every conversation, the books he loaned me, walkie-talkie jokes and each time he was the last one in the café at the end of the day. I can say all I like that I didn't do anything to make him think I wanted more than a friendship, but if that's true, then he's either incredibly dim or incredibly bold ... or I'm wrong and I did encourage him.

'You'll never guess what just happened,' I tell Daniel as soon as he walks in the door. Because I'm not guilty. Guilty people keep secrets. 'Leo just tried to kiss me.'

He throws his courier bag on the sofa under the window. 'Leo, the bloke who always wears tweed and plugs in his beard trimmer?' His words are light but his expression is frozen. It's the face he uses when he's working out a problem. *I'm the problem.*

'I know, can you believe it?' I blunder on, because I've started it now. 'I told him where to go, obviously.' Before I can stop myself, I pucker up for Daniel to kiss me hello.

We both know he hesitates. 'Why would he kiss you, Em?' he asks.

'I have no idea! What cheek, eh? I've only ever been friendly to him like I am with all the customers.'

'That is cheeky, rahly. The thing is, I've been friends with lots of women over the years and I've never thought it was okay to kiss one. Even before you and I were together, even when I was single. So it does make one wonder ...'

He leaves the question hanging between us. I can feel the slight relaxation I was just starting to feel slipping away. This would be one of those times when it would be nice to be very English so we could avoid a confrontation. But in that way we are alike. 'It makes one wonder what?' I challenge.

'Did you want him to kiss you?'

'Daniel, do you really think that of me? No, I did *not* want him to kiss me.'

'And you're sure? Because I know things haven't been easy lately. Between us, I mean, rahly. Maybe I haven't realised the full extent. You have been happy with me, haven't you? I mean, aside from the usual. I know I drive you mad at times, but I don't mean to. I try to be as good a partner for you as I can. I'm sorry, I'm still learning.'

Oh god, this is worse than if he'd angrily accused me of flirting with Leo. Which I'm pretty sure I haven't done. He can't think Leo's kissing me is somehow his fault.

I've loved Daniel nearly since our first date, in that way that's as sure as my love for our children. As sure as my breath. He's the answer when people ask how one knows when one is in love and the response is 'You just know'. There's something unassailable about the feeling, despite anything outside of us, even a stranger's kiss, or daily pressures or frustrations.

Maybe I've lost sight of that in the past year. I know I'll never let something so precious out of my sight again.

'I am sure,' I tell him. 'I didn't want it.' And I know what I'm saying is the truth, the whole truth and nothing but the truth, Your Honour. 'I only love you. I only want to be with you. Leo was out of line. Unprovoked.'

I'm not sure who goes in for the kiss first. But it's passionate and meaningful and I've missed it so much. I only know this is where I want to be. With Daniel by my side.

End of, as the kids say. Hopefully it is.

Chapter 22

Stop the Convict Café!!

Concerned neighbours: Don't let our homes be overrun by criminals!

Are you worried about the untrustworthy people lurking around the Second Chance Café day and night?

Do you want your children and grannies threatened and intimidated?

Would you like to have homeless people sleeping in your doorway??

HAVE YOUR SAY!!
Wednesday at 7pm
The Other Half Caff
Tea and cake will be served

When Barb's Convict Café leaflet turns up just after the constables' visit, it's the last straw. If that woman wants a fight, she's going to get one tonight.

Peering through the caff window, I'm pleased to see that complaining about my café hasn't drawn in quite the same crowd that the tombola did. Maybe Barb should be offering prizes, I think bitterly, as I approach the door. There are still fifteen or so people in there, though, and I'm going to have to face them. My anger has propelled me this far, but there's not quite enough petrol in the tank to get me over that threshold. Everyone inside wants our café closed down, and they don't look like they'll be shy about telling me so. Some are old, some are my age, and they probably all have different jobs, or no job, but they're all there for the same reason.

Barb spots me as soon as I get to the doorway. 'Didn't think you'd have the guts to show up,' she says loudly so that everyone turns to look.

'Is that her? It's her,' I hear a few people murmur.

'I wouldn't miss it,' I tell Barb as sweetly as I can. When she slowly reveals a yellow-toothed smile, I know she's been hoping I'd come. She wants to do this to my face and see me squirm. Well, she'll be disappointed because I might not look as tough as her, but I am not about to let some sour-faced bleached blonde harpy put me out of business.

A few of the men and women sitting at the Formica tables smile when I catch their eyes. That gives me the tiniest hope that this might not be as bad as I think it's going to be. Thinking positively (okay, grasping at straws), there might be some constructive criticism we can use to improve. What's that thing Joseph says? Learn from mistakes or you're doomed to repeat them. Or some such bollocks.

Then I notice a familiar face. 'Councillor, what are you doing here?' It's the councillor who drinks at Uncle Colin's, the man who okayed us to use Carlton Square for our wedding reception and who, after a bit of convincing by the vicar, let us have the lease on the café.

I guess I do know why he's here. 'You're here in an official capacity tonight?' I ask him.

'I'm here to listen,' he mumbles. He won't make eye contact with me or anyone else in the caff. He'd much rather be sipping a pint at his usual spot in the Cock and Crown.

This must be putting him in an awkward position. He's been one of my uncle's most consistent customers for years. Uncle Colin isn't the vindictive type, but he won't be happy if the councillor ruins his niece's business.

'Right, you lot.' When Barb claps her hands, the fat under her sleeveless arms jangles madly. 'The faster we get started, the faster you get tea and cake.'

A moan goes up across the caff as people realise their cuppa is dependent on their performance. Barb isn't doing any of this for free.

I wonder what does motivate her. She's been open here for as long as anyone remembers. If she didn't have a loyal customer base, she wouldn't have lasted. But if she's desperate enough to run down her competition, then she deserves to go out of business.

'As you know,' Barb addresses everyone, 'the Second

Chance Café over on Carlton Square has been nothing but trouble since it opened.'

Objection, supposition! I cross my arms. That's leading the witness, at least. Or leading the jury. Is there such a thing? I need to stop watching so many courtroom dramas.

'It causes congestion on the square. All those mums hanging about blocking the pavement with their pushchairs and prams.' She points to one older lady. 'Didn't you say you couldn't get by with your shopping trolley the other day?'

I feel like I recognise her. She doesn't look like she's related to Barb, although her face is just as lined, especially around her lips, from a lifetime of smoking fags. Where have I seen that hair? It's blonde like Barb's. Maybe they are related. But no, I've seen those dark roots somewhere and it wasn't in here.

'It's always chocka with fackin' babies,' the woman says. She's got no problem looking right at me. 'That lot stand around gassin' so nobody can get by. Ought to be closed down. It's disturbin' the peace and quiet of the neighbourhood.'

Suddenly I know exactly how I know her. She's that rude woman who accused us of trying to poison her with free tea and cake when we were handing out invitations to our opening party.

'It's only a narrow walkway,' Barb agrees, egging her on. 'And with those window boxes, now there's even less room.'

'But you killed all the flowers!' My little charm bracelet tinkles with the violence of my hand gesture.

'You are mad,' she says. 'I didn't do nothin', and that's not the biggest problem anyway. It's them delinquents you've got in there all the time.'

At this, everyone starts shouting out tales of how they've allegedly been accosted, threatened or sneezed at by someone from my café. The councillor tries a few times to make them take turns, but Barb has unleashed the rabble now and there's nothing stopping them.

'I had to go in the road with my grandson to get around everyone on the pavement, and I nearly tipped him out of his pushchair. He could have been killed if he'd fallen out and there'd been a car coming.'

We get about five cars driving into the square all day and they rarely get out of second gear. It wasn't a near-death experience.

'Bands of them roam through the square shouting and cursing at night,' another older lady says.

'But we close at five o'clock every day and I live on the square,' I tell her. 'Everybody goes home when we close. Or they go somewhere. I would have heard them if they were hanging out in the square.'

'Who are you to call me a liar, girl? You're the bloody liar here!'

'Now, come on,' the councillor says to her. 'There's no need for name-calling.'

Barb shoots him such a withering look that it stops the words on his tongue.

'I went by on my way from the Job Centre and when I got home, my phone was gone,' says one man who's probably not much older than me. He's pale and skinny and when he speaks his Adam's apple bobs up and down. 'It didn't just vanish into thin air.'

'Maybe you lost it,' I say.

'Maybe it got nicked by one of them when I went by,' he says.

'Maybe you want a new phone through your insurance,' comes a belligerent voice behind me.

Lou! I whip around to see her and Joseph standing in the doorway in front of a crowd of hooded teens. Near the back I spot Tinky Winky, the boy with the unfortunate tattoo who I interviewed. He returns my smile.

The delinquents are here. 'What are you doing here?'

'Well, someone needs to tell them how it is,' Lou says. They all shuffle into the already-crowded caff, between the tables and along the windows at the front. It looks like every one of the kids from upstairs is here, and maybe even a few extra. I'm sure I don't recognise one or two.

'Room for two more?' comes a wee voice from the back.

Elsie's got Carl by the hand. They've dressed up especially, Carl in a very smart tweed suit and Elsie in a pretty floral dress and little heels.

I feel the lump rising in my throat. I purposely didn't ask anyone to come tonight. It's not their job to fight my battles. Even Joseph and Lou. This is above their pay grade.

As the teens move along to make room for Carl and Elsie, Barb and the crowd are conspicuously silent as they gawp at us. I suppose we do make unlikely bedfellows – teens and OAPs and me and—'

'We're not late, are we?' Melody calls from the doorway. 'I told you we should have taken the Tube,' she says to Samantha.

'Emerald was late,' snitches Garnet.

'Only because I needed to put on my face,' she says, 'unlike some people.' She raises her eyebrow at Garnet's lack of slap.

'Some people don't need a lot of make-up,' she snaps back. 'Sorry if we're late, Emma.'

They're all here, ready to defend our café. 'Well, now I guess it's time to tell you our side of the story,' I say, looking pointedly at the councillor. He's the one who really needs convincing. 'I opened the café as a charity to train at-risk youth.' I cringe a little bit as I say this. It sounds so business-speaky now that I know the kids we so casually label. 'To train them in catering and hospitality so they can go on to better jobs and have a chance for their future. Joseph and Lou are the first people to come through the six-month training programme.'

Barb finally finds her voice. I knew it wouldn't be lost for long. 'That means they'll have another crop of losers there in a few months. Great.'

She does know how to push my buttons. 'They're not losers! I wish you'd stop being so horrible about everyone. They're kids. If you remember back to the dark ages, you might remember when you were one too.'

I think I catch the councillor sniggering, but I can't be sure because he covers his mouth.

'What about all the others?' Adam's apple says. He's got his hands clenched in his pockets. He's probably holding on to his wallet. 'Even if those two are okay, what about the others?' This raises approving murmurs from some of the tables.

'Are we allowed to answer?' Tinky Winky asks me from beneath his hood.

'Of course.'

At that, all the kids pull their hoods down, unzip their sweatshirts or pull them over their heads, and stand neatly dressed in button-down shirts and ties. A few could use an iron and one or two aren't quite tucked in, but the implication is unmistakeable before they even speak. Don't judge us by what you see. Look at what's inside.

Lou has peeled off her sweatshirt too. Her pale blue hair is swept back into a high, neat ponytail and the flowery tunic she's paired with her jeans makes her look older than seventeen.

Then Ice Lolly speaks. You remember Ice Lolly, the enormous fifteen-year-old with the spotty face and mini Afro and chain on his wallet, aka Martin? 'Yo, before the café we didn't have nowhere to go,' he says. 'We was harassed by the po-po just for standin' with our bluds doing nothin'. We're not doing nothin' wrong, just existing, but nobody sees that. Then Emma invited us to her café. She *invited* us. Us. Nobody ever does that. Now we have a nice place to go and we buy her drinks and cakes. She got wicked cakes, yo. And we don't cause no trouble.'

'May I say something?' Elsie asks, peering around from behind Ice Lolly. The kids move a little to make room for her at the front. 'We're the kind of people who should be afraid of these boys, don't you agree? I think I'm supposed to be the granny you mention in your leaflet.' At this, Barb looks slightly off-kilter. She might bully me, but she'll think twice about going up against Elsie. 'Well, we certainly ain't intimidated by these boys. They're always polite and respectful to everyone in the café. Yes, they're loud. What do you expect from teenage boys? Boys are loud and they're high-spirited and full of bravado. But that doesn't make them criminals.' Again she glares at Barb. 'That makes them boys.'

'And we're the mums with children who are supposed to be intimidated,' Samantha adds. 'We've got babies and children to protect. My son is in a wheelchair and my daughter's only fourteen months old. Do you think they intimidate us? Look at them,' she challenges the room. 'I don't mean through your biased eyes either. If they were dangerous, do you really think there'd be so many mums in the café? Use your common sense.'

They speak up, one after another, the mums – Melody, Emerald and Garnet – saying how much they appreciate finally having a safe and welcoming place to bring their children and meet other parents. But it's the boys who finally make my tears spill over. Sure, their language is rough, they say 'ain't' and 'nuffink' and pepper sentences with London slang, but their message is the same. They aren't bothering anyone, they're sorry that people are uncomfortable with their very existence, but they're not sorry for existing.

I'm so focussed on the boys that I only notice Daniel when he speaks. 'May I say something?'

I stare at him. 'What are *you* doing here?' As usual he's wearing his unique blend of old-man-in-the-countryside toff – yellow trousers, two-tone boat shoes, a stripy red work shirt and his navy jumper tied around his neck.

'We're on the same side, aren't we, Em?' He smiles. 'Let's do this together.' He excuses himself through everyone to take my hand, then says, 'Right, yah, I'm new to East London. Don't let my local accent fool you.' That raises a laugh. 'When I first met Emma, I'd never really even been here before. And I admit I was intimidated by everyone. It's not my cultural milieu, you see.'

God, will he ever stop using that word around normal people?!

'Before coming here, I wasn't used to people in East London. You sound different, you look different from West London, where I grew up.'

This draws snorts from Barb and a few of her customers. 'You all scared me, to be perfectly honest. Well, you would, wouldn't you? We're afraid of the unfamiliar, of things that look different, so I do understand how you feel. But Emma introduced me to her world and when I met everyone, I wasn't afraid anymore. So I guess what I'm saying is that once I let go of my prejudices I could see people for who they are. And I hope they see me that way too.'

I stretch up to kiss my husband. My unusually dressed, plummy-speaking, kind, wonderful and best of all, open-minded husband.

'All this is very moving,' Barb says. 'But I'm not buying these yobs-with-a-heart-of-gold stories. It's easy to dress up for a night and pretend you're not all a waste of space. You do it for court anyway, I'm guessing. But you're not fooling us. You'll be back to your normal ways as soon as you take off those ties.'

To their credit, the boys keep silent. I guess they're probably not surprised that even after all that, Barb and her kind won't give them a chance.

'Now, who wants tea?' she says. 'Not you lot. Clear off, if you don't mind. You've got your own poncy café. At least for the moment.'

She turns to look at the councillor.

I do the same.

He looks away from us both.

Chapter 23

'I think we convinced them,' Daniel says as I'm lying in bed that night staring at the ceiling. I've thought of at least half a dozen good comebacks to Barb's horrid words. Fat lot of good they're doing me here under the duvet.

I snuggle deeper into Daniel's side and let his arms close around me. 'I'm not sure we convinced anyone,' I murmur. 'It didn't seem to matter how many arguments we came up with or how persuasive the kids were. They were great, though, weren't they? To be honest it's the first time I've heard most of them speak.' I smile into the darkness. 'It gives me hope that we really can make a difference.' If I can get other people to remember that they're just normal kids, then maybe they'll have a chance. 'As long as the café stays open.'

'We'll make sure it does, Emma. Just let me know what I can do to help, okay? I meant what I said. It might be your café, but we're in this together.'

'Thank you. I know that. I guess the councillor will decide what to do based on tonight. I just hope we did enough.'

'He can't just close you down, though. Proper procedure must be followed.'

Dear, sweet Daniel. He still thinks East London works the way the rest of the city does. This is the borough where the government's community secretary had to take over the running of the council because it was so corrupt. We practically have the UN's blue hats here during elections. I know as well as Barb does that the councillor can do whatever he wants to.

The mums are abuzz over the meeting the next morning. You'd think they were modern-day Erin Brockoviches to hear them, fighting for the rights of the little people. Emerald and Garnet are bickering over who had the most persuasive argument, with Melody refusing to take sides as usual.

Only one person was conspicuously absent from Barb's last night. I doubt that's a coincidence after the other day. 'All right?' I ask Leo when he comes in. There are a lot of questions in those two little words.

'Yeah, fine,' he says. 'It sounds like you had an eventful night. Why didn't anyone tell us about the meeting? We'd have come to support you too.'

'Thanks, Lou arranged everything. I didn't expect anyone to come. I guess she figured you'd be busy.'

'So you didn't tell her not to say anything to me about coming?'

'No! Why would I?' Now why did I say that, when I know very well why? 'I think we're clear about ... the other night. It was a mistake. A misunderstanding, that's all. No hard feelings, right? So it's not awkward.'

'No, not at all,' he agrees.

It couldn't be more awkward.

'One thing, though,' he says. 'Could you please not tell your husband what happened? I feel like enough of an arse. I'd rather not have him know I've made a move on his wife. My ego is fragile enough without having to take that beating too.'

'Awkward,' I sing.

'You told him.'

'I'm sorry. I didn't want to keep it from him. Let me rephrase that. There was no reason to keep it from him.'

'So now he thinks I'm an arsehole too.' Leo strokes his beard.

'He probably does. But I don't. It was an honest mistake.'

I can't admit I might have had the tiniest hand in his actions. If I didn't encourage him, then I didn't discourage him either. That's just as bad and I'll have to live with that.

'And don't worry. Daniel isn't the kind of person to hold a grudge.'

'That's probably one of the reasons you love him.'

I nod. 'One of many.'

His expression is resigned as he makes his way upstairs to start work. I get the feeling our philosophy lessons are over, and I won't be surprised if Leo finds another café to work in. Somewhere with good cake where he hasn't kissed the owner.

I've got to own up to my part in this, because I'm not innocent. I didn't do much to discourage him when he got friendly. I got friendly too, and the attention felt good. I can make all the excuses I want. That was wrong. And it could have been catastrophic if Daniel wasn't so forthright and, ultimately, understanding. It's just one more reason to be so grateful for him.

I know as soon as I see the envelope from the council a few days later that we haven't heard the last of Barb and her complaints. I'd actually started to convince myself that everything would be okay. Stupid optimism.

I don't have to say anything when I bring it to Lou and Joseph, who are cleaning the Gaggia. In some ways I guess we've all been expecting it.

'You haven't opened it yet?' Lou says.

'I thought we should do it together. It affects all of us.'

'It might be good news,' says Joseph. 'Maybe there's no case against us. I mean, we know there isn't a case. She's just stirring up trouble. After everything we said, the council has to see that.'

I'm not as sure as Joseph seems to be.

There's a lot of legalese in the short letter – on the twelfth day of this and pursuant to that – but it boils down to the fact that the Carlton Square Residents Group has made a complaint against us for failing to curb the intimidation and violence that our customers are inflicting on residents. It's news to me that Carlton Square even has a residents group. If they do, Daniel and I haven't been invited.

The complaint will, the council goes on to say, mean that our business licence is under review.

'That's not good, boss. If they pull our licence, then we're ...'

'Out of business,' Lou finishes for him.

I look around our café. Auntie Rose is doing her morning reading group with the children, something with bears judging by the way she's holding up imaginary claws and baring her teeth. Emerald and Garnet are comparing the perfection of their manicures while Melody feeds her little one. And Carl is sitting alone in his booth looking sad that Elsie's not here.

What an intimidating bunch we make.

'Let's not say anything to anyone yet, okay? This is only a review. It might still come out okay.' Besides, I may know a way to make this whole issue go away. It's a long shot, but Barb isn't the only one around here who can mobilise support.

Nobody suspects what I'm planning when I invite everyone to the pub. Mum and Dad and Auntie Rose know about Barb's meeting, of course, but not about the council's letter or the licence review. They probably assume I just want some cheering up. Only Daniel knows everything. I rang him at work right after I opened the letter. 'Right,' he'd said, 'I don't want you to worry. I'm going to find out what the appeals process is, just in case it comes to that. I don't think it will, darling, rahly, but let's be prepared just in case. I'll tell you what I find out tonight, all right? I'll pick up something for supper on the way home. I can get take-away from The Enterprise. Now, Emma, I know you, and I don't want you to worry about this. I'm looking into the next steps so you don't have to. You will let me do that for you, won't you?'

'Of course I'll let you. Thank you, Daniel.'

'It's nothing, Emma. We're a team.'

It hasn't been easy pretending everything is normal when at this very moment people I don't know might be deciding whether we get to keep our café or not. I have to hope that they'll weigh up Barb and the residents group's charges against everything we said. But only the councillor was there to hear them. I'm not convinced that he'll put our side forward convincingly.

If he knows why we're in the Cock now, he's not letting on. Hunched over his pint as usual at the bar, his eyes barely flicker to us when we arrive. I knew he'd be here despite any discomfort he might have felt seeing me the other night at Barb's. He's a career councillor. If he avoided everyone who'd ever lodged a complaint against the council, he'd never leave his house. He's used to being a beer-soaked punching bag.

Daniel reaches for my hand. 'Is it okay to let them loose?' he calls to Uncle Colin behind the bar.

'Hang on, let me lock up the cat.' My uncle's pub cat is the orneriest animal you'll ever meet. Worst of all, he pretends he's not, just so he can lure unsuspecting people to stroke him, preferably on his tummy where he can employ his four deadly weapons at once. The old-timers might not like the recent influx of new residents into the neighbourhood, but the cat loves gentrification for the fresh supply of scratching posts.

Grace starts on her rounds of the tables as soon as she's free from the pushchair. She's sure to stop long enough at each one to catch everyone's eye and collect a smile before she moves on. Oscar, on the other hand, crawls straight into Mum's lap.

The vicar is at his favourite spot in the pub – the piano. There are two empty pint glasses and a whisky glass lined up along its top, just as I'd hoped. Not that I need him to be pissed for my plan to work, but it helps. The vicar is most persuasive when he's loosened up.

'How's business?' Uncle Colin asks, giving me the perfect opening to save Daniel having to prompt me like we practised. His look of relief is comic and would definitely raise eyebrows if my family weren't all looking at the twins.

'Interesting, actually, Uncle Colin. We've had some trouble with one of the local caff owners. She's made a formal complaint to the council.'

Now Mum and Dad and Auntie Rose and everyone is looking at me. 'What kind of complaint could they make against you?' Dad wants to know. He might normally be mild-mannered, but you don't want to mess with his family. I pull the letter from my pocket to show them all.

'What intimidation and violence?' Auntie Rose demands. 'It's a load of bollocks. Ignore it, me girl. They're just jealous.'

I suppress a giggle at that. It was exactly what she used to tell me every time I snivelled into her shoulder when the girls at school were being mean. I didn't believe her then either. 'I can't ignore it, Auntie Rose. The council is investigating. Our licence is under review.'

The vicar, who'd been tinkling quietly on the piano, stops playing. My whole family turns to look at the councillor, whose shoulders are shrunk even more into his suit jacket. Trying to make a smaller target, maybe.

'Councillor? Do you know anything about this?' my dad asks. But the councillor has survived the last five governments by only talking to his constituency if he absolutely has to. He's playing dead.

'Councillor.' The piano bench scrapes back as the vicar rises to his feet. 'I believe I heard Jack asking you a question. Jack, would you like to repeat it?'

Now Dad is wheeling toward the councillor too. 'I asked whether the councillor knows anything about this complaint against my daughter's café.'

'I'm sure he doesn't,' the vicar says. 'Because if he had even an inkling, he'd be the first person to want to sort it out. Our democracy functions on the rule of law, truth and justice, don't it, Councillor?'

Finally, the councillor turns around. 'I don't want any trouble. I'm only doing my job.'

'As you should,' the vicar says. 'As you absolutely should. We're just trying to help you evaluate your evidence. If there *is* any evidence against Emma's café, then it must be inaccurate, wouldn't you agree? Because otherwise you're saying that this fine young woman is running a business that's … what did the complaint allege? Intimidating and violent? That doesn't sound like our Emma at all, does it? Now, who's made this complaint?'

'The Carlton Square Residents Group,' I say, 'but it was started by the owner of The Other Half Caff.'

Uncle Colin stops stacking his glasses. 'You mean the caff up on the main road? Isn't that your wife, Councillor?'

We all stare between Uncle Colin and the councillor. I can't have heard him right. Who in their right mind would marry Barb?

'Is that true?' Dad asks him.

Uncle Colin answers instead of the councillor. 'I've run this pub for twenty years, Jack. If I don't know it, it ain't worth knowing.' He goes back to his glasses.

The vicar clamps a meaty hand on the councillor's shoulder. 'You're married to her? Up at the caff, the blonde one? Christ, mate, I'm sorry to hear that.'

The councillor accepts this sympathy with a resigned sigh.

'No wonder 'e's in here all the time,' Auntie Rose says.

'It's not really cricket, then, is it, being an interested party to the complainant,' the vicar continues. 'I don't see how you can be unbiased in such a situation as this. A declared interest, I believe it's called. If you have declared it, that is.' He looks to the councillor for confirmation.

Instead of answering, the councillor takes a long last sip of his pint, wipes his mouth on his hand and stands up. 'Right, that's me off.'

'Why the rush, Councillor?' I can't see whether the vicar's hand tightens on the man's shoulder, but he sits down again. 'I believe we've still got a situation to resolve.'

The councillor holds up his hands and addresses us for the first time. 'Look, try to understand. I'm a simple man. I don't bother anyone and I don't want anyone to bother me. I work all day and then I come in here for a few pints so I can face going home to 'er indoors. You think it's hard dealing with 'er at the caff? Try living with the woman. All I want is an easy life. If you want something different, then you try standing up to 'er.'

Finally, I find my voice. 'So you are going to close us down? This review is just a formality. You've already decided to do what your wife says.'

He looks at me with the watery blue stare of a PTSD victim. 'You have no idea. What do you think she did when I gave you the lease?'

'What did she do?' I whisper. Not that I want to give him flashbacks.

'Well, actually she stopped speaking to me, so it wasn't

too bad. But that's not what she's doing this time. Emma, please try to understand. I just want an easy home life. You can find another place for your café. I'm stuck with my wife till one of us dies. 'Er mum lived to ninety-nine.' He sighs. 'Actually, Colin, I will have another pint.'

'Well, Councillor,' says the vicar. 'I guess you need to ask yourself this: do you want an unhappy home life for a while or an unhappy life outside forever? I know what a smart man would choose.' His tone is friendly, but his meaning is crystal clear.

Chapter 24

The weather has turned decidedly summerlike and the café is buzzing. Ever since the teens took their stand at Barb's caff they've been more sociable. Carl and Elsie now know how to do fist bumps (better than I do) and a few of the boys even sit downstairs now when they've got girls with them. I'm not naïve enough to think they spend all their time sipping tea. They still have to walk a fine line between pissing off the local gangs and getting mixed up with them, and a few will be putting on their shirts and ties again to go to the same court as Lou did last month. But everyone rubs along pretty well in here.

After our talk with the councillor in the Cock, my parents think he'll drop the case against the café, but I'm not so sure. So when Lou hands me the council's letter with the morning's post, my heart leaps into my throat. Our future is literally in my hands.

Now that Lou is officially my business associate – dubbed Head of Training and Recruitment by Joseph – she's as tied up in its future as I am. We both know she doesn't really have enough work experience to get another job like she's got here now. It's only because I know she has so much more going for her in real life than she does on paper.

I don't worry so much about Joseph anymore. He's got the kind of belief in himself that's made millionaires out of barrow boys for centuries. That and the ability to work the Gaggia would get him another job.

'Open it,' Lou says. 'Whatever it says, we'll deal with it.'

'Together.'

'Right.'

'"Dear Mrs Billings,"' I read. '"Pursuant to the complaint made by the Carlton Square Residents Group on blah blah blah …" Let's see – here's their answer. "The council has reviewed the evidence presented and is *satisfied that the Second Chance Café and its owners and employees have no case to answer* in terms of the original complaint that its customers were inflicting intimidation and violence on residents. Case number blah blah blah is therefore closed to the satisfaction of the council and no further action will be taken." We're cleared. We don't have to close.'

I'm not sure who is more surprised when Lou launches

herself at me and we end up jumping up and down in each other's arms shouting 'We're cleared!' in the middle of the café.

Our excited shouting pulls everyone into our orbit, starting with Joseph, but before long Samantha, Emerald, Garnet and Melody close in for the group hug. The teens raise a smile but keep their distance. They might drink tea from dainty china cups and occasionally stick out a pinky finger, but they still have their reputations to think of.

'Thanks to you all,' I say. 'You too, boys. We've saved the café together!'

'Well done, us!' Elsie says from their booth. 'Power to the people.' She raises her hand in a Black Panther salute that sets the teens off into fits of laughter.

'Yo, Elsie, you're whack,' says one.

'Thank you, young man, I think you're whack too. Is that right?'

'Close enough,' I tell her. 'Can I get you anything else? Slice of cake? Zane's made a Victoria sponge.'

Carl hoots. 'Ha, the last thing my girl needs is cake!'

Instead of decking him, like I'd have done to Daniel if he ever tried telling me what I should or shouldn't be eating, Elsie pats Carl's arm. Here she is, an intelligent woman, career diplomat and speaker of multiple languages, and she's letting him talk to her like that? 'Carl, Elsie can eat—'

I start to say, but he starts talking over me. Sometimes his hearing's not too good.

'She might love it, but it don't love her. Not that there's anything wrong with the cake, mind you. It's wonderful.'

Elsie fiddles with the brooch at the neck of her frilly blouse. 'I'm afraid my digestion isn't what it used to be, though my sweet tooth is. I can't help myself, but I always pay for it later.'

'And then I'm without me girl.' Carl loops his arm over Elsie's shoulder.

'You mean you weren't in bed because of the cancer?' My voice dials down in volume as I slide towards the "C" word.

'Goodness, no, is that what you thought? No, I 'aven't got any of those symptoms at all. They've got me going in for blood tests every few months, but my GP thinks it's moving slowly because of my age. No, it's nothing as dramatic as that. I was indisposed through too much cake.'

'She gets the sugar shits,' Carl shouts, jerking his thumb at Elsie. I did mention that his hearing isn't very good, right?

'Carl, language, please,' she says. 'Maybe I'll just have a tiny sliver with my tea.'

There's one person who won't be celebrating the council's decision. Well, two if you include the councillor, who'll probably have to live at the Cock now that he's ruled against his wife. I'll stop by tonight to thank him personally, but first I've got someone else to see.

'Want me to come too?' Lou asks when she hears where I'm going.

'Thank you, no, I'd like to do this myself. If I'm not back in half an hour, though, ring the police, okay?'

'Ha ha, you joke but I'm keeping an eye on the time,' she says. 'Good luck.'

As usual, Barb spots me as soon as I get through the caff door. Her face remains absolutely impassive as she watches me approach the counter.

'Hello, Barb. I just got the letter. I assume you did too.' Though she'll have had more warning, what with being married to the judge in this case.

She holds up her identical letter. 'The fackin' coward wouldn't tell me to my face.'

Wow, he is afraid of her.

'You can save your gloating,' she adds. 'This ain't over.'

'I'm not here to gloat, Barb. But I do want to know why. Why do you hate us so much? Have I ever done anything to you?'

When she scoffs, the lines between her eyebrows get deeper. 'I don't hate you. Is that what you think, that this is personal? You're such a typical whinger, bringing it all round to you.' She shrugs. 'I want the lease on the building. Simple as. I'd have 'ad it too if your friends hadn't threatened my husband.'

'Only slightly more than you did,' I say, shaking my head. 'I've seen your customers during busy times, Barb, and I can tell you that my café is too big for you. I doubt you'd really want to run up and down those stairs all the time.'

'You daft cow. I don't want your poncy café. I said I want the lease. Me husband could have given it to me for nothing.'

'But if you don't want to move your caff there, I don't see ...'

'Move me caff? Why the fack would I do that? My customers 'ave been coming 'ere for over thirty years and are very happy, thank you very much.'

I look around at the dirty yellow walls and faded menu specials that are probably anything but special. There's a layer of grime and hopelessness covering everything, but she's right. Her customers, mostly tradesmen and local business owners, do seem happy enough. 'You just want my café gone?'

'Got it in one,' she says. 'You're not as dim as you look.' She turns to a customer who's come to the counter. 'Keep your wig on, I'm talking. Go sit down.'

The customer does as he's told, folding his large frame into one of the battered wooden chairs to wait until Barb is ready to serve him. I'll say this, she's got her customers well-trained.

'If you don't mind me saying, Barb, if you closed me down, then my customers probably wouldn't come here.' They're not overly keen on being mistreated and she doesn't have enough electrical sockets for the freelancers anyway. Even if she put a power station in the back, I can't see her letting Leo and his friends monopolise a table all day.

She snorts. 'I don't want 'em! A bunch of screaming babies, hipsters and delinquents.'

'Then what's your problem, if you're not after my customers?'

'I don't want you after mine either.'

Now it's my turn to snort, but she seems to be perfectly serious. 'Your customers don't strike me as the china cup latte and chai tea crowd, Barb. You serve hot food and we don't. We've got sandwiches and cakes and that's it.'

'So far,' she says. 'What 'appens when you start serving cooked breakfast?'

'That'll never happen,' I say. For one thing I wouldn't want the cloying stench of fry-ups hanging in the air like it is in here.

'Everyone wants a cooked breakfast and a hot dinner.'

'If that's true, then they'd have to come here to get it. I've got no interest in being a caff, Barb. My business is hot drinks and cakes and a few sandwiches. So if you don't want my customers and I don't want yours, and we serve totally different food, do you really have to keep going through all the trouble to try to turf me out?'

'How much do you charge for a pot of tea?' she asks, even though her spy already gave her that information.

'Which flavour?'

'Fackin' 'ell, regular tea,' she says.

When I tell her two-fifty she says, 'Disgraceful. It's not worth more than a quid.'

'We have china pots and cups,' I point out, 'but I take your point. I'd never charge less than two pounds for a pot.'

'Promise two-fifty. None of my lot would be stupid enough to pay that.'

'Two-fifty, then,' I say, feeling like a very lightweight East London gangster, price-fixing pots of English Breakfast tea. 'And I won't have any cooked food either. I'd have to hire a cook to do that and I'd rather spend the extra money training more kids. So you're going to keep your ... policy about parents with pushchairs?'

'Won't have 'em in my caff.'

'Then it sounds like we don't overlap at all, Barb. Do you think we can let each other alone now? You're welcome to come to the café any time you like, you know.'

'Pssh, as if I'd ever spend two-fifty for a fackin' pot of tea.'

But she nods once, ever so slightly, before turning to the table where the builder is patiently waiting. 'What do you want?' she barks at him.

Chapter 25

'Yo, boss, you think we've got enough cake?' Joseph surveys the sea of baked goods laid out on pretty plates and stands along the bar top. He's got his hair gelled straight up off the top of his head in a wavy black wedge, and he even has a new bow tie – a trend he's embraced from the freelancers. 'We could feed East London on these, yeah.'

I let Zane go overboard on the cakes, but it's important to be *abundant* when having a party to celebrate your business's six-month anniversary.

Joseph and Lou are behind the bar working the Gaggia with barista skills that would make Pablo proud. It's hard to remember why we were so afraid of that machine. I guess we speak the same language now.

'Not like this, like this,' Joseph tells the boy who's holding the little metal pitcher under the steamer.

'Like this?' the boy says. His big eyes never leave his instructor's, which couldn't make Joseph happier.

'No, like this. Listen. Can you hear it?' Joseph catches Lou's eye over the boy's head. 'Listen to the bean.'

'Don't be an arsehole to the new kid,' Lou says. 'You were just as hopeless when you started.'

'Yo, Professor, what else do you need?' Tinky Winky says as he carries more clean crockery from the kitchen. 'The teacups are dried off.'

Joseph nods. 'And the plates? Top and bottom? Well done, blud. Strong attention to detail. Go see if anyone wants more hot water for their teapots.'

You heard right. Tinky Winky is our newest trainee, along with the boy trying to work the Gaggia, who was referred by Mrs Boggis-Stanton. I might have been too harsh about her over Lou. She did reopen the complaint against Lou's foster parents. It took several visits and they finally interviewed all the kids without the adults there to intimidate them, and just last week they ruled that the children should be placed with new foster families. It means a lot of upheaval for them, but hopefully they'll end up being looked after by people who care about them. I know that Mrs Boggis-Stanton will do everything she can to make sure they do.

I just wish they could all stay together. It's going to be hard for Lou to be away from them. Although her birthday is next month, so she'll be old enough to live on her own anyway. She can't wait for that.

I wish we could all stay together too, but I'll have to get used to saying goodbye to the trainees, since that is the whole point of the café.

Joseph will go off to his new job next week, working for one of the restaurant chains where they do breakfast from the four corners of the world, all with poncy names like the Barbary Toast. Barb would probably spit on the floor if she was ever dragged into one, but I've got no doubt that Joseph will rise quickly and have collected at least three new job titles by Christmas.

One of Mrs Ishtiaque's ladies saunters up to the counter, where Lou is slicing Zane's newest cake – peanut butter and jelly. I know what Auntie Rose will say about it, but it's got a certain something.

'Are you enjoying your job?' she asks as Lou carefully tries to cut perfectly even slices. She glances at the woman in her bright orange saree.

'It's great,' says Lou, eying the cake again. 'Do you enjoy being my customer?'

'It is very nice being your customer. I think you are being a very good waitress.'

Lou smiles at that. 'And you are a very good customer. Now bugger off, please, so I can cut this.'

'I am buggering off!' The woman waves cheerily over her shoulder.

Lou winks at me. 'Teaching them the local vernacular,' she says.

Who'd have imagined a year ago, when this was just a closed-down smelly old pub, that it would become someplace where so many people could come to feel at home? I'm thinking about Uncle Colin's pub, as I often do, and that time I wished for the café to have the same kind of camaraderie. I got my wish.

Six months ago these were all strangers. I'd never even laid eyes on Mrs Ishtiaque's ladies or, if I had, I didn't distinguish them from the other women I passed every day. Same goes for the teenagers – who were only faceless hoodies I avoided on the street – or the hipsters whose beards I mocked. Now they're all as familiar to me, and to each other, as long-time friends – real people, not just the stereotypes that are too easy to ignore or fear or mock.

I watch the vicar as he talks with Carl and Elsie and Mrs Delaney. I know he'll be sad when Mrs Delaney moves to Spain, but that lovely old couple will keep him from getting too lonely without her. He wouldn't hear of accepting my thanks when I told him about the councillor's decision. It's part of his job, he says, to look after his flock.

'Gawd, tell me you're not blubbing again,' Kelly says,

handing me one of the paper serviettes from beside the Gaggia. 'You're supposed to be happy.'

'I am happy,' I tell her. 'It's just hit me that everything's about to change, I guess. Joseph's leaving, and Mrs Delaney ... and you.'

'I'm not leaving for months.'

'But then I'll hardly ever see you. I'm going to miss you, that's all.'

She rolls her eyes. I did tell you she doesn't show her emotions very much. 'Give me your phone.'

'Why?'

'Just give it here. It's your usual password?'

I'm so predictable. She taps a few buttons before handing my phone back. Then she takes hers out.

My phone rings. 'Answer it,' she says. 'The green button.'

When I slide the button, Kelly's face appears on my screen. 'Happy now?' virtual Kelly says. 'You can see me any time you want. It's Facetime. Now will you pull yourself together and enjoy your party?'

But I'm not looking at my screen. 'I love you,' I tell my real best friend.

'I love you too, you daft thing.' Then she hangs up and puts her arm round my shoulders.

'Who wants more cake?' Joseph calls out to the crowd.

'We'll miss you, Joseph,' Melody calls back with a catch

in her voice. She's been overly emotional lately, ever since she and her daughter finally decided to call time on the breastfeeding. Now Melody is talking about having another baby. Her poor boobs just don't get a break.

'Only because you're getting free cake,' Joseph says.

'To Joseph!' Tinky Winky booms.

'The Professor,' Lou says as Joseph beams. 'Our first graduate.'

'The first of many. Hip hip—'

'Hooray!' Everyone shouts, and all their voices – from the teens to the OAPs, the mums, the freelancers, my family, the ladies in their bright sarees and our kindly corrupt vicar – merge into one.

'What is meaning hooray?' I hear one of the ladies ask in the silent second that follows.

'Just be cheering,' Mrs Ishtiaque says. 'It means our café is wonderful.'

Acknowledgements

I was in the middle of writing this novel when I noticed a new coffee shop near my house: Second Shot Coffee. The name was similar to my book title so I went inside, where I discovered that not only do they make great coffee, they're a social enterprise that trains people affected by homelessness and helps them go on to work. It's life imitating art imitating life!

So, if you're on Bethnal Green Road, do stop by the shop, have a delicious coffee and support a great cause: www.facebook.com/secondshotcoffee

I'd like to say a huge thank you to Second Shot Coffee's owner, Julius Ibrahim, who very kindly let me pick his brains about opening the café. Any factual errors about setting up and running such an endeavour are mine alone.

Thank you too to my wonderful editors, Charlotte and Caz, whose belief in Lilly's books means so much to me. Thanks to my copyeditor, the wonderfully OCD Lucy York. We've been together now for years and you still always impress me with your attention to detail. Thank you to Sam, HarperImpulse's fantastic social media ninja, for putting Lilly's books so firmly in the spotlight, and to all the bloggers and readers who take the time to read them. To all my author friends, old and new, so many of whom said wonderful things about the books and who helped spread the word. With a special mention for the HarperImpulse authors – what a lovely bunch you are! The support from you all has meant the world to me.

Finally, as always, thanks to my agent, Caroline, and to my husband, Andrew, for being so enthusiastic about the new pen-named books. You're both contractually obliged to be my cheerleaders, but I love knowing that you'd do it anyway!

TRINITY UNITED CHURCH
NORTH BAY, ONTARIO